Praise for "A Life Earthbound"

"Jennings did a great job of pulling me in to Rhia's story and making me feel with her even as Rhia built walls to protect her heart from feeling too much."

– *A.D. Trosper, author* –

"This story tugs at the heartstrings and I am glad to have read it... Katie Jennings is a very talented writer..."

– *Natalie Gibson, author* –

"*A Life Earthbound* is a coming of age story of a young girl and hard working young woman that must battle with her emotions and determine what she truly wants in life. A must read."

– *D. Martinez, reader* –

"*A Life Earthbound* gives you so much more information on what is was like in the beginning and after Capri was taken. I would definitely recommend reading the books in order. It is so nice when the pieces fall in place from each book!"

– *Jenny, reader* –

"*A Life Earthbound* gives you a deeper understanding of what life was like for Rhia, and I was totally mesmerized by the true love that Liam felt for her. I have really enjoyed this series of books!"

– *Angela, reader* –

Also By Katie Jennings

The Dryad Quartet Series
Breath of Air
Firefight in Darkness
Of Water and Madness

The Vasser Legacy Series
When Empires Fall
Rise of the Notorious
Coming Spring 2013

THIRD OF THE DRYAD QUARTET

KATIE JENNINGS

Cover design by Katie Jennings
Interior book and eBook design by Blue Harvest Creative
www.blueharvestcreative.com

A LIFE EARTHBOUND

Published by
Sapphire Royale Publishing

ISBN-13: 978-0615720401
ISBN-10: 0615720404

Visit the author at:

www.katieajennings.com
www.facebook.com/katieajennings
www.twitter.com/dryadquartet
www.katieajennings.wordpress.com

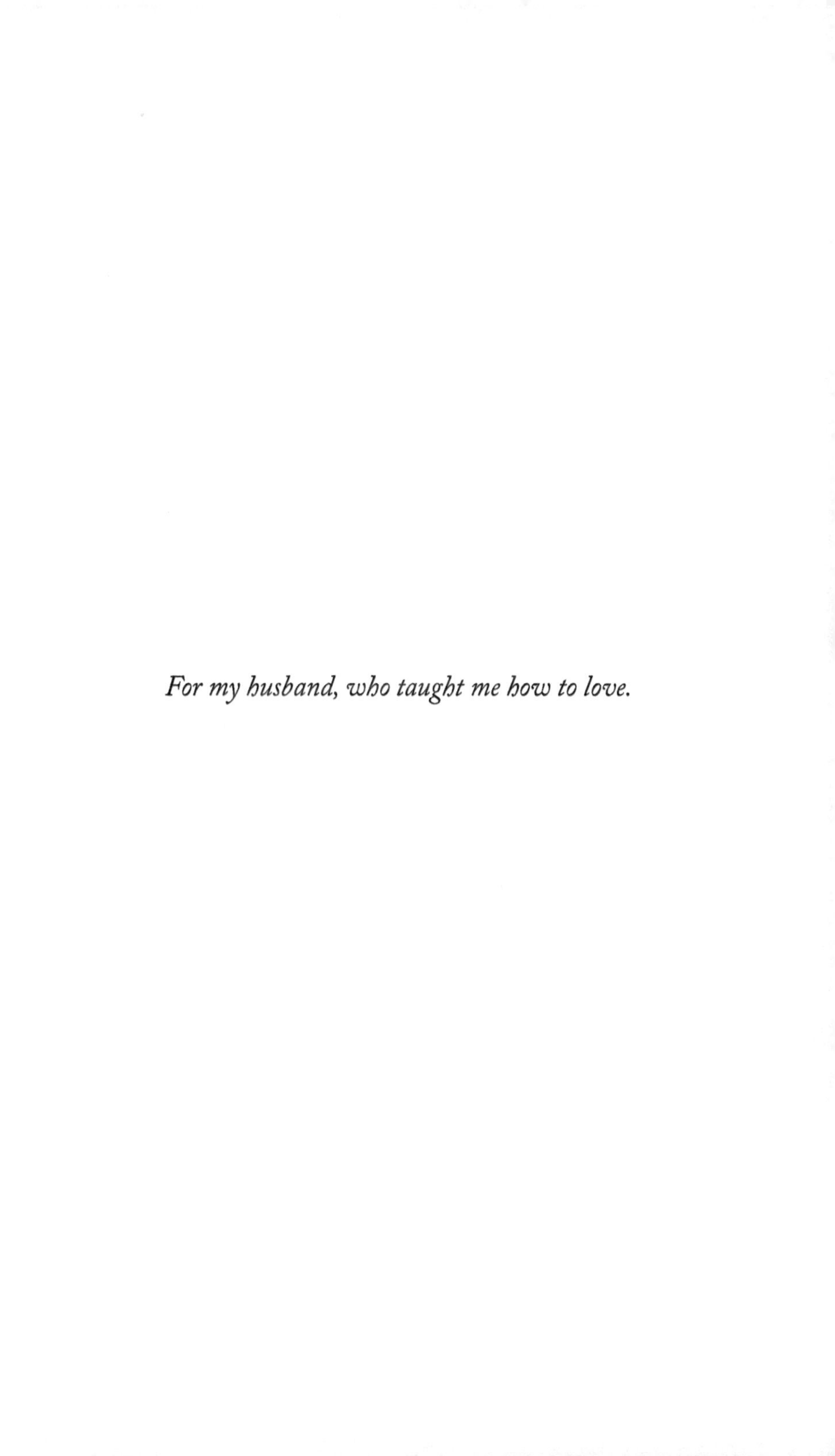

For my husband, who taught me how to love.

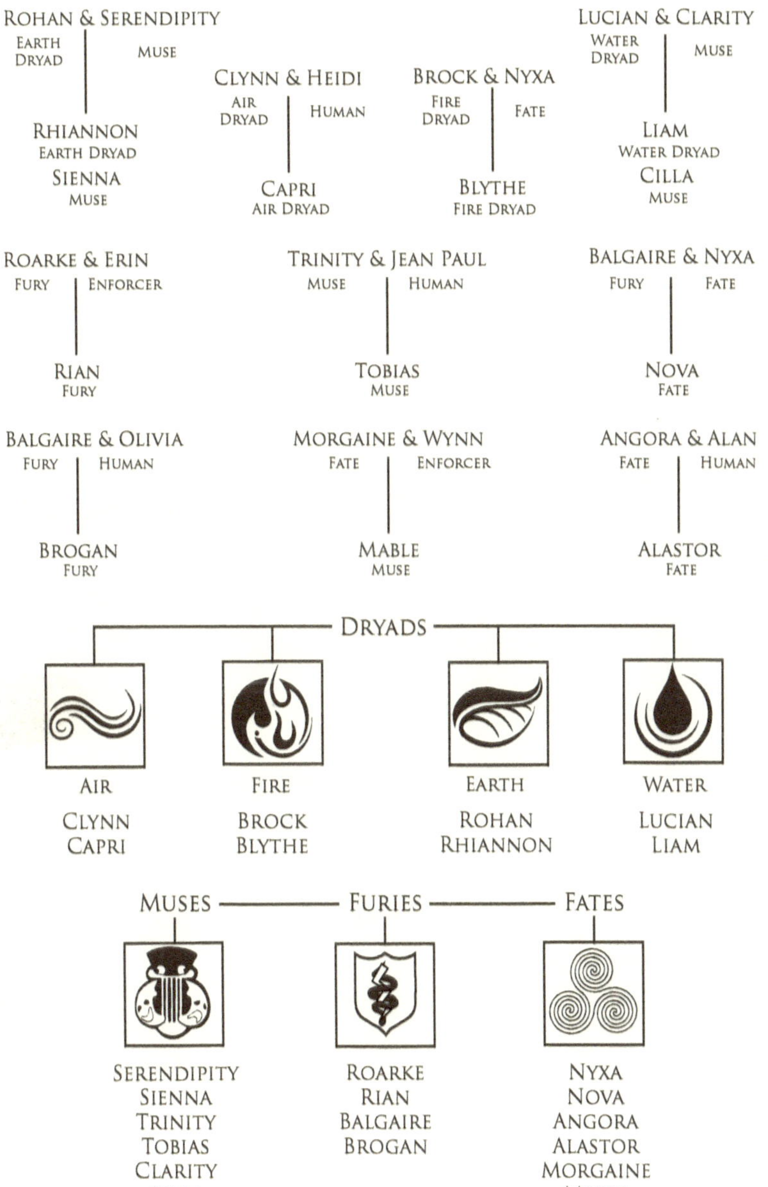

Thea & Sebastian
Mother Earth & Father Sky
Rohan & Serendipity
Earth Dryad
Muse
Rhiannon
Earth Dryad
Sienna
Muse
Clynn & Heidi
Air Dryad
Human
Capri
Air Dryad
Brock & Nyxa
Fire Dryad
Fate
Blythe
Fire Dryad
Lucian & Clarity
Water Dryad
Muse
Liam
Water Dryad
Cilla
Muse
Roarke & Erin
Fury
Enforcer
Rian
Fury
Trinity & Jean Paul
Muse
Human
Tobias
Muse
Balgaire & Nyxa
Fury
Fate
Nova
Fate
Balgaire & Olivia
Fury
Human
Brogan
Fury
Morgaine & Wynn
Fate
Enforcer
Mable
Muse
Angora & Alan
Fate
Human
Alastor
Fate
Dryads
Air
Clynn
Capri
Fire
Brock
Blythe
Earth
Rohan
Rhiannon
Water
Lucian
Liam
Muses
Furies
Fates
Serendipity
Sienna
Trinity
Tobias
Clarity
Cilla
Roarke
Rian
Balgaire
Brogan
Nyxa
Nova
Angora
Alastor
Morgaine
Mable

Prologue

She's only a bird in a gilded cage,
A beautiful sight to see.
You may think she's happy and free from care,
She's not, though she seems to be.

Her name was Rhiannon, and she was Earth.

To the casual observer, her life appeared to be as flawless as a Kinkade landscape: every minute detail portrayed with clarity and precision, and not a smudge or flyspeck in sight. Order was everything, and as such nothing was sloppy, excessive or done in haste.

But what they didn't know and what they couldn't see was her world had long ago turned into a gilded cage– enclosing her in a prison in which she remained trapped. It was her burden...and her gift.

But she didn't concern herself with the gilded cage now. Rather, she thought of those who resided within it with her and what the events over the last twenty-four hours would ultimately bring. Murder, in its most brutal form, had landed right on their doorstep…

The wind tore through the valley and swept past the barley, bending the thin stalks so that the entire field shivered in golden waves. She walked through this yellowed sea, the barley grazing her fingertips as the setting sun glowed warm upon her face. Dark hills and trees graced the horizon in front of her, while for acres everywhere else, the field of gold reigned.

This was nature's beauty; the glory of the Earth and what she could create. She was in tune with herself here and centered in her element. Her long, dark hair flew back from her face, and she spread her arms wide to embrace the wind and to feel the moving sea of barley against her legs.

The brief taste of freedom nearly sated her, but she knew it wasn't enough. And at the rate things were rapidly crumbling, who knew if she would ever be free.

There was blood on someone's hands and part of her couldn't help but wonder...but no, he wouldn't do something so drastic, not for her. When they had been children he'd sworn to protect her, to save her no matter what. Had all the years of promising finally come true in one cruel, brutal act of devotion?

She supposed at this point nothing could be ruled out. Including the notion that Liam had resorted to murder.

Chapter One

September 4th, 1990
Euphora

It was the absence of crying that alarmed those who witnessed her birth.

She emerged into the world without so much as a peep, and as Thea held the tiny baby in her arms, she realized with curiosity that the child was in perfect health. Not that there had been a doubt, the entire pregnancy had been a breeze with no complications. The baby had hardly kicked, never turned or twisted, and had remained in relative harmony.

But to not even wail or gurgle as tiny lungs gulped in air for the first time…that was just odd. And yet, as Thea would come to understand through the years, this was just who Rhiannon was. She never spoke unless words were necessary and it would never occur to her to complain or disobey her elders. She was the ideal child–perfect in every way.

"Why isn't she crying? Is something wrong?" Serendipity huffed, out of breath and miserable as she lay on the bed.

Thea turned and smiled. "She is just a quiet baby. You should be pleased." She began to hand the bundled child to Serendipity, who batted her away with a frustrated groan. "You don't wish to hold your daughter?"

"I've just been through six hours of labor, Thea, I'm exhausted. Take her to Rohan. Let him deal with her. I need to rest." Serendipity rolled over on her side and Clarity proceeded to cover her face with a damp cloth fragranced with subtle lavender to urge her into sleep.

"Six hours is nothing," Thea muttered under her breath as she swept from the room, tiny Rhiannon tucked in a soft, green blanket in her arms.

She'd been delivering babies on Euphora for centuries. It still amazed her to see mothers who cared so little for the miracle they had just borne once labor was over. It was rare, but not unheard of. But Serendipity had always been a selfish creature.

Life was precious, and a child was a gift, not a burden. If she had been able to have children herself, she was certain she would have had several. She smiled sadly at the thought, knowing Sebastian would have loved to have children as well. But it wasn't her destiny to bear children, only to watch over those who could.

She paused outside the room where Rohan was anxiously waiting and glanced down at the baby. She looked so peaceful with her eyes still closed. Her breathing was calm and steady, and her head was already graced with dark wisps of hair. She would look just like her father, but only time would tell who she would become as a woman.

Pressing a soft kiss to the child's forehead, Thea opened the door and stepped inside. Rohan was standing in front of the window and Lucian was sitting in the chair beside him reading a book. Upon hearing her, Rohan whirled around, his normally placid and serious face twisted with nerves and anticipation. His dark green eyes shot immediately to the bundle in Thea's arms, and she was pleased to see them fill with joy.

"Is that her? Is that my Rhiannon?" he managed, stepping forward, his hands clenched behind his back as though afraid to reach out and touch her. Lucian stood up and grinned, patting Rohan on the back.

"She's beautiful." Lucian beamed, taking a peek around Thea's arms.

Thea just smiled. "Take your daughter, Rohan," she ordered, holding the child out for him.

He hesitated, shooting a nervous glance to Lucian, who nodded reassuringly. With all the care in the world, he accepted his daughter in his arms and walked over to the chair, sitting down carefully, his eyes never leaving her face. She was, as Lucian had declared, beautiful. And she had come from him. It took all he had to hold back astonished and disbelieving tears.

Thea eyed Lucian expectantly. "You should go and get Liam from the nursery, introduce him to the baby."

He nodded and disappeared out the door. Thea followed, hoping to give the new father a moment alone with the child.

Rohan sat still as a statue, afraid to move or disturb the tiny creature he had helped bring into this world. She fit so delicately in his hands and the crook of his arm. He watched her breathe slowly and peacefully, his mind consumed with wonder and that special something reserved for new fathers. She would need him to guide her, to protect her and to be there for her. And he would do his best to give her the finest life he could, structured and ordered and secure, just as his childhood had been. Under his instruction, she would grow into not only a fine young woman, but the best Earth Dryad Euphora had ever seen.

"Rhiannon…" he murmured, leaning in to press his lips to her forehead. "You are my heart."

A tear escaped and slipped down his cheek. He shut his eyes against the emotion, afraid to embrace it. He wasn't an emotional man but nothing had moved him like this moment of holding his daughter in his hands.

When Lucian returned, he held his sleepy, year and a half old son in his arms. Liam yawned hugely, then rubbed his eyes and stared up owlishly at his father, before looking curiously toward the new baby.

Lucian grinned, his eyes sparkling with delight. "Liam, this is Rhiannon."

He walked over to where Rohan still sat with the baby and held Liam close so he could get a glimpse of her. Liam leaned over, fighting for a better look while keeping a tight grip on his father's shirt, his bright blue eyes wide with wonder.

Rohan watched Liam stare down at his daughter and managed a smile.

"You take care of my little girl, Liam. Be nice to her always."

Liam nodded as he reached out with his finger to gently touch Rhiannon's cheek.

"Boot-ful," he announced, turning back to grin at his father. It was a word that he had heard Lucian use time and time again to describe his mother and this was his first time trying it out.

Lucian laughed and Rohan joined in despite himself.

Pleased to have made the adults smile, Liam beamed at them and repeated himself. As he stared back down at Rhiannon, he knew, even then, that it was true.

The smell of grass and wildflowers filled the air, mixing subtly with the unmistakable scent of baby powder and fresh linen. The lovely, white blanket they rested on crunched upon the grass and a cool, gentle wind caressed the air. A buttercup yellow butterfly landed breezily on the linen, as if momentarily resting its wings. Rhiannon's arm reached out, pure curiosity, to try and touch the newcomer.

When it flew away on a light gust of wind, escaping her still pudgy baby's fingers, she merely watched it go, wondering if would return to visit again.

Beside her, Liam was busy breaking apart graham crackers and methodically making a pile for each of them. He was wearing his favorite denim overalls with a sunny yellow t-shirt, which he had already cheerfully smudged with ketchup at lunch.

His favorite time of the day was being outside and he adored taking care of the baby. He accepted what his young mind thought of as his responsibility with eager enthusiasm, and he took it upon himself to ensure the baby was happy and entertained.

He looked up from separating the crackers to watch her and she smiled at him. He smiled back, easy as rain.

Rhiannon was prettily dressed in a tea green dress with just enough skirt to hide her diaper. In her already generous dark hair was a matching green bow, complete with a plastic lady bug charm.

She was only a year old.

Seated a few yards away were their mothers, busily knitting and gossiping. It was a bright, cheerful sunny day, as it always was on Euphora. And for now, life was peaceful.

"Did you hear the racket the little thing made coming out? I thought my ears might bleed!" Serendipity chuckled, shaking her head. "And she's only gotten worse these last few months."

Clarity sighed, her fingers busily shifting yarn. "Why in the world did you offer to assist Nyxa during her labor in the first place?"

"I didn't offer, Thea coerced me into it. She seemed to think Nyxa and I would bond over the experience." She sent a frosty, meaningful glare to Clarity to emphasize her point. "That woman is insane. Why Brock puts up with her, I will never understand."

"She was the best he could do after you dumped him." Giggling, Clarity patted her friend's arm. "He's never gotten over you, you know."

"Don't I know it." Rolling her eyes, but smirking with pleasure, Serendipity reached for her glass of peach tea and took a generous sip. "But he's distracted now with that little hellion daughter of his. God, I am so glad Rhiannon doesn't cry like that little brat. A year old and Rhiannon's hardly cried once. Sometimes I wonder if something's wrong with her..."

"Oh, be thankful, Serendipity," Clarity demanded, glancing over at the babies. "Liam is a good child, too."

"Yes. I can say with full confidence that I made the right choice in having Rohan's child instead of Brock's." Serendipity visibly shuddered, shaking her head. "Earth Dryads have always been more centered and mature. I don't know what I would do with a Fire Dryad for a child."

"And your father never approved of Brock, so that was really never going anywhere anyway."

"True. Rohan was the perfect suitor. Albeit quite boring in comparison, but he's a good father and he will always be faithful to me. I wouldn't have those same assurances with Brock." Her eyes lit up as she leaned in conspiratorially to her friend. "I heard Thea mention something to Sebastian about how she caught Brock smuggling in demon weapons. Can you imagine? What in the world he needs those for is beyond me..."

"Maybe he's going to challenge Rohan to a duel and win you back." Clarity winked and tossed back her luxurious mane of strawberry blonde hair.

"Perhaps." Amused, Serendipity leaned back in her chair and resumed knitting.

Trinity, the third Muse, appeared behind them and took a seat at the small table, her eyes dancing.

"Did you girls hear about Clynn?" she asked excitedly, eager to spread the latest gossip.

Serendipity eyed her friend. "No, what happened?"

"He just went to Thea and told her he wants to marry a human girl! He even threatened to leave Euphora for good if she refuses to let him."

"Interesting…who is this girl? Is she of proper pedigree?" Serendipity asked, setting aside her knitting.

"No, that's just it!" Trinity gushed. "She's just some girl that works at a coffee shop. She's basically poor and worthless as far as human society goes. Can you imagine?"

"Clynn has always been a bit weird," Clarity chimed in. "I'm sure the idea of marrying someone beneath him doesn't faze him."

"Yes, but you know how Thea is," Trinity continued. "If we're going to choose a human for our mate, they have to be of importance in some way. Like that Enforcer I told you both about, the tall, dark and handsome one."

"Oh yes, he sounds most agreeable." Clarity nodded in approval.

"You just have to tell him your intentions, Trinity," Serendipity advised. "Or perhaps your father can arrange the marriage for you."

"I didn't even think of that," Trinity mused, though her eyes narrowed. "But that hasn't been done in some time."

"Please, my parents' marriage was arranged," Clarity declared, chin up proudly. "If you recall, my father was a very talented French painter and it was my grandfather who petitioned him for marriage to my mother. Unfortunately, he died young so I really don't remember him. But I like to think that I am more in tune with our work because of my artistic roots."

"That is definitely true," Serendipity agreed. "I, for one, think that arranged marriages are a splendid idea. It takes all the messiness out of selecting a proper husband. There's little emotion involved and it's really like a business transaction. In fact, my marriage was essentially arranged."

"Except that Rohan worships the ground you walk on," Trinity said, rolling her eyes.

"This may be true but our relationship is still very much business. As is yours, Clarity."

"Lucian is kind." Clarity ran her hands through her hair as she eyed her friends knowingly. "You remember when we were teens, he and I made a promise that if we didn't find anyone else by our twentieth birthday, that we would get married. And so it happened."

"I have considered arranging Rhiannon's marriage. The best thing for a child is direction and structure, and I plan on giving Rhiannon both of those things."

"You rebelled for years after being beholden to your parents' structure, Serendipity," Trinity reminded her friend. "Don't you worry she will do the same?"

"Not my daughter," Serendipity said assuredly, daring them both to dispute her. "I will mold her into the perfect woman and guide her to the perfect marriage. One sniff about rebelling and I will squash those hopes immediately."

Clarity glanced over at Trinity, both looking wary. "You don't think that's a bit harsh?"

Serendipity scoffed as if she couldn't believe they were disagreeing with her. "Not at all. She will benefit from my instruction and Rohan's as well."

"If you say so." Trinity glanced up as Rohan and Lucian strolled down the pathway, heading straight for the babies. Both men crouched down beside the children, smiling.

"You save some graham crackers for me?" Lucian cheerfully asked Liam.

"Nope! All mine." Liam grinned up at his father.

Rohan watched Rhiannon, admiring her. She just watched him back, eyes already as green as grass. It amazed him how docile she was, how calm and easygoing. And when she looked at him as she was doing now, he swore her little mind was working through all manner of thoughts and observations.

"We're still waiting for her to say her first word," Rohan told Lucian, looking worried. "Thea says she should have at least said something by now, but she's convinced Rhiannon is just quiet by nature."

"Be happy she's so quiet," Lucian chuckled with a grin. "Liam does nothing but ramble on all night and day, don't you, boyo?"

Liam beamed and then happily began to make farm animal noises. Lucian glanced back at Rohan, eyebrows raised. "See?"

Rohan smiled and then looked down at Rhiannon. She was watching Liam with serious eyes, as if pondering the strange noises. He watched as her mouth opened and he heard her say something so quiet he could barely make it out.

"Wait, I think she just said something." Rohan knelt down closer to her. Lucian put a hand on Liam's shoulder, encouraging him to be quiet. "What did you say, Rhiannon?"

She looked up at her father and then back to Liam.

"Lee-um," she said, so soft it was barely a word.

"Liam?" Rohan choked out, astonished. He stared wide eyed at Lucian. "She just said Liam."

Lucian ruffled his son's hair and smiled. "Did you hear that?"

Liam's eyes widened as understanding came to him. When she said his name again, he burst into raucous laughter and leapt up to dance in place.

"That's me, that's me!" he boasted, excited when his father lifted him into his arms.

"Can you say her name?" Lucian asked, kissing his son's nose.

"Ree-ah..." Liam attempted, his face screwed up in concentration. Lucian just laughed and held him close.

"Rhia is good, boyo. Rhia is real good."

Liam tried the name out again, deciding he liked it.

Rohan watched his daughter, tears in his eyes. "Incredible," he mumbled, his head shaking.

Rhiannon only continued to sit quietly, looking at those around her as if nothing extraordinary had happened at all.

Her fingers itched to touch, grazing lightly over glass and fragranced silk, marveling at the loveliness of it all. Her mother's dressing table, covered by dozens of perfumes, powders, jeweled boxes and silk flowers…it was like something out of a fairytale; a little girl's dream come true.

Sunlight poured through the window, filtering through gauzy silk curtains. It shimmered and sparkled over the glass bottles, giving everything a rosy glow.

This was her favorite place in the castle. Her parents' room and the dressing table with its soft, plush stool and pink silks draped everywhere. And, the best part was, it smelled exactly like her mother.

The mirror above the dressing table was broad with an elegant, gilded frame. It was attached to the glass table, which had legs in the shape of scrolls with floral accents.

Rhiannon sat tentatively on the stool, knowing her mother was in the bathroom taking one of her hour long baths with all the frothy scented bubbles. Glancing around, her eyes caught her reflection in the mirror over the table, and she briefly stared, lost in thought.

Where her mother had long, generously curled hair the color of honey, Rhiannon's hair was stick straight and bark brown. Where her mother's eyes were clear and blue as the morning sky, her own eyes seemed a dull green. Her mother's face was heart-shaped and beautiful, while Rhiannon's cheeks were still chubby in a rounded face with no trace of beauty she could see in her four years of age.

Reaching carefully, she lifted the top from one of the bottles, pulling it toward her to smell. With a gentle sigh she set it back down in its exact place, knowing her mother would notice if it had been moved. Then she reached for her mother's powder with its lovely puff. She glanced up at the mirror and pretended to put it on, mimicking her mother as she had often watched her. Next she reached for one of Serendipity's many lovely scarves.

Draping it over her shoulders she looked back in the mirror, wondering if she'd look like her mother now. But, no, she still didn't.

Putting the scarf back, she cautiously opened one of the many jeweled boxes, lifting out a glittering, diamond-encrusted necklace. She held it to her neck, watching the light catch and imagined getting ready for a lavish party. Her mother always smiled when there was a party to attend, and her father always wore a suit and looked so handsome.

Thinking of him, she put the necklace away, slipped off the stool and tiptoed toward his solid oak dresser, where he kept his bottles of cologne, cuff links, watches and cigars. She sniffed one of the colognes, relishing what she recognized as his scent. She replaced the bottle delicately, then wandered over to sit on her parents' giant four-poster bed to wait for her mother to finish her bath so they could go downstairs for dinner.

She glanced around the room, content; comforted by the surroundings of her parents. Her mother's tidy silk draperies in cool pastels, and her father's oak furniture and bookcase housing his favorite novels. She'd looked through them before, at least the ones she could reach, but she'd only flipped through the pages, unable to understand most of the words. But doing so was like spending time with him and that was something she cherished.

Soon her mother would be done with her bath and would begin primping at the dressing table. She always said it was necessary for a woman to look her absolute best when in the presence of others and that proper manners were of vital importance. Rhiannon learned early on that her mother didn't tolerate dirty hands or wrinkled clothes.

She imagined herself growing up to be just like her mother; tall, slender, beautiful…to her, her mother was perfect.

Sometimes, Rhiannon looked at the other children with their parents–especially Capri with her mother, and she wondered why hers acted so different. Heidi was always holding Capri, always kissing her and tickling her. Her own mother never did anything like that. But she was beautiful, so maybe she wasn't supposed to.

Inspired, Rhiannon slid off the bed and padded back to the dressing table, eyeing herself in the mirror again. Maybe if she could make herself more beautiful, like her mother, then maybe her mother would kiss and hug her. And maybe her father would swing her up and spin her around the way she'd seen Lucian do with Liam. Liam had laughed and laughed, and his father had smiled so brightly. Her father never smiled like that.

She heard her mother pull the drain on the bath. She hurried to sit back on the bed, content with the hope that one day she would be beautiful enough to be loved.

Chapter Two

A few days after her fourth birthday, her education began.

Not only was she taught general studies such as writing, reading, mathematics, science, and the history of humans and Euphora, but she would also begin her lessons with her father on how to use her Dryad powers.

Though she didn't show it, Rhiannon was thrilled to finally get the chance to learn. For a year she had watched Liam studying in the classroom the Muses used for teaching, while she herself had been forced to sit with the babies. She was more than ready to put her already active mind to use.

For centuries, the Muses were responsible for educating the children of Euphora in general subjects. They utilized a room on the second floor of the castle with big, airy windows that let in lots of natural light. Scattered throughout the room were desks and tables, the walls lined with bookcases filled with art books, history, literature, math, science, and more.

Depending on the amount of students, either one, two, or all three of the Muses would participate in instructing the children. Currently there were only four students so Serendipity was the only teacher.

She led Rhiannon into the classroom, pointing at one of the desks in the front.

"Sit," she quietly ordered. Rhiannon obeyed without a word, taking her seat and looking around in wonder. Her serious eyes took in every detail, from the view of the courtyard through the windows, to the stone walls covered with lovely landscape paintings, to the sturdy oak wood of the desk and chair she sat in. In front of her was a stack of blank paper and a wood pencil sharpened to a fine point.

She heard the door open behind her, but refrained from turning around. She was too focused on learning to think about anything else.

When Liam sat at a desk a couple of feet away from her, she glanced over despite herself.

"Hi, Rhia," he greeted happily, setting down his bag filled with books, papers, pencils and some toys he'd managed to sneak past his father's watchful eye. He began tapping his hands on the desk, full of boundless energy.

Rhiannon just watched him, noting how his messy, black curls fell over his face, thinking he should trim them. He had peanut butter smudged on his cheek, probably from breakfast, that needed to be cleaned off. And all the noise he was making was going to attract the attention of her mother, who would scold him.

Agitated, she sat rigid in her seat, trying not to think of those things. But her neat and orderly mind couldn't shut out the noise, so she turned and shushed him, her finger pointed and held against her lips like she'd seen her mother do so many times.

He stopped and grinned at her. "I want to learn to play the drums," he announced, his fingers itching to start again. But she only stared at him, her face serious, and he looked away, hurt by her disinterest.

"Sit up straight, Liam, and pull out your homework," Serendipity ordered, her voice as smooth as whipped cream but the message firm. She glided past, her eyes noticing everything, including her daughter's rigid back and primly folded hands on the surface of her desk. She pursed her mouth, noting a few strands of Rhiannon's hair had slipped from its hair clip. "Fix your hair, Rhiannon."

Standing in front of her daughter's desk, Serendipity watched as Rhiannon hurriedly fixed her hair. Moments later, she looked up with eager eyes, hoping she had met her mother's expectations. When Serendipity nodded slightly, Rhiannon felt relief course through her. She wasn't in trouble after all.

Just then, Brogan and Rian entered the classroom, the last two old enough to be taught. Rian was already seven years old, the oldest of all the children on Euphora, and Brogan was four, same as Rhiannon.

"Have a seat, boys," Serendipity chimed, watching as the two took the remaining desks behind Rhiannon and Liam.

Rian dutifully pulled out his homework. Brogan sat still as a frightened statue, his dark eyes big as saucers. It was his first day of school, too.

"Rian, please pull out your math book and begin working on your multiplication tables. Liam, begin reading the short story *The Cat and the Hare* on page 176 of your English book." Serendipity stood, watching as the two boys got to work. Nodding, she looked down at her daughter.

"Rhiannon, I want you and Brogan to come with me over to the workstation under the window. We're going to work on your writing skills today."

Without a word, Rhiannon slid from her chair and neatly gathered up her paper and her pencil, then walked purposefully toward the large, round table under the window. She took a seat in one of the small chairs, tucking her skirt underneath her to avoid wrinkles before folding her hands in her lap and waiting patiently.

Brogan glanced nervously at Rian, who nodded at him in reassurance. He trudged over toward Rhiannon, only to have Serendipity clear her throat and point at the paper and pencil that he had forgotten at his desk. Blushing, he raced back to gather them and then sat across from Rhiannon, his eyes cast downward.

Rhiannon watched him curiously, wondering why he was so nervous when she felt so eager.

Serendipity strolled over and sat with them, and began her careful instruction.

While other children may have noticed a difference between the studious way their parent talked with them as a teacher, versus the gentle, persuasive way they talked with them as a parent, Rhiannon noticed no such difference.

Her mother was her usual self–cool, removed, stern and critical. She possessed a heartbreaking face but her eyes were sharp more often than soft. And although her voice could sound as enchanting as the chiming of a bell, it could also cut to the bone when she was disappointed.

Serendipity never raised her voice, never cried and rarely smiled unless it was a brief curving of her mouth. But despite this, Rhiannon wanted nothing more than to emulate her mother in every way. In fact, she wanted to *be* her mother because that was all she knew.

After a few hours, Serendipity released them for lunch, the day's lesson finished.

Liam waited for Rhiannon to gather up her things and slip them into the bag her mother had given her. When she finished, she spotted Liam waiting by the door for her, his own bag slung over his shoulder and a goofy grin on his face.

Unable to help it, she smiled back, feeling pleased at completing her writing assignments well. She skipped toward him, feeling genuinely happy.

"Walk, Rhiannon," Serendipity scolded, crossing her arms and eyeing her daughter. Rhiannon slowed to a walk, feeling repentant as she glanced back at her mother briefly before disappearing out the door into the hallway.

They headed down to the dining hall together. Liam was rattling on about how Rhiannon was going to love being in class and if she needed any help that he could help her. Then he launched into a discussion of the stories he'd read that day and how he could read them to her if she'd like.

Quiet as always, she merely listened and sat down with him at the table, content to let him do all the talking.

As she listened, her eyes watched the fairies.

Hundreds of them flew around her, nothing more than glowing golden lights most commonly confused with fireflies. As they zipped across the surface of the dining table, various dishes and food items appeared, transported from the kitchen.

Sometimes Rhiannon would sneak into the kitchen, fascinated to watch them work. She loved it there, especially the small greenhouse that was connected to it that housed the vegetable and herb garden. She was fascinated with the fairies, even though most of the others never even noticed them.

She felt as if she had a secret friendship with them, even though they couldn't speak her language nor did they pay any attention to her.

"Thank you," she whispered as the fairies finished laying out lunch. And then they disappeared, off to clean the castle or wash the linens or prepare bread for that evening's dinner.

"You know they don't understand you, right?" Liam told her with a laugh.

Rhiannon nodded, knowing he wouldn't understand. She liked thanking them. Her mother had raised her with impeccable manners and it was always proper to thank those who served you, even though Serendipity never took her manners quite this far. Rhiannon silently hoped that one day her mother would see her doing it and then would praise her for being so considerate.

Tucking her thought away, she reached for a ham sandwich and an apple as Brock entered the room, Blythe on his hip.

"But I want chocolate cake!" Blythe was yelling at the top of her lungs, tears already in her eyes.

Brock just laughed. "Babycakes, you ain't getting chocolate cake until dessert. You'll have to settle for some applesauce and a cheese sandwich until then."

She pouted, but quieted down. She really liked cheese sandwiches and the thought distracted her from the chocolate cake.

Brock sat her down beside Liam and then took the seat beside her. He fixed her a plate and with a loving smile, he tucked her napkin into the collar of her bright orange shirt, then placed a quick kiss on her nose. She giggled and dug into her sandwich.

Rhiannon watched out of the corner of her eye, feeling an emotion she couldn't describe rush through her. Years later, she'd understand it was envy. Pure, yet undeniably healthy, envy.

As if to further perpetuate this strange feeling she had, her own father entered the dining hall, looking distracted and stressed. He sat down across the table from her and hurriedly grabbed a turkey sandwich and a scoop of potato salad. Without even acknowledging anyone else, he began to eat in fast gulps, as though he were late for something.

"Looks like you're getting some gray hairs there, Rohan," Brock commented, smirking in between bites of his giant roast beef sub.

Rohan glared, his green eyes sharp with disdain. "Some of us take our work seriously, Brock. Gray hairs are only an occupational hazard."

Brock chuckled, shaking his head as he took another bite of his sandwich. As he swallowed, he looked back over at Rohan, a dangerous fire in his eyes even though his lips were still curved. "Betcha my girl doesn't like screwing an old man. Tell me, does Serendipity ever call out my name while you're fumbling around in the dark, knowing, as you do, that you can never be me?"

Rohan paled as his eyes widened and shot to his daughter, who was watching him curiously. He turned back to Brock, furious.

"There are children present!" he managed, fighting to hold back the urge to throttle the man then and there. How dare he say such disgusting, vile filth in the presence of the children?

"That's enough, Brock," Serendipity said sternly as she entered the room, having heard the exchange between her husband and her ex-lover. She glided along, taking a seat beside Rohan, her cool blue eyes on Brock.

Brock watched her, unable to hide the lust in his eyes.

"I apologize, Serendipity." He bowed his head slightly, although it appeared more as a challenge than in repentance.

She tilted her head so she was looking down at him, her lips parted slightly as she let out a soft sigh. It was also a challenge and the message was understood. There was still fire between them, although neither would do anything about it. They both did their best to assure themselves that they were long past their desire for each other.

Turning to her husband, Serendipity patted his arm.

"Calm down, Rohan. Your daughter does not need to see you losing your temper," she said coolly as she spooned salad onto her plate. She drizzled it with a meager amount of balsamic dressing and then poured herself a small glass of fruit juice.

Rhiannon watched her mother's every movement, noting how she held the juice pitcher, how she held her fork, how she looked when she chewed. She was determined to emulate her.

Liam had already turned to Blythe and was busy tickling her. When Rhiannon noticed, she shifted away from them, feeling lost and excluded.

Three days later, she stood in the Greenhouse, mesmerized.

Her father's work area was referred to as the Greenhouse, even though it was not a house for growing plants. On the contrary, he referred to it as a house for growing the Earth.

It was a rectangular structure attached to the far east side of the castle, with glass walls and a steeply arched glass roof with a few panels pushed open to the sky, letting in glowing rays of sunlight. Ivy crawled up the walls on the outside, spreading its thin, leafy arms greedily across the glass, covering nearly half of the building.

On the inside, stepping stones were laid across the ground with bright green moss lining the spaces between. There were small, verdant fruit trees lining the walls and various plants growing in pots scattered throughout. Her father's many experiments and projects were also housed here, including his dabbling in new breeds of trees and crops. On three separate corkboards were his charts and graphs showing animal migration patterns, earthquake data and monthly plans, and his hundreds of detailed, scientific drawings of his creations. There was a drafting table in the corner, covered with his latest work.

In the middle of the room was a small pond that appeared bottomless, its dark depths a mystery to her. It was lined with stones, almost more like a well. It showed her father a scale model of the Earth so he could do his work.

She'd been here only a few times before, but today was the first day he was going to begin teaching her how to use her powers. She was even more excited than she had been attending class for the first time. This was, as her father stressed to her, the most important role she would ever have in this life.

"Come here, Rhiannon." He motioned toward the board with his latest drawings on it. One of the drawings she noticed as she approached was of a lovely, vivid purple flower.

He pointed at the flower drawing and glanced at her, his eyes patient.

"This is a new breed of flower I've designed. It's in the viola family. I've developed it to have larger petals and leaves enriched with additional vitamin A, vitamin C and antioxidants. The viola species is used for medicinal purposes and I have created this breed to be much more potent for that use," he explained, watching her closely. "I am going to show you today how to create it, and how we can select where they will grow. Are you ready?"

She nodded, her hands politely clasped in front of her. He led the way toward a small table near the pond that held a good-sized ceramic pot filled with rich, moist soil.

There was a chair beside the table, and without a word he lifted her up and set her on it so she could see the pot more clearly. The thrill she felt at having him hold her, even though it was brief, stayed with her as she watched avidly.

"I want you to watch me first and then I will show you," he instructed as he held out his hands inches above the soil. He closed his eyes and concentrated. Rhiannon kept her eyes glued to the soil, eager to watch the flower bloom.

A few seconds later, green tendrils slowly crept out of the dirt, spiraling skyward. Leaves began to bud and sprout from the stems, soft and diamond shaped. Rohan opened his eyes and examined the progress of his creation. They seemed to brighten to a more lucid, vivid green–almost as if they were glowing, as he continued to direct the growth of the plant.

Suddenly, a final stem rose from the ground, a bud appearing at the tip, and Rhiannon watched eagerly as the bud began to open, almost in a dance as it swayed and curved into its final position. The petals opened to reveal a glorious, vivid purple flower, complete with tiny black dots and a yellow core. The petals were diamond-shaped, matching the leaves.

Rhiannon stared in fascination, even after Rohan was done. He watched his daughter's fingers twitch, and could tell she was eager to touch it but would not do so without permission.

"You can touch the flower, Rhiannon," he said, smiling at the pleasure in her eyes.

She reached out tentatively and brushed her fingertips over the purple petals in a caress.

"I want to know how," she said, looking at him with eyes much too serious for a girl so young. "Please. Teach me."

He nodded. "Hold your hands over the soil."

She did as he requested, her eyes still on his.

"I want you to close your eyes and imagine you are inside the dirt, burrowed deep down where it's dark and moist. Imagine the seed growing out of nothing." He paused for a moment, waiting for her. "Have you got it?"

She nodded, her eyes closed in complete concentration.

"Good. Now imagine the stems growing from the seed. Guide them up to the surface, but go slow, don't rush. Nature prefers to take her time."

Rhiannon felt the odd sensation of power tingling in her arms, pulsating deep within and surging out of the palm of her hand. Even though visibly it appeared as though nothing was happening, in her mind's eye she pictured the seed and its subtle progress of becoming a lovely flower.

When she opened her eyes, her flower sat next to her father's. It was slightly smaller and the petals were odd sizes, but otherwise it was a perfect replica.

Concerned with the defects in the flower, she focused harder, wanting to make it perfect. Rohan watched in amazement at her attention to detail and marveled at his daughter's determination. He had been blessed with a prodigy and her ambition humbled him.

"Excellent," he said when she'd finished and glanced up at him expectantly. A tiny smile graced her face at earning his praise.

Lifting her down from the chair, he set aside their flowers and led her over to the pond.

"Now that you've seen how we create one flower, let me show you how we transplant them." He stopped in front of the pond and held out his hands, knowing Rhiannon would stand patiently at his side and watch.

Summoning the power deep within, he beckoned a smooth orb from the depths of the water. It seemed to appear from nothing and then rose, glasslike and spinning, into the air over the water. It was nearly the same diameter as the little pond, roughly three feet, and as it spun it began to take on the appearance of the world. Continents appeared, green and brown, while the oceans turned blue and the clouds wisped over. When it was complete, the globe ceased to spin and sat still, hovering over the pond.

Rohan glanced down at his daughter, pleased at the wonder on her face. She looked as though he had performed a miracle, and nothing had ever made him feel more important.

"The point of using the globe, Rhiannon, is that it allows us to monitor everything we do for the Earth. We not only use it to plant and grow flora or plant life, but we can also keep track of and maintain the fauna, or animal life. This will be your most useful tool, once you are ready for it. All the charts, the drawings, the planning…none of it matters without this." Inspired, he smiled at her, earning a small smile in return as he lifted his arms again and, using his hands, spun the globe around until China was visible. "Now, let's go ahead and plant these violets."

Rhiannon watched in astonishment as her father pointed his index finger, barely a few inches above the surface of the globe, and tiny white lights the size of grains of sand materialized from the tip of his finger and floated toward the land. As each light landed on the surface, it stayed lit, showing where he had planted the seeds. After placing at least forty separate lights, he pulled his hand away and examined his work.

"Each of the lights is a cluster of seeds, specifically the seed I just showed you how to create. Our greatest tool, other than the globe, is our mind. We use it to create and to imagine our gift as we improve the world." He tilted his head down to look at her, his eyes serious. "Our work is very important. Everything we do affects the ecosystem of our planet and must all be for the purpose of maintaining balance. We have been entrusted by Thea and our creator to carry out this responsibility." He saw her nod seriously and he hoped he wasn't overloading her. But then again, she had already proven herself to be more proficient than he had been at her age. "I know it's a lot to handle right now, but you have years to learn and to practice your craft. And one day you will take over and run all of this on your own." He spread his arms out, motioning to the entire Greenhouse.

"Can you show me more?" she asked politely.

He nodded. "Would you like to see how we make an earthquake?"

"Yes," she replied, her demeanor calm and reserved while on the inside she was jumping with the childlike enthusiasm she wasn't allowed to show.

Hours later, after he'd walked her through everything there was about being an Earth Dryad and helped her practice using her powers, Rohan looked at his daughter and knew she was going to be excellent. She had so much promise, such natural ability and intelligence, that he was struck blind with pride.

But, in his usual manner, he kept his comments to himself and set aside emotion for the sake of keeping things tidy and neat, as he preferred. His own father had been strict with him, stern and all-knowing. He intended to do the same with his own child, guiding her with a strong hand down the path to success.

Yet even he, a man reserved, grounded, and cautious with his mind and most especially his heart, could see the longing in his daughter's eyes as she stared out the glass walls of the Greenhouse.

Lucian was chasing Liam in the courtyard, bubbles floating all around them as they ran, both grinning and laughing.

Lucian gripped his son around the waist and lifted him high up into the air, spinning him around before nimbly setting him on his shoulders.

Rhiannon watched them with somber eyes, silently wishing she could play, too. But there was work to be done and play would always take second place.

Though he didn't expect it, Rohan's gut clenched and his heart ached as he watched his daughter. He knew he could never give her that kind of affection, could never play with her like that. He just didn't know how. He loved her with a depth so great it filled and enriched his very soul, but he lacked the power to show emotion. He wasn't the kind to laugh easily, nor smile with true joy, or even love with explosive passion.

And though it pained him, he knew that in the end Rhiannon was destined to grow up to be just like him. He only hoped she learned to cope with the emptiness of a cold heart better than he did.

Chapter Three

Laughter rang out through the misty morning air, joining in with the cheerful sound of birds basking in another beautiful day. Sunlight poured through the vast trees and shone upon the cobblestone walkway and grass in hazy pools of golden light.

The flowers were in glorious bloom, the scents carrying on the air, light and fresh. Plump honeybees and delicate butterflies drifted from plant to plant, content in this peaceful paradise.

As Rhiannon walked holding Capri's tiny hand, she took a deep breath to inhale the glory of it all. This was her home and she loved it with all her heart. This was what she knew and she couldn't imagine life where the humans lived. At the tender age of five, she preferred Euphora and the safety of the walls that one day she'd consider her cage.

But until then, she was content to stroll along with Capri, who was like her little sister. Kind, gentle Capri, with her slightly curled strands of pale blonde hair and her wide gray eyes, so sweet and shy, with a mouth that was almost always smiling. Rhiannon adored her and found herself constantly seeking to be in the younger girl's presence, if only because she brought comfort.

Ahead of them, Blythe and Liam skipped and chased each other, laughing loudly and calling out, teasing and taunting. It was a game they knew well, something that seemed to bond them together in a way that had made Rhiannon feel like an outsider until Capri came along.

While Blythe and Liam were both energetic, spontaneous and loud, Rhiannon and Capri were both subdued, thoughtful and shy. And it appealed to Rhiannon's sense of responsibility to be in charge of Capri while they played together, at least the rare times she was given permission to take a break from her studies and join in.

But today she was with them, and her heart felt included enough to be satisfied.

"Let's play hide and seek!" Blythe shouted suddenly, whirling around to face the others.

"Yeah!" Liam exclaimed, tapping Blythe's shoulder. "And you're it!"

"Okay, but you better choose a good spot 'cause I'm the best seeker there is!" she announced as she danced off to a nearby tree, pressing her face against it with her arms covering her head. She began to count, her high-pitched voice almost screaming, just to be sure they heard her.

Rhiannon watched as Liam bolted away, off to the far left corner of the courtyard. She paused for a moment, distracted as she spotted her mother and Thea strolling down the cobblestone pathway, heading out to handle a food delivery in the meadow. Though her eyes followed her mother, Serendipity did not glance over, but instead continued her conversation with Thea, oblivious at how desperate her own child was for her attention.

Pushing thoughts of her mother away, Rhiannon anxiously chewed her bottom lip, wondering where she should hide and whether or not to take Capri with her.

Capri looked at her for instruction and Rhiannon decided to hide with her. They'd find a good spot and hopefully Blythe would find Liam first.

Her heart pounding with excitement and adrenaline, Rhiannon walked swiftly over to Thea's rose garden. Large rose bushes were clumped together, filled with fragrant red, pink and yellow blooms. Crouching behind one of the bushes with Capri, Rhiannon put her finger to her lips, urging her friend to be quiet.

Rhiannon held Capri's hand, anxiously waiting for Blythe to finish counting. Her entire body quivered and she shut her eyes to fight the urge to give up and run away. This was what playing was, and even though she didn't know much about it, she wanted desperately to be included.

"Ready or not, here I come!" Blythe shrieked, a giggle escaping her throat as she whirled around and scanned the gardens, searching for her friends. Then she was on the hunt.

Rhiannon could hear Blythe tromping around through the shrubs, examining every good hiding place as she went. When the sounds got louder, she knew Blythe was heading in their direction.

She met Capri's eyes, and had to bite back a smile and a giggle as they heard Blythe coming closer. Capri looked away, however, distracted by one of the pink roses in front of her. Her hand reached out, and before Rhiannon could pull it back, Blythe jumped out at them and yelled "Gotcha!"

Startled, Capri's hand instinctively clamped around the stem of the rose. She looked down at her hand, feeling the sharp and sudden pain, and spotted the blood. With a terrified glance up at Rhiannon, her eyes began to well with tears.

Blythe, not noticing what had happened, skipped off cheerfully and called for Liam to come out.

Rhiannon stared at Capri, not knowing what to do as her friend began to cry. Frightened, she stood up and looked around, and saw Heidi nearby, trimming roses and putting them in a basket.

The woman turned in Rhiannon's direction, her soft brown eyes honing in as she heard her daughter crying.

Within seconds Heidi was lifting Capri into her arms, cooing and smiling, relieved it was only a tiny prick from a thorn, and not something much worse. With a kind smile, she patted Rhiannon's head and carried Capri away, kissing her tear stained cheeks and holding her close, making light of the situation to calm her daughter down.

Trembling, Rhiannon watched Heidi and Capri disappear inside the castle, her heart still thudding in her chest. She stared at the roses and without thinking she gripped one of the stems hard, letting the thorns pierce her skin.

Her brows creased together with pain as she pulled her hand away, staring numbly at the blood that now dripped from several cuts on her skin.

She didn't know what had driven her to do it, but seeing the way Capri's mother had swept her away, holding her and kissing her, had struck a chord within her. This was, although she didn't know it, an experiment.

Holding her hand out, her face expressionless and her eyes dry as the desert, she headed off to where she had seen her mother go with Thea. She saw the two women standing beside the large oak tree, taking inventory on a few crates that had been dropped off by a couple of Enforcers.

The pain in her hand barely registered as she walked through the meadow, her eyes on her mother, her mind blank.

Serendipity turned as Rhiannon approached, her hand pressed against the small of her back as she supported her heavily pregnant belly. When she saw the blood on her daughter's hand, she let out an impatient hiss.

"What did you do, Rhiannon?" Serendipity scolded, her ice blue eyes sharp as glass. "You shouldn't be so careless."

Thea looked over and watched the situation unfold with troubled eyes. She could see exactly what the young Earth Dryad was doing. She was testing the waters and hoping for a result that would, unfortunately, never occur.

Serendipity rolled her eyes at Thea and grimaced. "I'll be right back."

Thea just nodded, biting her tongue. She wanted to scold the young mother for being so heartless. But she knew it wouldn't do any good. It was Serendipity's nature to act that way and she was unlikely to see past her selfish ways for years to come.

Serendipity grabbed Rhiannon's wrist and pulled her through the meadow and into the courtyard, her pace brisk despite her pregnancy. Rhiannon fell into step beside her, fighting against the disappointment she felt.

They headed into the castle and up to her parents' room, where Serendipity shut the door behind them and ushered Rhiannon into the bathroom.

With a heavy sigh, she opened the cabinet and pulled out bandages and ointment, and set them on the counter. Crossing her arms, she turned to her daughter, her face grim.

"Wash your hand with soap," she ordered.

Rhiannon did as she was told, biting back against the pain from the cuts on her hand. When she was finished, she toweled her hand off and stared at her mother.

"Now put ointment on the cuts so they don't get infected."

Rhiannon had a hard time gripping the tube of disinfectant, but she managed to squeeze a tiny bit onto her hand. She spread it around and winced as it burned, but still she did not cry.

"Put the bandage over it," Serendipity instructed, her voice even, but tinged with irritation. "This should teach you to be more careful, Rhiannon. I don't have time to deal with you getting hurt. Next time, you can come up here and do this yourself."

Rhiannon bandaged her cuts, and nodded solemnly. She believed every word her mother said and blamed her own foolishness. She shouldn't have bothered her mother and it was stupid to cut herself on purpose.

Serendipity swept from the room, leaving behind the vivid scent of sweet pea and vanilla.

Rhiannon never asked her mother for anything ever again.

When her little sister was born, Rhiannon saw a side of her father she'd never seen before.

She watched him warily, nervous at his agitation and fear as he paced back and forth in the guest room a few doors away from where Serendipity was currently giving birth. Lucian was there, offering words of comfort as the hours stretched on, seemingly endless.

"It won't be much longer now," Lucian said reassuringly, sitting beside Rhiannon on the bed and resting his hand lightly on her shoulder. She stared curiously at his hand, not sure why the gesture hurt more than comforted.

"It's been nearly twelve hours," Rohan groaned, running his hands through his slightly graying hair, his eyes meeting his friend's. "When Rhiannon was born, it took half that. Something must be wrong."

"Nothing is wrong, twelve hours is still fairly normal," Lucian insisted, motioning with his eyes to Rhiannon so Rohan wouldn't alarm her. "Everything will be fine."

Nodding but still anxious, Rohan began pacing again. He stopped in his tracks as a sudden loud, shrieking cry pierced through the stone walls, echoing down the corridor and filling the castle. Alarmed, he whirled around, his eyes frantic. "What was that?"

Lucian grinned, standing up to pat his friend on the back. "That's probably your new daughter."

Rohan looked dumbfounded. "But..." He glanced at Rhiannon, who was sitting patiently and quietly on the bed, watching him. He was about to remind Lucian that when Rhiannon had been born there had been no shrieking cry. But then he realized that his daughter was just unique that way. In fact, now that he thought of it, had he ever really heard or seen his little girl cry?

His thoughts were disrupted as Thea suddenly walked in, a pink bundle in her arms. She smiled at Rohan and handed him the baby, wiping the sweat from her brow, clearly exhausted.

"Mom and the baby are both fine," Thea assured him, watching as he held his new daughter. She noted he seemed distracted and unsure, and that he kept looking at Rhiannon instead of the new baby.

"I want to see my wife," he said, pushing the baby back into Thea's arms. "She might need me."

He left the room swiftly, leaving Thea and Lucian alone with the baby and Rhiannon.

Sighing, Thea met eyes with Lucian. "Let me guess. He's worried because this time it took twice as long to deliver the baby as it had the first time?"

Lucian smiled and nodded. "I tried to tell him that twelve hours isn't all that odd, but he worries nonetheless."

Shaking her head, Thea turned to face Rhiannon. "Would you like to meet your new sister?"

The little girl nodded, waiting good-naturedly for Thea to take a seat beside her and to shift the baby up so she could see.

"This is Sierra. She is a Muse, like your mother."

Rhiannon looked, but did not touch. The first thing she noticed was that she had blonde hair, the same color as their mother's. Jealousy over that settled dully in her stomach. And when the baby opened her eyes, they were the same clear blue as Serendipity's. Rhiannon's heart ached.

She knew she should be happy about having a little sister, but instead she felt confused and hurt.

Awhile later, Rohan led Rhiannon in to see her mother and told her to sit in the wooden chair beside the bed. He had the baby in his arms and went to give her to his wife.

"I'm too exhausted to hold the baby, Rohan. Set her in the crib under the window, that's what it's there for," Serendipity snapped, reaching for a cold compress to put over her aching temple. Labor had given her an intense headache.

He paused and eyed her as if seeing her for the first time.

"You wouldn't hold Rhiannon either," he murmured, more to himself than to her, as he straightened and turned away, gently placing the baby in the wooden crib. He looked down at his new daughter, wondering what his prim and proper wife would do if he just started shouting at her and screaming all the things he'd wanted to say for the last several years, to release all his frustration in one giant tirade. But he knew he couldn't, especially not with Rhiannon in the room. He would be reserved and courteous as always, and keep his comments to himself.

But part of him, somewhere deep inside the locked doors of his heart, began to wonder what it was about Serendipity that kept him bound as if by chains, unable to ever break free.

"I'm a knight, come to save the three princesses from evil!"

"Nuh uh, Liam, I'm not a princess!" Blythe challenged, rearing up to her fullest height, chest puffed out arrogantly. "I'm a witch, but a good one, who uses her powers to also save the helpless princesses!"

"Then we ride together on horses, across the land to get to the castle where the princesses are being held hostage!" Liam pranced around as if on horseback, with Blythe behind him making appropriate galloping noises.

Under the cool, dappled shade of a nearby tree, Rhiannon sat on a white blanket with Capri, braiding flowers into crowns.

She watched Blythe and Liam race around the courtyard, confronting imaginary enemies and battling them with pretend weaponry, crying out war chants as they went.

She was content to rest in the shade with Capri, who was nestled in her lap and leaning against her chest comfortably, her little fingers playing with one of the pink flowers. Around them, the day was sunny and beautiful, as always.

Liam pretended to gallop toward where they were sitting, a big grin on his face. "Don't worry, princesses, we will save you!" he declared before racing off to fight a battle Blythe was engaged in.

Capri giggled and pointed after Liam, looking up at Rhiannon with bright eyes. "Hero!" she called out, her expression adoring and sweet.

Rhiannon smiled in return, pressing a neat kiss to the top of Capri's head. "Yes, Liam is our hero."

On impulse, she hugged Capri, relishing in the simplicity of the love she felt for her. She'd never been affectionate with anyone before, but with Capri it was easy and came naturally.

She spotted a little boy walking toward them, about Liam's age, his chin held so high in the air it almost appeared as though he were looking up at something. But in reality, he was staring down his nose at everything in his path. He approached Liam and Blythe, who both whirled around.

"Hi there!" Blythe greeted, racing toward the newcomer excitedly. "Who are you?"

Liam followed her, coming to a stop in front of the new boy, not quite as excited as Blythe was. Being the only male Dryad made him naturally protective of the girls and defensive when it came to other boys being around.

The newcomer sneered at Blythe, his sandy colored cap of hair glinting bronze in the sunlight. He was about Liam's height, but rail thin with knobby knees and expensive, formal looking clothing. His hair was combed neatly to the side, not a strand out of place, and his dark blue shorts were pressed and stark against his pristine white button-up shirt.

Rhiannon thought his face looked as though he'd tasted something sour, because his nose and mouth puckered together and his light eyebrows creased over his eyes in distaste.

"My name is Michael," he announced, adding as much authority to his voice as he could. "My father is an Enforcer. We are here on business. Who are you?"

"I'm Blythe," she greeted, although she was looking at the boy as if he were an alien. "So you're a human?"

"Thankfully. I would hate to be a freak like you."

She wasn't used to someone being unabashedly mean to her and she almost missed the context of his comment. But when Liam jolted forward defensively, they all understood what he had meant.

"We are not freaks!" Liam shouted, glaring at the boy angrily.

Michael just smiled haughtily, as if these simpletons had no clue just how superior he was to them.

"You keep telling yourself that, but it doesn't change anything," he huffed, rolling his eyes.

"So you don't have any powers?" Blythe asked inquisitively, her hands on her hips as she stared him down.

He responded to her question with a glare. "I can shoot a gun."

"What's a gun?"

Again, he rolled his eyes. "Too important for you to understand."

"You know what I can do?" She grinned wickedly as she stalked right up to him, getting in his face. She was shorter than him, but daring all the same. She saw him retreat slightly, clearly unnerved by her. "I can shoot fire out of my hands."

"So?" he responded, attempting to sneer again even though there was fear in his eyes.

"So, you wanna see?" she taunted, holding up her hands, palms facing him.

"*Don't!*" he shrieked, backing away and tripping over his own feet, falling to the ground. "I'll tell my father on you!"

Blythe doubled over with laughter, and Liam joined in, both amused by the terrified expression on Michael's face.

"You're gonna run and tell your daddy?" Blythe teased with a grin.

"Shut up!" Scrambling to his feet, Michael lunged toward Blythe, only to have Liam intersect him and push him back to the ground.

"Go away!" Liam shouted, his chest heaving, anger taking control of him.

From beneath the tree, Rhiannon watched the whole scene unfold. Seeing Liam so valiantly defend them all excited her for reasons she couldn't explain. He really was a hero.

Michael brushed at his pants as he sat on the ground, looking humiliated and furious. His eyes shot over and landed on Rhiannon and Capri, who sat in silence beneath the tree.

"What are you looking at?" he snarled, getting to his feet. "You're all nothing but freaks!"

Then he took off toward the castle, where his father was inside meeting with Thea.

Capri looked up at Rhiannon once more, this time her lips pursed in a pout and her eyebrows furrowed.

"Mean," she said quietly, pointing after Michael's retreating figure.

Rhiannon sighed and nodded as she clutched Capri tighter to her, needing comfort.

Yes, there was no doubt in her mind that Michael was a downright, mean little boy.

Chapter Four

It had taken her weeks to perfect her creation, but now that it was done, she was immensely proud of it. It was a lovely, pale pink lily with black spotted petals and a long, tall stem brimming with slender leaves. She'd grown it just as her father had taught her, and put it in a ceramic pot she'd found in the greenhouse.

She hoped her mother would like it.

It was Serendipity's birthday, and there was going to be a big party that night in celebration. Knowing her mother would spend hours at her dressing table, Rhiannon strategically placed the flower amongst her mother's various perfumes and oils.

Then she sat back and waited.

That was nearly an hour ago, and although Serendipity was seated at her dressing table applying her creams and powders, she had yet to comment or even notice the flower.

So Rhiannon waited some more.

Rohan was standing in front of his dresser, putting on a hunter green tie, his elegant fingers expertly sliding along the silk material. Rhiannon's eyes followed the movement of his hands, enchanted.

In her eyes, he was the most handsome of all the men on Euphora, including Sebastian. Her father looked tall and trim in his expertly tailored black suit, gold cufflinks and waves of bark brown hair feathered with strands of gray at his temples. He had a dignified face, tanned and classically handsome, with wise and intelligent eyes.

But there was something wrong with him that she couldn't quite place, and because of her youth had no hope of possibly understanding. But it was still there, and because she was so closely in tune with him, she could sense it as clearly as she could sense her own secret feelings.

"You shouldn't wear that tie, Rohan, it doesn't suit you. Put on the blue one," Serendipity remarked, her eyes flashing at him in the mirror over her dressing table.

His hands paused as he was looping the tie, and his eyes met hers in his own mirror over his dresser. There was a momentary heartbeat of silence as her parents stared each other down. Rhiannon sat between them, anxious and confused.

Then it passed. Rohan removed the tie, opened the drawer in his dresser and put it away. He grabbed the sapphire tie his wife insisted upon and dutifully put it on without saying a word.

Pleased, Serendipity smiled primly and began to powder her face.

"I do hope that Burke brings little Michael along tonight. He is such a bright boy, so much potential," she commented, reaching for her mascara.

"Yes, dear," Rohan replied, his voice hollow and void of emotion as he straightened the tie.

"And there had better be enough champagne and caviar to go around. I would just die of embarrassment if Burke caught us unprepared. He said he might bring along a few more of the lead Enforcers for us to meet. I just love meeting new people. Oh, and Trinity is about to burst, I can't believe she hasn't had that child yet. Thank God I didn't get so huge when I had the girls, how embarrassing to walk around like a cow. Poor thing looks miserable."

"Mmm hmm."

Rohan sat beside Rhiannon to put on his shiny, black dress shoes. She watched him intently, enjoying the scent of his cologne. She wanted to reach out to him, to have him hold her, but she knew if she tried he would just pat her arm and walk away. It was just his way.

Serendipity spritzed on her signature scent of luxurious sweet pea perfume and rose to her feet, elegant in a draping, off the shoulder gown the color of a delicate pink rose.

She looked at her daughter in irritation. "How many times have I told you to be careful how you sit on your dresses? Stand up, let me make sure you haven't wrinkled it."

Rhiannon climbed off the bed, brushing at the skirt of her light green tea dress.

Serendipity gripped her arm and whipped her around to examine the back of the skirt, brushing at it with her hand. Seeing no wrinkles, she released Rhiannon and turned to Rohan.

"Come. Let's go." She glided to the door and stood beside it, waiting for him to open it for her. He did so, and she strolled out into the corridor, stopping again for him to join her.

Rohan motioned to his daughter. "Come along, Rhiannon."

She walked, head down, into the hallway. Before her father closed the door, she stared back inside, wondering if she should ask her mother about the gift she had neglected to notice.

But before she could decide, her father shut the door. Her heart broke; another fresh crack to join the sea of fractures that were already slowly but surely breaking her down.

She sat beneath her favorite tree in the courtyard, her knees pressed up against her chest and her chin resting on them. Her eyes felt hot and heavy, an unfamiliar sensation. The disappointment still lingered, even though she fought to push it away.

In the distance, everyone danced and celebrated. Her mother glided along the dance floor, arm-in-arm with a man Rhiannon didn't recognize, while her father spoke with Clynn at one of the tables. There were many people she didn't know, most of them humans involved in some way with Euphora or with the Enforcers.

She had managed to slip away and even though she was afraid of being scolded, she was tired and didn't want to be there anymore.

There was a rustling noise behind her and she whirled around to see Liam approach, smiling at her.

"Why are you over here?" he asked, plopping down on the grass beside her, his sky blue dress shirt already smudged with food.

She eyed him thoughtfully and shrugged.

He frowned. Her eyes were glassy and bright, and her brow was creased in a way he wasn't used to seeing. "You look sad, Rhia."

She shrugged again, looking away from him.

"Tell me."

Biting her lip, she gripped her knees tighter to her chest, rocking back and forth as she debated whether or not to speak. She'd gone so long without saying anything that it was hard to find the words.

When she didn't respond, Liam shifted closer and put his arm around her shoulders. Then he placed a tiny kiss upon the top of her head–just like he'd seen his father do with his mother when she was sad.

Rhiannon stiffened, unused to the closeness and affection, unsure what to do in response.

He continued to hold her and she gradually began to calm down. When she tried to speak, her voice was so quiet it was barely more than a whisper.

"What?" he asked, unable to hear her.

She stared at him, her eyes huge and her lips trembling. But still no tears fell.

"She didn't see my gift," she repeated, a bit louder. Saying the words aloud and admitting the problem hurt just as bad as keeping it inside.

Liam smiled sympathetically. "Your mom?"

Rhiannon nodded.

Unsure how to help, Liam squeezed her tighter and smiled brightly. "Maybe she'll see it later."

She nodded again, though it did give her some hope. She smiled slightly and looked at him again. He was so nice and easy to be around, at least when he wasn't with Blythe. The Fire Dryad was a bit too rambunctious for Rhiannon to handle and was often intimidating. But Liam…he was kind.

Feeling better, she rested her cheek against her knees and gazed at him, her jade eyes seeing him as if for the first time. Along with the sliver of hope he'd given her, one of the tiny cracks in her child's heart was slowly beginning to mend.

Almost a month later, Euphora would be rocked by a terrible, devastating tragedy.

Rhiannon had no way of knowing how life-altering the night would be as she sat in the parlor, watching her parents socialize once again in their stylish clothes, her mother adorned with glittering jewels. Serendipity laughed beautifully, and as she did so the diamonds at her ears and neck caught fire in the golden light of the chandelier.

Rhiannon sat alone on a bench in the corner, watching the party unfold. She liked watching people, how they moved, how they spoke, the subtle nuances she was still so unfamiliar with.

But she absorbed it all. Filing it away in tidy compartments in her mind to use later. She had an excellent memory. She had already breezed through the alphabet and could recall exactly how to pronounce a word after only hearing it once.

What she saw next she made sure to tuck away, not because it had anything to do with her, but because it had to do with her closest and dearest friend. She was inordinately protective where tiny Capri was concerned.

Capri had a flower clutched in her hand as she slipped away from her mother. She walked up to Rian, one of the Furies, and held out the flower to him as a gift. He pretended not to see her and turned his head away, ignoring her.

Capri pouted, clearly unsure why he wasn't seeing her. Hanging her head, she turned around and sniffled, tears beginning to run down her face.

She went back to her mother, who immediately lifted her into her arms and comforted her, cooing and shushing as Capri began to cry.

"Poor thing, I'll take her for a walk outside, calm her down." Heidi smiled apologetically to her husband, kissing his cheek before leaving the room with Capri in her arms.

Rhiannon watched them go, then turned and stared at Rian. To her surprise she saw him watching Heidi and Capri with a blank expression. She filed this away as well.

Just then, Blythe appeared and took a seat beside Rhiannon on the bench, her own face scrunched together and tears on her cheeks. She sniffled and kicked her legs, restless.

"I can't find my daddy," she announced, sulking.

Rhiannon wasn't sure what to say. She hadn't seen Brock all night.

"No one has seen him, I asked," Blythe went on, still kicking her legs, more fervently now. Rhiannon felt anxious watching Blythe's agitated energy, her hands clenching uncomfortably in her lap.

Getting no response from Rhiannon, Blythe sniffled again and started to move away, only to have Nyxa suddenly rush up and glare at her.

"Where is your father?" she asked in a heated voice.

Blythe looked at her mother and shook her head. "*I don't know*!" she shrieked, upset and tired and cranky.

"Shush!" Nyxa grabbed Blythe's arm, pulling her to her feet. "Be quiet, you're disrupting everyone. God, when I find him I'm going to kill him. How dare he be so late?"

Rhiannon's eyes widened as she watched Nyxa's grip tighten on Blythe who began to cry, sobbing loudly and howling for her father. Embarrassed and uncomfortable, Rhiannon shifted away, wondering if she should leave. Nyxa scolded Blythe, her voice raising as she hissed at her to be quiet.

Suddenly, the Fury Balgaire bolted through the parlor doors, his face strained and pale, his dark eyes frantic.

"We're being attacked!" he growled, glaring at everyone. For a moment, everyone stood in silent and collective shock. And then, just as swiftly, pandemonium reigned.

The adults in the room began to move all at once. Sebastian ordered the men to follow Balgaire to defend the castle. Thea hurriedly instructed the Muses and the Fates to take all of the children upstairs to the Muses' tower, where the babies were sleeping with the fairies.

Rhiannon's head darted back and forth, watching everything and wondering what was happening. Confusion and fear crept through her but she was too scared to move.

Beside her, Nyxa pulled the sobbing Blythe into her arms, panic in her eyes. She put a hand on Rhiannon's shoulder and pulled her along, making her way out of the parlor with the other women.

Behind them, Rhiannon saw her mother with the other two Muses, looking more annoyed than scared.

"This is probably all some big misunderstanding," she said as the group of them walked down the corridor to the Muses' tower. "A shame to disrupt the party this way."

Clarity grabbed Liam's hand firmly and despite Serendipity's lack of concern, she looked terrified.

"I don't think Balgaire would misinterpret something like this," Clarity said nervously. Trinity nodded in agreement, clutching her newborn son Tobias in her arms.

Blythe was crying soundlessly, the adults' alarm scaring her into silence. Her bottom lip trembled as she nuzzled against her mother.

Nyxa still had her hand on Rhiannon's shoulder as they raced up the stairs and then entered the tower, locking the door behind them.

She let go then, taking Blythe and sitting down on one of the plush sofas, her face intense with warring emotions. Rhiannon was left standing in limbo, not sure what to do. Her own mother glided past and sat imperiously on a separate sofa, crossing her legs and pursing her lips, as if this entire commotion was created just to inconvenience her.

Clarity sat beside Serendipity, ushering Liam to sit. His eyes were huge and glassy, his face pale. Beside them were two cradles, holding Sierra and Clarity's newest daughter, Cilla.

The other two Fates sat with Nyxa, looking agitated and nervous. The only one left standing was Rhiannon.

She glanced around and realized that Capri and Heidi weren't there. Then she remembered they went outside just before Balgaire had rushed in. Where could they be?

She wanted to ask her mother why they weren't in the tower but then a loud explosion outside rocked the castle walls and trembled the floor.

Rhiannon hurriedly went over to her mother and crouched beside her, reaching out to hold a fold of Serendipity's skirt. She closed her eyes tight, more frightened than she had ever been in her life.

She could hear the babies whimpering and crying, and Blythe was still asking for her father. At every sound of explosion or gunfire, Liam asked his mother what it was. But she had no answers. None of them knew what was going on. All they could do was wait.

The minutes ticked by, and after what seemed like forever, the noises outside stopped. Silence hung heavy, cloaking them all in a shroud of uncertainty and tentative hope.

Moments later, there was a knock on the door. Trinity ran to open it, letting Lucian inside. Apprehensively, they all turned to face him.

"It's over," he reassured them. But there was something dark in his voice and a numb sadness in his eyes that meant there was bad news. When he spoke again, his voice cracked and his composure wavered. "We lost Heidi and Capri."

"What? How?" Serendipity asked as all of the women rose to their feet in disbelief.

His eyes flicked over to his own son. "Someone let in a group of demons, and they ran into Heidi and Capri in the courtyard. Heidi…she didn't make it. And they took Capri. We don't know where. We're going to send out a search group as soon as possible to try and find her."

"Who let in the demons?" Clarity asked her husband, her hand clenched tightly on Liam's shoulder.

Lucian watched her for a moment, unsure how to phrase his answer. "Well…it appears as if...at least Balgaire is saying ...that he witnessed the demons being let in by…Brock."

"*What!*" Nyxa shrieked, setting Blythe down on the floor as she rushed up to Lucian, getting in his face. "You think Brock is behind this?"

"We don't know anything for certain," he corrected, trying to reassure her.

Serendipity stared at him, her eyes hard as stone. "Brock isn't that stupid," she declared, tilting her head up defiantly.

Nyxa rounded on Serendipity. "This is none of your business, bitch!" she growled, fury in her eyes.

Serendipity glared at the other women in disgust. "Control yourself, Nyxa. There are children present."

Nyxa trembled with anger and a deeply rooted, jealous hatred but Serendipity brushed her off like an annoying fly.

"Where is Rohan?" she asked Lucian.

"He should be on his way up, he was with Clynn. In fact, I should probably go down to him." Distracted, Lucian started to turn around to leave, only to whirl around and walk to his son, pulling Liam into his arms tightly. "I love you."

"I love you too, daddy," Liam replied, scared at the anguish on his father's face.

With that, Lucian swept from the room just as Rohan came in, looking disheveled, his face stone cold.

"Rohan, is it true that Brock is responsible?" Serendipity demanded to know.

He stared at her, his rage barely controlled. "It looks that way."

"I'm going downstairs to find out for myself," she huffed, pushing past him and leaving the tower. Nyxa followed her, along with a few of the other women.

To Rhiannon's surprise, her father stepped forward and lifted her up into his arms, clutching her against him as he buried his face in her hair.

"My heart," he whispered, tears suddenly falling down his face. She clung to him, unsure what was happening, but thrilled all the same.

He sat down on the sofa with her still in his arms and rocked back and forth, grief and rage taking over. Never in his life had he seen such pain, such agony, as like what he had seen on Clynn's face moments before. It had quite literally staggered him, destroying his steel resolve. The only thing that reassured him of anything was to hold his own daughter, and to know that at least it wasn't his child who was taken that night.

Days later, Brock was banished.

It had taken awhile for Rhiannon to adjust to the fact that Capri was gone and that Heidi was dead. It didn't seem real to her. She kept thinking she'd see her little friend wander out from behind one of the jasmine bushes in the courtyard with a smile as sweet as honey on her face.

She knew she would probably never see Capri again. Her grief left her feeling closed off with no idea how to release it. Instead, she retreated within herself, her heart shattering more while her mind tried to shut out the pain in an effort to survive.

Her father barely let her out of his sight the days following the raid, and while she was delighted with his attention, she was also perplexed by it. He was acting as though she was in danger, as if the demons might return and take her like they'd taken Capri. The idea of it terrified her so much she could barely sleep.

On the day of Brock's banishment, everyone gathered in the courtyard to say their goodbyes.

Sebastian and Thea hung back, standing in front of the entrance doors to Euphora, watching the scene unfold with livid expressions. Brock had been proven guilty not only by Balgaire as an eyewitness, but one of the demons had named Brock as the man who'd led them there. It had been enough, coupled with the lack of an alibi and his history of dealing demon weaponry, to declare him responsible.

Nyxa was sobbing and snarling at the same time, her grief and fury so great she could barely contain herself. Brock gripped her tightly in his arms, still in disbelief.

From where she sat under a nearby tree, Rhiannon watched them with quiet eyes. Liam was beside her, both of them too young to fully understand the implications of what was happening. All they knew was that Blythe's father had to leave because he had done a very bad thing.

They watched Blythe hug her father for the last time, her piercing cries echoing throughout the courtyard. Her face was red and tear streaked, and all Brock could do was try and comfort her as he pulled her into his arms.

Nearby, Serendipity and Rohan stood hand-in-hand, both staring at Brock with cold and distrustful expressions. They wholeheartedly believed in his guilt and though Serendipity may have loved him once, this one act had shattered her image of him.

Lucian was with Clynn, who was staring at Brock with empty eyes. Neither of them could believe that Brock was guilty, but the proof was too damning to question. They would have never thought that their lifelong friend, their brother, would do something like this. But there was nothing they could do now except mourn what was lost.

Rhiannon turned to Liam, unable to watch anymore. He looked at her and smiled, earning a tentative smile back.

"Want to see something cool?" he asked her, holding out his hand. She nodded and he proceeded to produce a bubble out of thin air that hovered just inches over his hand. It glistened in the sunlight, all shades of purples, blues, and vivid pinks. She stared at it in wonder, her fingers aching to touch it. But she knew what happened when you touched bubbles…they popped, and she didn't want to destroy his creation.

He lifted the bubble into the air so it could float, and they both watched it fall to the grass, bursting as it hit one of the blades.

With a giggle, he looked at her again. "You should make something."

She bit her lip, wondering if she should. But he was looking at her expectantly, so she held out her hands just above the grass and moments later a green stem emerged, rising up into the air and sprouting leaves. A single bloom opened into a vivid blue daisy.

He stared at her in amazement, never having seen her create anything before. "That's cool," he told her, reaching out to touch the daisy.

As he was marveling at her flower, Brock was leaving Euphora and the courtyard was silent except for Blythe's whimpering sobs.

Within moments, Rohan and Lucian appeared beside where she and Liam were seated. Her father lifted her up into his arms, prepared to carry her away.

Although she didn't know why, she did not want to leave Liam. She wanted nothing more than to stay with him, and the need for it was so great that she did something she had never done before.

"No!" she cried out, straining against her father's arms and reaching toward Liam, who got to his feet and stood, his eyes wide. Lucian placed his hand on his son's shoulder as the two of them watched.

Dumbfounded, Rohan pulled Rhiannon away from him so he could look her in the eye. He had never seen her act this way. "What is it?"

"I want to stay with him!" She struggled against him again, but he only held her tighter.

"You can see Liam later. I want you upstairs where it's safe. Brock may retaliate against us. I can't have you out here unguarded."

He braced her on his hip and began to walk toward the castle. Unable to do more, she just looked over his shoulder at Liam and Lucian.

Although she didn't know it, this was the beginning of Euphora shifting from her home and her safe haven, to becoming her gilded prison.

Chapter Five

She watched them through the glass walls of the Greenhouse with empty eyes.

Lucian with Blythe and Liam, all racing around playing together, so carefree. Despite a deep, hidden longing to join them, she knew now that she did not belong. She was an outsider to their cheerful trio; the lonely one.

She was eight years old.

Since Capri had been taken, nothing had been the same. She had lost her dearest, sweetest friend, and the loss had taken its toll on her. She couldn't be around Liam and Blythe without Capri being there; they were too much for her to handle at the same time so she shied away. Her refusal to play and distant attitude confused Liam and irritated Blythe. Whatever small friendship she'd had with the Fire Dryad had slowly dissipated into a steady dislike that had at some point turned mutual.

Despite how hard he tried, Liam could not bring the two of them together as they had once been. Instead he had become the go between and the middle man; a shaky bridge that clung with all its might to not collapse under the pressure.

Rhiannon dealt with a pressure all her own, one that the others could never understand.

"Rhiannon, come here and concentrate, please," Rohan urged her. He was standing before the globe over the tiny pond, planning shifts in the Earth's crust.

She wandered over to him, looking repentant.

"Sorry, father," she apologized, lifting her hands and focusing on the globe.

"Now, as we've been practicing, locate the fault line and trace it with your finger."

She ran her finger along a fault line in the sea near Japan. It highlighted with white light at her touch, outlining the length of the entire line.

"Now hold your hands over the line and shift the plates. Be sure to concentrate."

Closing her eyes, she felt the power surge through her arms and into her hands, and then push through to her palms. Using it, she moved her hands as if she were physically moving the plates, and she could feel it happen within her. The small earthquake, while barely felt by humans, rocked her down to her core, the sensation both thrilling and daunting.

Finished, she pulled her hands away and stared at him. He nodded at her.

"Good." He began to locate the next fault line due for a shift, when he noticed his daughter staring outside the glass walls again. Noticing she was watching Liam and Blythe playing, he felt a tinge of regret for restricting her so much. But in the end he knew he was doing what was best.

She was the brightest of all the Dryad children, and of all the children on Euphora, second only maybe to Roarke's son, Rian. He attributed it largely due to his and his wife's stern and dedicated approach to her education. She spent half of her day excelling at her general studies and her afternoons were spent with him in the Greenhouse. He had to admit, she was already beyond his level when he had been her age. But he'd known that from the minute he'd first introduced her to her powers.

One day, she'd be the best Dryad Euphora had ever seen.

Determined to distract her from the other children, he put the globe back into the pond and shut everything down. He smiled when she looked at him questionably.

"I'd like to take you somewhere, Rhiannon. It's time I showed you the world outside of Euphora."

She couldn't hide the smile that graced her face, excitement rising in her. "Okay."

Seeing her smile, which was much too rare these days, warmed his heart.

He led the way out into the courtyard, where they walked side-by-side down the cobblestone path and headed toward the meadow and the giant oak tree that would transport them away from Euphora.

Rhiannon walked quickly, eager to go, forgetting all about Liam, Blythe and Lucian. The longing was pushed aside and replaced by her impatience to see what she hadn't yet seen in person.

Rohan pressed his hand against the wrought iron gates, which melted away at his touch. He led her into the meadow, his head up and his back straight as always. She chanced a glance at him, marveling at how handsome he was.

When they reached the tree, he reached for her hand and placed it gently on the bark.

"Keep your hand pressed firmly against the tree," he instructed, placing his own hand on it as well. With a deep breath, he closed his eyes. "Take me to barley field, Swan Valley, Bonneville County, Idaho."

Rhiannon kept her eyes on her father as the tree began to glow with golden light. She had seen others coming and going before so she expected this. She was just happy to finally be going somewhere herself.

It happened so fast she barely had time to blink and suddenly they were no longer on Euphora. A mist surrounded them out of nowhere and just as suddenly disappeared, leaving them standing in the most beautiful field she had ever seen.

The sun was setting, its golden rays blanketing the area with warm light and casting a yellow glow upon the field of grain. She gaped around her, taking it all in, not wanting to miss a single detail.

The field was acres and acres wide, so that all the way to the horizon there was nothing but barley. Behind them were more trees and sloping hills, with the last dying rays of the sun filtering through them. Off in the distance, she could see a red farmhouse, standing alone.

And further in the distance, dark gray and blue storm clouds raged. Thunder rumbled faintly as the clouds churned.

"My father used to bring me here when I was a boy," Rohan shared with her, taking her hand. "What do you think?"

"It's amazing," she replied, her voice soft as she continued to stare around her, breathless.

"Come on, let's walk." His hand still holding hers, he led her through the field. She reached out and touched the barley as they walked, mesmerized by the golden tips of grain and the way the entire mass waved in the wind.

The air felt different here than it did at home, almost as if electricity were sparking around her, brought on by the approaching storm. Wind the likes of which she'd never experienced whipped around her, sending her hair flying. It was exhilarating.

"Everything you see is the reality of what we do," he said, motioning with his free arm. "The trees, the barley, the soil, the mountains...this is the beauty of what we create, and when all is balanced, this is the result."

She stared in wonder, feeling small and important all at once. It was one thing to look at the globe, but to actually be there experiencing the glory of it fascinated her.

"Humans have several important uses for barley. It is important that it's always able to grow here and that the harvest occurs every year. You see, while the Water Dryads ensure that the Earth is watered, we ensure that the soil is fertile enough to grow. Without the combination, none of this would be possible."

"And without air, water would have no clouds to be carried in to water the soil," Rhiannon added, glancing up at him thoughtfully.

He smiled. "Exactly. And sometimes when the flora becomes too exhausting for an ecosystem to handle, fire comes through and clears it out to prepare the cycle to start all over again."

Rohan watched his daughter as she looked around, her innocence and beauty striking him all at once. Even though she was only eight years old, she was already pretty and neat as a pin. Her clothes were modest and pressed and her face was always clean. Her rich, earthy eyes brimmed with a serious intelligence that he wondered if she had inherited from him. And as she grew older, she had begun to lose the childish chubbiness in her face, revealing her true beauty.

Her sister Sierra had already proved to be the exact opposite. She was three years old and was already selfish and grabby. He loved both of his children, but Rhiannon was closest to his heart. Serendipity had warmed up to the idea of motherhood after the birth of Sierra, but that was because Sierra was a Muse and her legacy rested with the child. It pained him to see that his wife remained cold with their oldest daughter, critical and discerning as always.

A flock of birds soared out of the trees and into the sky, fluttering overhead, startling him out of his reverie. He watched them fade into the horizon and his thoughts turned to Clynn and Capri.

It had been three years since that terrible day and his friend had still not fully recovered from his depression. Sometimes he wondered if Clynn would ever be the same again, but he reminded himself that if the same thing had happened to him, he would perish into nothingness, unable to cope.

The thought of losing his wife, the woman he'd loved his whole life, the most beautiful creature he'd ever laid eyes upon… if he didn't have her, he would be empty.

And the thought of losing Rhiannon…that would be like having his heart ripped from his chest and ground into nothing but dust.

Her hand swiped diligently across the paper as she wrote, filling in numbers in the boxes to complete the multiplication table.

Behind her, she heard shuffling and muffled giggling, which annoyed her. They were goofing off again and disrupting everyone, as usual.

She glanced over her shoulder and gave Blythe and Liam an irritated look. Blythe just stuck her tongue out, which caused Liam to laugh behind his hands.

"Settle down and get back to work," Serendipity scolded, gliding past them and approaching Rhiannon's desk. Stopping, she held out hand. "Let me see."

Rhiannon gave her paper to her mother, her eyes lowered.

Serendipity perused her daughter's work, pleased that the girl's answers were not only correct, but written with clear, precise handwriting. Without a word, she set the paper back down on the desk and moved on to where the Furies were sitting.

Rhiannon exhaled and then returned to her work. She'd grown accustomed to receiving silence instead of praise from her mother.

An hour later, they were dismissed for the day. Rhiannon neatly stowed her papers, books, and pencils into her bag. Behind her she could hear Liam and Blythe chattering loudly as they stuffed their bags and raced out of the room, excited to play in the courtyard. Rian helped Brogan put away his things and then the two of them left without a word.

Knowing the Furies would be heading outside as well, Rhiannon left the room and eagerly went to the dining hall. She looked forward to seeing the fairies laying out the food for lunch. She took a seat, thanking the fairies as she always did, and then selected a turkey sandwich and juice.

She enjoyed being the first one there, when it was still quiet and calm. She enjoyed the solitude and the silence of an empty room, where she could sit alone with her thoughts, with no distractions or disruptions.

At least, until the others came in.

She heard the laughter first, making her defensive and she fought back the instinctive envy. Instead, she sat straight and cocked her chin ever so slightly, pretending not to care.

Blythe rushed into the room ahead of Liam, racing around the table to take a seat across but down a ways from where Rhiannon was sitting. Her hair was a wild poof of vivid red, and she was panting and out of breath from being chased. Her grin was a mile wide as she beamed at Liam, who collapsed into the chair beside her.

"I beat you!" she declared, clapping her hands joyfully. Liam glared at her, clutching his stomach and gasping for air.

"You…cheated," he managed, punching her in the arm weakly.

She punched him back and they began a shoving match right at the dining table, laughing and smiling.

Rhiannon just rolled her eyes and turned away.

When she finished eating, she got to her feet and started to leave, only to stop when Liam called out to her.

"You should come play with us, Rhia," he said, his goofy smile bright and charming as he ran a hand through his tangled mass of dark curls. "My dad's putting up a swing for us outside, you gotta come try it!"

She looked over her shoulder at him, her head almost shaking before she decided. But her instinct told her to say no and so she did. She didn't have time to play on a swing.

Seeing his face fall, disappointed yet again by her refusal, she turned and swiftly left the room, wanting to get as far away from him as possible. It hurt to see him look like that, so she did the only thing that she knew worked: she fled, and tried to forget.

She started walking down the corridor toward the Greenhouse where her father was waiting for her, only to stop dead in her tracks when she saw a man and a young boy walking through the atrium toward her.

She recognized the boy as Michael, even though it had been awhile since she'd last seen him. His father had brought him by a few times over the last couple of years, but he never stayed long. He didn't get along with any of the children except the Furies, and she was certain they only put up with him because they were told to.

His father, Burke Callahan, had been successfully rising through the ranks of the Enforcers, swiftly becoming one of the best. He frequented Euphora to visit with the Furies and with Thea, making sure they knew he was reliable and trustworthy.

As they approached, Rhiannon clutched her bag and waited.

Burke was a tall man, lean but fit, with big hands and a slender face topped with cropped brown hair. He had sharp brown eyes that were deceptively framed with smile lines, and a mouth that was just as quick to grin. But while he appeared friendly on the outside, inside he was a well oiled demon fighting machine, gritty, precise and effective.

He smiled politely as he passed her, nodding in greeting. His son sneered in superiority, which she expected.

They brushed past her and continued down the corridor to the Furies' office, and as they continued she could hear Burke instructing his son.

"One day you'll be an Enforcer too, champ, and you'll be the best there is. I'm going to make it happen for you, you hear? Just do as I say and we will be on top, father and son. The Callahan name will go down in infamy."

"Yes, father." Michael's response reminded her alarmingly of herself.

He doesn't sound very happy, she thought as she turned in the opposite direction toward the Greenhouse. Did he even want to be an Enforcer?

She thought of her own father. He had always told her about her future as an Earth Dryad and how important she was to the world. But he had never asked her if that was what she wanted.

In some of the books she read, they told of what humans did, how some of them became teachers, doctors or athletes. Did she have the choice to be something else, too?

With that question nagging her, she entered the Greenhouse and spotted her father, working over his drafting table on a new fern he was designing.

She debated whether or not to ask, wondering if he would be angry with her. But it seemed like a reasonable question to her, and her curiosity was so great she needed to know.

When he heard her come in, he straightened and turned around. "How was class, Rhiannon?"

"Fine," she responded, as she always did. He nodded and rose to his feet, glancing one last time at his drawing and making a few quick notations.

She clenched her hands behind her back and tried to find the right words to say.

"I was wondering…" she began, her chest constricting from nerves and her clasped hands trembling slightly. He turned to face her, removing the reading glasses he'd taken to wearing recently.

"About what?"

Biting her lip, she took a deep breath. "Do we ever have the choice to…not be a Dryad?"

Taken aback, he wondered if he had heard her correctly.

"Choice, Rhiannon?"

Seeing his confusion, she tried to elaborate. "I read that humans can become teachers or doctors…they have choices. Do we have a choice, too?"

"Why in the world would you want something different?" he asked, alarmed and wondering where this came from. "It is our duty to be Dryads. What we do is crucial to the survival of this planet, Rhiannon. We don't have the luxury of a choice."

Wishing she hadn't asked, Rhiannon nodded solemnly. Of course he was right, she should have known that.

Feeling he'd gotten his point across, Rohan motioned her to look at his charts on redwood growth in the Sierra Nevada Mountains.

She listened as he explained the importance of repairing the damage to an area that had been burned by human carelessness just a year before. Re-growth and mending the damaged trees was imperative for this endangered species of tree to survive.

Although she listened, part of her was busy wondering why she hadn't felt like a prisoner before in her own home, duty bound to serve Euphora simply because of who and what she was.

After seeing her father's reaction, Rhiannon never again questioned why she had to be a Dryad. She merely accepted and moved on.

She wandered through the courtyard while everyone else went to dinner.

Lucian had hung the brand new swing from one of the large, overhanging trees, and it sat oddly still and silent after hours of cheerful activity.

Rhiannon approached it, tentatively touching the rope with her fingertips, yearning to swing on it. Just one swing, just one chance to feel her belly flop and the wind rush past her hair and to see the ground fall away from under her…just one chance to be a child.

Pulling her hand away, she turned her back on the swing and left, her father's voice in her head telling her that she didn't have a choice. She had work to do.

Chapter Six

If I endeavor to undeceive people as to the rest of his conduct, who will believe me? The general prejudice against Mr. Darcy is so violent that it would be the death of half the good people in Meryton, to attempt to place him in an amiable light.

Rhiannon set the book aside thoughtfully. She hadn't expected anything in *Pride and Prejudice* to relate to her, but low and behold, something had. But was she really as bad as cold, discerning, overly critical Mr. Darcy?

The answer was simple: of course she was.

At thirteen, she was well aware by now of her own attributes and faults, and perhaps having a more conscientious mind meant that she not only saw shortcomings in others, but she saw her own as well. It was both the blessing and the curse of being a Virgo.

Shutting the book, she pulled out her notebook and opened it to the list of notes she had already begun taking on the book. She was doing a comparative essay on the differences between *Pride and Prejudice* and *Wuthering Heights*, two of her mother's favorite novels. Not that it was the reason she was doing the essay, she reminded herself. She was merely interested in exploring two of the earliest female authors who had managed to stake their claim in the vaults of time and history. Amongst humans, Jane Austen and Emily Bronte were infamous. It pleased her to explore the differences in their characters, writing styles, and storylines, citing what was good and bad about each. She was, if nothing else, an excellent critic.

She had already finished *Wuthering Heights* and had decided both Kathy and Heathcliff were overly selfish, aggressive, and vindictive. However, she appreciated the fact that their flaws made them real, a rarity sometimes in fiction. And although she found she couldn't sympathize with their inherent obsession with each other, she could still see how it made an interesting story.

In her orderly way, she noted the quote, hoping to use it in her comparison later. Mr. Darcy was certainly much more of a gentleman than Heathcliff and she found him much more interesting as a character. He had a proper way about him, even if he was a bit curt at times. And despite his wealth and position, he was somewhat of an outsider simply because of the way he was. Rhiannon certainly could sympathize with that.

There was a noise behind her, disrupting the silence of the classroom. She turned her head slightly to see what it was.

She wasn't the least bit surprised to see her prissy little sister, now eight years old, sitting in her chair while Tobias, one of the other Muses, crouched on the floor to pick up her books that she had more than likely knocked to the ground herself.

"Good boy," Sierra preened as Tobias set her books back on the desk before returning to his chair beside her.

It disgusted Rhiannon to see the way her sister acted, especially toward the young boy, who was obviously pining for her attention. Sierra, with her fluttering blue eyes and wavy mane of honey blonde hair, was downright insufferable, selfish and vain. She got nearly everything she wanted and was given much less grief than Rhiannon had been given by their mother. As the second child, the youngest and a Muse, she was clearly Serendipity's favorite. Rhiannon had long ago accepted that fact.

The classroom was at full capacity now and required that all three adult Muses teach. Dividing the students by age, Serendipity continued to teach the older students, while Clarity taught the younger Fates and Trinity taught the younger Muses.

Rhiannon still sat in the front of the room at her single desk and kept to herself. Though she maintained a polite friendship with Liam she didn't spend time with him. His time was generally monopolized by Blythe, who was a regular hell raiser.

The two of them were constantly getting into trouble. Whether it was camping out in the woods at night or stealing sweets from the kitchens, they were both frequently being reprimanded and given chores to do as punishment, although that didn't stop them. Lucian was at his wit's end, but he was either wise enough or foolish enough to chock it up to kids being kids.

Rhiannon couldn't understand why they enjoyed getting into trouble all the time. She always followed the rules and disobeying her parents had never even occurred to her. Why go through the stress of breaking rules when it was so much easier to just follow them?

She returned to her note taking, her neatly manicured fingers pressing her mechanical pencil against the lined paper with precise, neat cursive.

"Rhiannon," her mother said, approaching her. Rhiannon looked up with a polite expression.

Brogan was standing beside Serendipity, looking awkward and shy.

"Brogan needs help with an algebra problem. I need you to show him how to do it. I'm just too busy at the moment," Serendipity ordered, motioning Brogan to drag a chair over to Rhiannon's desk and to sit with her.

Rhiannon nodded as her mother walked away, and then turned to smile politely at Brogan.

"What problem is it?" she asked, watching as he sat beside her, his black curled hair hiding his face as he flipped open his book and searched for the page he needed.

When he found it, he nudged the book toward her, chancing a look up to meet her eyes. She studied him for a moment, realizing she'd never really spoken to him before.

He had a youthful and poetically handsome face, with dark brown eyes and pale skin over hollowed cheekbones and full lips that were always set in a firm, serious line. He rarely spoke, and then it was only when he was spoken to. Brogan had always been overshadowed by his fellow Fury, Rian, and was hardly noticed by anyone. Rhiannon had noticed him, though, and wondered if she was the only one, other than Rian, who ever had.

She looked at problem, which he had circled in the book. The fact that he'd written in the book irritated her for a brief moment, but she knew it wasn't worth mentioning.

Taking out a piece of paper, she neatly wrote out the equation. "What you need to do is simplify the equation," she told him, looking up to make sure he was paying attention. He was leaning over, his eyes glued to the paper attentively. Pleased, she continued, "The first thing you do is see if you have any like terms. $5x^2$, $-2x^2$, and x^2 are all alike, so we can combine those to equal $4x^2$."

She wrote down the new term beneath the full equation. "Now 3x is the only term of its type, so we leave that one alone. And then we add the constants, which equal 6, and put it all together."

Completing the simplified equation, she smiled at him, meeting his eyes. He smiled in response.

"Thank you," he said quietly, his voice surprisingly deep, yet soft as she had expected. He gathered up his book and the paper and started to stand, only to turn back around and look at her with hopeful eyes. "Actually, can you help me with this other problem, too?"

Although she had her own work to do, she decided to help him, realizing she enjoyed it more than she'd expected. He seemed nice and his presence was strangely calming.

"Okay."

He sat beside her and they continued to work together. She did most of the talking even though the conversation didn't stray from algebra. But she found herself relaxing in his company and the end of class came faster than normal.

"Thanks again." He brushed back his hair as he stood, awkwardly grabbing his book and papers.

"You're welcome," Rhiannon replied, smiling at him. He hesitated a moment before jerking around and heading back to his desk so he could gather the rest of his books.

She let out a sigh and began to put away her own books, slipping them into her bag as she rose to her feet.

She turned to leave and saw Blythe and Liam play wrestling with each other, both laughing and grinning like fools. Jealousy shot through her but she pushed it aside, instead choosing to feel annoyance over their childishness. Rhiannon watched them leave, making sure to follow several steps behind. She'd learned long ago that it was easier to avoid the two of them when they were together.

She followed them to the dining hall for lunch and took her usual seat. The fairies were just finishing up setting out the food and she thanked them before they left.

Reaching for a tuna sandwich on rye, she diligently laid her napkin in her lap and took a small nibble of the sandwich, careful not to get mayonnaise or tuna on her lips.

She heard a noise and glanced over her shoulder and saw Brogan pulling out the chair next to her. He smiled shyly.

"Can I sit here?" he hesitated, looking hopeful and nervous all at once.

She almost said no since she preferred to eat lunch alone. But something in his eyes reminded her of herself so she nodded and motioned for him to sit.

He reached for a sandwich and took a big bite, earning a look from her. He wasn't even using his napkin, she noted with dismay, pondering if she should suggest it to him. But before she could, he tilted his head and looked at her, his dark curls falling over his forehead.

"You're really good at everything, huh?" he said, his dark eyes watching her with admiration. She'd never had anyone look at her that way.

"Not really." She pursed her lips, not wanting to sound conceited. "I'm sure I'm not any better than you or the others."

He chuckled, shaking his head and turning back to his sandwich. He took a bite and chewed thoughtfully, then gulped and turned back to her. "No, I think you're the smartest one out of all of us."

"Surely there's–"

"No." He shook his head again, this time fervently enough so that his hair shook with him. "You're brilliant."

She stared at him, startled by his assertive tone. She wasn't that smart…

"Well, I got an A- on my essay on the benefits of organic farming and using weed suppressive cover crops versus typical herbicides…but really I think the low grade was because I went over the ten page limit and wrote twenty one pages, though I would think that a longer, more solid essay would be better than a shorter one that was missing key information. Oh, and I'm pretty sure I forgot to number one of the pages, so that was also probably another reason points were docked. So, you see, I'm not that smart."

He just smiled, slow and knowing, and she shook her head at him. "What?"

"I like the way you talk," he told her, blushing a little around his neck, as if he hadn't meant to say the words aloud. She bit her lip, wondering what to say in return.

Just then, she felt someone watching her. Turning her head she saw Liam staring, his brows creased in both confusion and irritation. She glanced around, wondering if he was really staring at her, but when she met his eyes she felt an uneasiness rise within her. What was his problem?

Then she realized that he wasn't just staring at her, he was glaring at Brogan, too. Was Liam jealous or something?

Annoyed, she bristled in her chair and pursed her lips. She was perfectly allowed to have a friend, if that's what Brogan was going to be.

Deciding to ignore Liam, she turned back to Brogan and smiled.

"So, what's it like being a Fury?" she asked, resting her elbow on the table and her chin in her hand, purposefully turning away from Liam.

Brogan had also noticed Liam staring, and he looked uncomfortable. "Um…it's alright, I guess," he answered, focusing on what was left of his sandwich.

"What kinds of things are you learning?" she pressed, curious and eager to know him better.

"All kinds of stuff…how to detect demons, how to use different kinds of weapons…"

"Do you enjoy it?"

He chewed his bottom lip anxiously before speaking. "It's okay. I don't have a choice though, you know? My father's counting on me to learn all of it." He glanced up to meet her eyes and smiled sadly. "Rian's better than me and I know I'm disappointing my father, but I just don't think I'm cut out for being a Fury."

"You still have time," she assured him, smiling sympathetically. "I'm sure Rian will help you if you ask him."

"Yeah, maybe." He shrugged, but his lips curved slightly. "I don't know why I've never talked to you before. It's…nice."

"Yes, it is nice," she agreed with a smile. Then she glanced at her watch and sighed. "I have to go. My father's waiting for me."

"Okay. Bye." He watched her stand up and pull her bag over her shoulder.

"Goodbye," she replied as she left, walking swiftly. She was already a few minutes behind schedule, which made her ridiculously anxious. Punctuality was almost as important to her as breathing.

She started down the corridor, but stopped when she heard someone following her. Whirling around, she spotted Liam, purposefully charging toward her.

She stared at him warily.

"Rhia, was he bothering you?" Liam asked, motioning to the dining hall, his eyes fierce.

"What? No, of course not," she replied, tilting her head up haughtily. "We were just having a nice conversation."

"Are you sure? Because you can tell me," he insisted, his hands clenched into fists at his sides. She eyed him apprehensively, wondering if he really would go to blows with someone over her. "I'll tell him off for you, Rhia. And if he bothers you again, I'll protect you."

Insult warred with the dark, primal delight she felt at his words. Choosing indignation, she crossed her arms tightly over her chest and stared him down.

"I don't need a hero, Liam, I can take care of myself. And I will speak with whomever I please. I'm allowed to have a friend too, you know."

He looked ashamed and seeing this gave her pleasure. She was glad he understood her.

"Okay," he replied, brushing a hand through his tangled mass of black curls and hanging his head. When he glanced at her a few seconds later, he had a goofy grin and his eyes lit up with their usual cheerfulness. "I was just worried about you. We hardly ever hang out or talk anymore. I guess I just wanted to remind you that I'm still here."

"I've been busy," she replied, annoyed at the strange feelings she felt when he grinned at her that way.

"You're too serious and smart for your own good, Rhia," he teased, casually stuffing his hands into the pockets of his faded jeans. "You need to get out more, have some fun."

"I don't have time." She glanced down at her watch again and nearly had a heart attack. "Oh, no! I'm two minutes late, I have to go."

Without glancing back, she raced away. Liam watched her go, amused and confused at why seeing her with the Fury had bothered him so much.

Pushing the thought away, he began to whistle and casually strolled back to the dining hall, content in the knowledge that everything worked itself out in time.

That night at dinner, two very strange things happened.

Rhiannon sat beside her father as always and quietly ate her dinner while those around her bustled with conversation. Over the years, she'd taken to observing and listening instead of talking, which gave her the advantage of knowing almost everything that was going on.

She knew Blythe had been caught trying to sneak away from Euphora again and she was being punished by having to scrub the floors in the corridor. She also knew that Roarke had narrowly escaped with his life in a recent tussle with some uncooperative demons in New York City and he had a fresh scar on his face to prove it. She heard Clynn complaining to Lucian about a storm system they were working on and how Liam had accidentally added too much water, causing flash floods that would have to be corrected before entire towns were washed away.

But the most intriguing thing she noticed was that she was getting a lot more attention than she used to.

Liam kept glancing at her, trying to meet her eyes. When he managed to catch her attention, he made a funny face that made her smile involuntarily before looking away.

And just when she thought the coast was clear to continue her observations, she caught Brogan watching her as well, smiling at her shyly when she noticed him.

This was most curious. She had been virtually unnoticed her entire life and now two boys were suddenly adamant about getting her attention. Even her father noticed, and he protectively hovered over her, trying to be subtle even though she could see the difference in his demeanor. She was completely puzzled. What was it that was suddenly different about her and why all of a sudden had she become someone worth noticing?

That night, she sat in her room at her dressing table, staring at her reflection. She didn't look any different than she had the day before. She still had the same long, straight, bark colored hair, the same almond shaped, sage green eyes and the same rounded face with cheekbones that were just beginning to show.

Out of pure curiosity, she reached for the makeup set her mother had given her for her birthday and opened it hesitantly. She had hardly seen the need to wear makeup, had deemed it impractical and useless, but perhaps it wasn't so bad…

She lifted one of the large brushes and dabbed it in the blush, then brushed it on the hollows of her cheeks. She examined herself, wondering if it really had done much.

Deciding to try something else, she reached for the eyeliner and smudged it behind her lashes, darkening her eyes. Adding some shimmering eyeshadow and black mascara, she sat back and took looked at herself in the mirror once more.

This time, the difference surprised her. She looked years older; more mature and even kind of beautiful. Her lips tugged into a smile, even though she tried to fight it back, turning her head to admire herself at different angles.

Maybe she really was worth looking at, she thought, tugging at her still slightly chubby cheeks and eyeing her slightly too small ears critically. She wasn't stunning, but maybe she was...pretty.

Deciding she was being foolish, she went to her bathroom and rinsed the makeup off. Drying her skin with a hand towel, she stared at her reflection once again, feeling confused.

Deep down she knew the only reason she had bothered with the makeup at all was because of Liam. The way he'd smiled at her earlier that day had sent her heart fluttering, as much as she'd tried to deny it to herself.

But perhaps the weirdest part and what was really bothering her the most was that she'd known him her entire life. They were raised together, and although she didn't think of him as her brother the way Blythe did, she still knew him. It wasn't like he'd dropped out of the sky all of a sudden; he had always been around.

So what had suddenly changed? When had he gone from being a nice boy who smiled at her every once in awhile, to suddenly giving her strange and unfamiliar feelings? Feelings that she tried to convince herself she wasn't feeling, but knew she couldn't deny. They were buried deep, but they existed. Despite how long she'd practiced closing her heart to emotion, to steeling herself against the threat of others having any hold over her like her parents had, she still found herself unable to resist him.

And then there was Brogan, who she had been surprised to find so agreeable. There was something relaxing about being around him and his obvious admiration for her was undeniably flattering. But he was a Fury, and it was an unspoken rule that the Dryads were not to socialize much with them. Not that she'd discovered the reason, but it made her wonder why others feared them. Brogan seemed perfectly fine; albeit a bit shy, but still very kind and polite. Perhaps he was just different than the other Furies, and therefore maybe the rule didn't apply to him. She would have to find out.

Folding the hand towel neatly, she hung it back up and walked to her bed, where she folded back the covers and fluffed up her hypo-allergenic pillows. She crawled under her linen sheets and turned off her bedside lamp, trying to convince herself that the odd events of the day were just getting to her, and that tomorrow everything would be back to normal.

She had to believe it, had to know that she still had some semblance of control over both her mind and her carefully protected heart.

Chapter Seven

The garden room had always been one of her favorite places in the castle, with its enormous skylights open to the heavens and the all encompassing presence of Earth. It was really more of an enchanted forest than a room, despite the practical furnishings and mirrors Thea used for day-to-day operations. Plants and trees of all types lined the walls, bursting through the cracks in the stone floor and climbing the enormous Greek columns that held up the tall glass ceiling.

Perhaps it was because her element was so heavily present that she felt drawn to this room. Or maybe it was because during most of her childhood when she couldn't play in the courtyard because her father deemed it unsafe or because Blythe and Liam were there, Thea would let her come to the garden room and play with the animals.

It was a simple thing and Thea had not minded one bit, but Rhiannon still felt humbled and in awe every opportunity she had to come in and just sit.

Thea kept all kinds of animals, mostly for companionship. Her newest addition was a young wolf named

Bane, barely more than four months old, who Thea had rescued from an uncertain, motherless fate in the Alaskan wilderness. Rhiannon had already fallen in love with him.

She sat with him, petting his scruffy silver fur and admiring his golden eyes. He was surprisingly docile for a wolf, but maybe that was her power over him. Because in the same way that Air Dryads could charm birds, Rhiannon connected with most other animals, especially those most linked with the soil and the trees.

The room was empty except for herself and the animals, which was how she liked it. Thea and Sebastian had left on a trip with the Furies and would be gone for awhile, hopefully giving her plenty of time alone.

She just hoped her mother wouldn't catch her. Even though Thea was adamant about Rhiannon being allowed in the room whenever she wanted, she knew her mother would expect her to be studying.

And while she knew there was studying to be done, she rationalized that sitting in the garden room and basking in the essence of the Earth element was a good way to hone her powers even further. Surely her mother couldn't argue with that.

Reaching for the rope toy Thea had got for Bane, Rhiannon tossed it across the room and watched him race to fetch it. He lumbered back with it in his mouth, tail wagging cheerfully. She laughed and played tug of war with him, enjoying herself for the first time in…well, longer than she could even remember.

Out in the corridor, Liam walked, his hands tucked in his pockets and his mind focused on figuring out how to convince his dad to let him go to California to go fishing. His dad had been iffy about the idea, but he was slowly bringing him around. He didn't see what the big deal about it was; it wasn't like he was gonna kill the fish or anything. He just wanted to catch a few and release them back into the lake. No harm, no foul.

Thinking if he brought up the idea of a father and son camping trip that maybe his dad would loosen up about it, Liam grinned and mentally patted himself on the back. He'd drop a few hints about wanting to do manly stuff like hiking, making campfires, cooking hot dogs and telling scary stories. His dad would then come up with the idea, and bam! Fishing in the Sierras!

Distracted, he almost didn't hear the sound. It was faint and distant and something he had never heard before.

It was laughter, though for the life of him he couldn't figure out who it was.

Intrigued, he followed the sound, stopping outside the closed door to Thea's garden room. He pressed his ear against the solid wood and listened intently. Hearing the sound again, he slowly and silently eased the door open, peering inside.

What he saw made his heart leap into his throat and quite literally stopped his breath. The sight of her, sitting on the stone floor with her long, dark hair spilling over her shoulders, her face glowing with laughter and her eyes filled with a joy he had never before seen shook him to the core.

The only thought that managed to race through his mind was: *when had Rhia become so beautiful?*

She was playing with what at first glance he assumed was a big gray dog, but when the dog turned and stared at him, a growl rising from deep within its throat as it bared its teeth, he froze. It wasn't a dog…it was a wolf. Fear almost had him charging into the room to rescue her.

Rhiannon's head whipped around at Bane's growl, and she caught sight of Liam in the doorway.

All she could do was stare, unsure and wary. He was watching her with the strangest look on his face; a look she had never seen before. When he smiled, she felt more at ease, but the memory of that look stayed with her.

"Hi." He edged into the room, shutting the door, his eyes flicking apprehensively to the wolf.

Sensing his fear, Rhiannon rubbed her hands up and down Bane's fur, her mind urging him to calm. She felt him relax under her hands, and he turned and licked her cheek lovingly.

"Can I come closer?" Liam asked.

Rhiannon nodded, keeping Bane close for comfort. Seeing Liam sent off sparks within her that were not welcome.

He crouched down and sat beside her, his eyes never leaving her face. She felt exposed and strange, as if he was seeing her for the first time.

"What are you doing in here?"

She bit her lip, hoping her voice didn't betray her nerves. "Thea lets me come in here sometimes."

"I never knew that." He grinned, casually brushing back his hair and resting his arms on his knees. He glanced around the room. He had been inside many times, but had never lingered more than a few minutes. "So is that your pet wolf?"

She shook her head as she looked at Bane, who decided to lay down in front of her with his head resting on his paws. "No, he's Thea's."

"He seems to like you a lot." Liam watched the way she was petting the wolf with slender, delicate hands. "What's his name?"

"Bane." She chanced a glance at him, her eyes deep pools of green, full of intelligence and uncertainty. He found it impossible to look away. "Why are you here?"

"I heard you laughing, from the corridor," he said softly, his smile fading and wonder replacing it. "It's been years since I've heard you laugh, Rhia."

Had it really been that long, she thought sadly, her heart aching even as her face remained carefully blank. Shrugging, she started to turn away; that look had returned to his eyes, making her uncomfortable.

Before she could move, his hand reached out and touched hers. She stared at it dully. The warm and soft feel of his skin against hers sent tingles up her arm.

Meeting his eyes again, her heart pounded loudly. She took in all the details of his face, a face she knew nearly as well as her own. His mass of black curls that fell across his forehead and hid his ears, his sapphire eyes flanked by dark eyelashes, his long face with a strong, slightly cleft chin and his goofy, crooked grin.

It alarmed her that he wasn't smiling at her now. Instead he was just staring at her, as if he really was seeing her for the first time.

And when he spoke, she could feel a tremor race through her body.

"You're so pretty," he murmured, awe in his eyes.

She blushed, but didn't look away, knowing she would lose control if she did.

"Do you mean that?" she heard herself ask, the question rising from the uncertainty in her heart. This was practically a dream, sitting here with him holding her hand, telling her she was pretty…when had this become her reality?

"Of course I do," he told her, looking baffled. "Why would I make that up?"

"I don't know." Fighting for control and trying to maintain an air of distance, she started to pull her hand away, but he only held it tighter.

"Don't," he asserted, loosening his grip when he sensed her uneasiness. "Smile, Rhia. Please smile for me."

Despite her instincts telling her to run and not look back, to escape while she had a chance…her mouth did the exact opposite. It slowly curved and she smiled the most genuine smile she had ever smiled in her life.

And it was at that moment that his heart locked its sights on her, and her alone, and refused to let go.

"Can I…can I kiss you?" he managed, already reaching out with his free hand, aching to touch her hair.

She started to shake her head, felt the movement happening, even as she leaned into him, her eyes closing as his lips met hers. Her heart was pounding at full speed, and the shivers that had been a mild inconvenience before were now shimmering through her in wild waves, sending her mind reeling with hopes and fears and uncertainties…but in her heart she felt delirious joy.

She could smell his soap, and the syrup from the pancakes he'd had for breakfast. His lips were soft as they inexpertly pressed against hers, neither of them sure exactly how to kiss.

His hand touched her hair lightly, brushing through the dark strands, pulling her scent in until he was lost in her.

When she pulled away, her eyes fluttered open and she let out a long breath, her lips slightly parted and her brow creased with confusion and dozens of other feelings she had no concept of.

In response to her uncertainty, his smile bloomed wide and bright enough to blind her.

Neither of them could find a single word to say, so they simply sat in awed and confused silence, drinking in the complicated teenage emotions that were starting to emerge within them both.

At her request, they met in secret.

It wasn't that she was ashamed; she was just worried about her parents. She knew her mother would disapprove and she was certain her father would think her too young to be spending time with a boy this way. The truth was, she probably was too young, but she rationalized the entire situation away as an emotional experiment. She was simply testing the waters of exposing her heart, little by little, to someone she was learning to trust. Certainly there was nothing wrong with branching away from her comfort zone for once, even if it was a bit unconventional for her.

And yet, while she criticized and berated herself when she was alone, trying to convince herself that she was being a fool and that she should end this and retreat back into her carefully constructed shell, when she was with him, her mind forgot about everything except him.

Liam's casual, carefree attitude toward life should have irritated her structured sensibilities, but instead it fascinated her. How anyone could look at life and shrug off the bad times and cheer on the good times was mind boggling to her. She was constantly preparing for the worst, and then worrying over the best, wondering when the ground was going to fall out from beneath her.

But Liam was the poster boy for optimism, full of wild and crazy dreams, and hopes and desires. He rambled on for hours about how he wanted to climb Mount Everest, and shrugged off her insistent reminders of the dangers, difficulty, and years of preparation involved in such a task. He just smiled in that way he had and told her to stop worrying.

Where he was a glass half full kind of person, she was constantly worrying over her half empty glass. She believed absolutely nothing she heard, and only half of what she saw, while Liam had an unwavering faith in others that she deemed blissfully ignorant. He rarely questioned anything, and she did nothing but question.

And yet, despite how radically different they were, they found comfort with each other. It was as if they balanced their two extremes when they were together.

During most days, especially when they were in class together, she acted like nothing had changed. But he couldn't resist sending a smile in her direction, or watching her with his chin in his hand while he was supposed to be working on an assignment. More than once, Serendipity had scolded him for being distracted. Although, she thought he was simply daydreaming, not eyeing her oldest daughter.

But any chance he got, Liam sought her out, sometimes in the kitchens or walking through the back gardens, and they would steal away to someplace private to be alone.

The library was a favorite of hers, as she liked to read and was slowly but surely convincing him of the joys of literature. She loved to sit with him in the corner, surrounded by gigantic fluffy pillows, him laying on his back with her perched gracefully beside him, reading him passages from her favorite novels.

And on this particular afternoon, that was exactly what they did.

"This Emma girl sounds pretty full of herself," Liam commented, grinning up at her, his hands tucked behind his head as he lay back against the pillows.

Rhiannon glanced at him from behind the book. "She has her faults, certainly, but she also knows when she's right."

"I can tell you right now, without even knowing the ending, that she's wrong about this Mr. Martin guy."

Fighting back a grin, Rhiannon eyed him inquiringly. "And why do you say that?"

"Because." Liam sat up on one elbow, running his free hand carelessly through his hair. "He actually loves Harriet. Yeah, he's goofy and poor, but he's a good guy."

"But the point is that Emma sees that he is less than what Harriet should be looking for. Hence why she suggests Mr. Elton, who is wealthy, established in the community, and more than agreeable."

"Nah, he's boring. I don't get the sense that he actually cares about Harriet. He wants someone else."

Because Liam was surprisingly intuitive when it came to the motives of the characters, Rhiannon was impressed. Despite how much he goofed off in class, he had a surprisingly avid and quick mind that had an excellent grasp on human emotions.

"Even if Mr. Elton doesn't care for Harriet the way Mr. Martin does, Mr. Elton can still provide a better life for her, not to mention a better social standing that will benefit their children and grandchildren," Rhiannon pointed out, earning a sardonic glance.

"Yeah, but she won't be as happy. She should stick to the guy she loves, not the one who's rich."

"This may surprise your romantic heart, Liam," Rhiannon began, smiling despite herself. "But marriage is not all about love. Many people get married for social or financial reasons."

"Why anyone would want to do that is beyond me." He frowned, shaking his head. "Losing out on love just to marry for status?"

"It may sound foolish to you, but it's quite common." Closing the book, she glanced at her watch. "I really should get going, my father is expecting me."

She started to rise to her feet, only to have him pull her down to the pillows with him. Startling even herself, she let out a quick giggle that she hadn't even realized was inside of her.

Liam's heart swelled at the sound of it. He looked at her a bit shyly, but with budding confidence, and stroked his hand through her hair. "Give me one more minute, Rhia," he said softly, pressing his lips to hers, reveling in her taste. He may have been young, but he knew his own heart enough to know it wanted only her.

Her pulse jumped in that still unfamiliar way, giving her a moment of hesitation and distress, but still underneath it all it was simple delight.

"I have to go," she murmured against his mouth, smiling even as she pulled away.

"Duty calls, as usual," he grumbled, though his expression was playful.

She stood and stared down at him as she brushed at her skirt. "Duty will always be calling, Liam. I just choose to listen when it does."

She swept from the room, leaving behind the distinctive scent of sage and vanilla. He laid back down on the pillows and closed his eyes, his mouth curving in a contented and lazy smile.

Riding on the bliss from being with Liam, Rhiannon headed to the Greenhouse, clutching the novel *Emma* to her chest like it was her most treasured possession.

She felt lighter and freer than she had in ages, and couldn't believe her own daring at pursuing whatever it was she was doing with Liam. But in her mind she was just experimenting, and as her father was apt to say, experiments were key to creating anything worthwhile.

As she turned the corner, stepping into the Greenhouse with her lips still curved in a smile, she spotted her father standing over his drawings, scrawling rapid notations in his small, precise handwriting. He was too involved in what he was doing to look at her.

He waved his free hand in the air absently. "Get to work on the population charts, Rhiannon."

His voice was distracted and curt, and she felt her smile vanish in an instant as she realized he was in one of his moods. It was rare for her father to be anything but civil and polite with her, but when he was irritated or upset he was downright unpleasant to be around.

Determined not to interrupt him, she hung her bag up on the coat rack and stowed the book away without a sound. She went to one of her father's large boards covered in charts, and selected the one on animal populations. Unpinning it, she brought it with her to her work table, took a seat and began to update the chart.

The Greenhouse was silent enough to hear a pin drop, and she soon lost herself in her work.

Roughly an hour later, her father pushed away from his drafting board, grabbed the large vellum sheet he'd been drawing on, and swiftly tore it in half.

She glanced up, startled, and watched with wary eyes as he tore the paper up again, and again, until nothing was left but shreds. His face was cold and calculating, his eyes hard as steel, and she felt a shiver race down her spine. This mood was a particularly bad one…

Without saying a word, he grabbed another sheet of paper and slammed it down on the surface of his table. He whirled around suddenly and stalked toward her, his arms crossed over his chest as he stopped in front of her. When she met his eyes she felt her entire body freeze from his stare.

"Let me see the chart," he said sternly, holding out his hand. She lowered her eyes and handed it to him, her heart thudding in her chest.

Rohan looked at the chart, but his eyes could hardly focus on the paper. This was merely a way to distract himself from his frustration. He knew he could trust Rhiannon to be thorough and precise with her work, but he had to do something to take his mind off the impending anniversary just days away…

Handing it back to her, he crossed his arms again and took a deep breath. She accepted the chart numbly, still refusing to meet his eyes.

"Look at me, Rhiannon," he ordered, part of him knowing he was being too hard on her, while the rest of him embraced his role as both educator and father. She tilted her head up, her eyes slowly rising. "You only have a year or so left of study with your mother, and then you will be in here with me full time. But it is imperative that you start taking on more responsibilities now. I'm going to entrust you with a very important project, and I need you to devote yourself to it. We can't afford to have any mistakes."

Rhiannon nodded, her eyes serious and her face carefully blank.

"Good." With a heavy sigh, he pulled his glasses from his face and rubbed his eyes, taking a seat in the chair beside her. It was clear something was weighing on his mind.

"Is something wrong?" she asked, concern for him flashing through her before she could stop herself.

For a moment he didn't say anything, he just studied her. She had changed from a child into a young, beautiful woman, although she would always be his little girl. He knew he was strict at times but he also knew his influence had helped her grow into the intelligent and independent woman she had become.

But wasn't it chance that she was still with him at all? And every year when summer was in full swing, he was reminded that his friend Clynn had not been so lucky and there was a daughter who didn't get the chance to grow up like Rhiannon.

That was the source of his anxiety, of his frustration and his lack of focus. And it was the reminder that his daughter was still here, and that she needed him to guide her.

"It's nothing, Rhiannon," he assured her, trying to smile. It wasn't easy for him but he knew it would comfort her. "Let me show you what I have in mind for this project."

He pushed away his thoughts and tried to focus on the present, and not dwell on the past and what couldn't be undone.

Chapter Eight

June fourth marked the eight year anniversary of the night she lost Capri.

It was always a melancholy day on Euphora, the memory of that terrible night was on everyone's mind. The adults had made it a tradition to venture out to the cliffs and toss a wreath of white and pink lilies into the ocean, in memory of both mother and daughter.

Though they didn't join in, Rhiannon and Liam held their own small memorial together this year in the courtyard. They braided a crown of tiny flowers and grass, and laid it gently beside the jasmine bush where Capri had last been seen. It broke her heart to return to that spot, even more so now that her memory of Capri was shadowed and gray, her face losing clarity with time. But she would never forget just how sweet her friend had been, or how her disappearance had essentially destroyed what was between the three Dryads left behind.

She sat in class later that morning, putting the final touches on her comparative essay on *Pride and Prejudice* and *Wuthering Heights*. She was perusing it for spelling and grammatical errors when she heard someone approach and sit beside her. Turning from her paper, she saw Brogan. Her smile was automatic and becoming easier for her now. That, she knew, was a welcome result of her ongoing experiment.

"Hello."

"Hi." He looked a little worse for wear, as if he hadn't slept at all the night before. There were shadows under his eyes, and his face was a bit paler than usual.

"Are you alright?" she asked, her brow creasing in concern as her smile faded.

"Oh…yeah, I'm okay," he replied, chuckling to himself and averting his gaze from her, clearly embarrassed that she had noticed. When she said nothing, he chanced a peek at her, seeing she didn't believe him. With a heavy sigh, he said, "I was up half the night practicing with this new weapon that we got…you see, Rian's already a pro with it, and I know my father's counting on me to do well also, so I stayed up to practice. It was just so hard to get the hang of, and I couldn't hit any of the same targets that Rian had hit so easily…but I'll just have to practice some more, I guess." He smiled again, shrugging.

Rhiannon looked over his shoulder to where Rian was sitting, back rigidly straight as his hand cruised over his paper diligently. Her dislike for him was obvious in her eyes.

"He should be offering to help you, Brogan," she insisted, turning back to him. "Instead he sits there like he's above everyone else. It's revolting."

"Rian doesn't think that way, not at all," Brogan insisted defensively, his dark, poetic eyes hardening. "He doesn't know I'm struggling so much. I…haven't told him."

"But surely he sees you–"

"No…Roarke has been giving him special training because he's going to be the Head Fury when his dad retires. So he hasn't been around very much. It's just been my father and me."

"I see…" Because she did, she smiled at him again in reassurance. "Just keep working at it, you'll be fine."

"I hope so." He chuckled, more relaxed. "Anyway, I was wondering if you could proofread my essay? It's not that long, but I'm an awful speller and…"

"I'd love to." She accepted his paper, grimacing at the sight of his chicken scratch handwriting. This was going to be…interesting. "What's it about?"

He flushed, looking embarrassed. "Well, you recommended that book *To Kill a Mockingbird*, so I read it and wrote about Boo Radley."

"I knew you'd like his character." She nodded, proud of him. "He's one of the most interesting characters in all of literature and by far one of my favorites."

"I guess I related to him a bit, is all." Brogan shrugged, pleased to have made her happy. "He didn't want to be in the limelight, but he still wanted to help people, ya know? He was lonely, but at the same time he didn't know how to live being around other people."

"I can't wait to read your interpretation," Rhiannon said as she tucked his essay into her notebook, along with her own papers, keeping them organized and straight.

Over the last few weeks since Brogan had first spoken to her, she'd taken a strong liking to him, much to her surprise. It wasn't what she felt with Liam…with Brogan it was more like discovering a long lost friend whose soul so closely mirrored your own in both desires and fears that when you talked with them, it was like looking into a mirror. He was soft spoken and usually let her do most of the talking, but she felt akin to him in a way, like he was the brother she'd never had as a child.

It made her sad to think about how he had been there all along and that they could have helped each other through the hard times.

She hoped this was the beginning of a long and fulfilling friendship. Because in her heart, she knew she desperately needed a friend.

That night, she lay with Liam under the stars.

They snuck out after dinner, pretending to go to sleep, and instead brought a blanket and some cookies to a secret, tucked away grassy area in the far corner of the courtyard. When they had been children, it had been a favorite spot for them to play. Now it was hardly used, except when they wanted to steal away for awhile.

She didn't think she had ever laughed so much in her entire life as she did that night. Her hands were cupped over her mouth to stifle the sound, afraid someone would hear, even as Liam continued to crack jokes about everyone and everything.

"Did you see Balgaire's face when Roarke spilled his drink all over his new leather shoes? I swear I saw his eye twitch, he was gonna blow a lid or something."

Rhiannon let out a stream of giggles, recalling Balgaire's sour reaction perfectly.

"I think his eye did twitch!" she managed, covering her mouth again as she burst into more laughter.

Liam just laid back and enjoyed the sound.

When she was finished, she sighed, her hands falling to her sides. Liam reached for her hand and held it in his own.

Above them, the stars rioted against the night sky. It was a new moon, so the courtyard was virtually pitch black except for the candle Rhiannon had dutifully remembered to bring, along with the crisp, clean cotton blanket and the napkins to go with the cookies Liam had nabbed from the kitchen.

She turned to look at him, incredibly relaxed despite everything. June fourth had always been a hard day for her, but this year…having Liam by her side made it a lot easier to handle.

"Do you remember what Capri looked like?" she asked, her voice sober and quiet. She saw him take a deep breath and close his eyes, as if trying to picture her.

"Kind of..." he replied, opening his eyes to look at her. "I miss her, though."

"Me too." Feeling sad, she bit her lip and looked back up at the stars. "Do you think she's out there somewhere?"

"I like to think so." He continued to watch her as he squeezed her hand. "I bet she's living on some exotic island, where they wear coconuts as clothing and lay on the beach all day and dance around a bonfire at night. And she probably has a pet orangutan, one of those big orange ones. His name is Charlie, and he plays the drums while she dances, carefree and happy with her island family."

Her eyes suddenly felt hot and heavy as she listened to his words, knowing with her practical heart that none of it could possibly be true. But that didn't stop it from being extraordinary.

"I wish she had never been taken," she said before she could stop herself, her heart aching, the tears just hiding behind her eyes, not yet ready to fall. "Things were easier back then."

"Things don't have to be hard now, Rhia," Liam insisted, sitting up to stare down at her. "I bet if you and Blythe gave it another shot, you'd be best friends. Then all three of us could be together again."

She shook her head, not wanting to look at him. "That will never happen, Liam, and you know it."

"What makes you say that? You haven't even tried."

"I can't handle the two of you together," she said coldly, sitting up. "I'm nothing like her."

"So what? You and I are nothing alike, but we get along."

"Blythe's bossy, loud and obnoxious," Rhiannon began, ticking off the qualities on her fingers. "She likes to put people on the spot and doesn't respect anyone's opinion other than her own. And she's incredibly selfish and has absolutely no manners."

Liam's normally soft and dreamy eyes hardened, and Rhiannon was sorry to see it, though she knew she wouldn't take back what she said. She knew she was right about

Blythe; she had always been an excellent judge of character, and Blythe was an open book.

"You know what Blythe says about you, Rhia?" Liam charged, upset as always to be thrust in between the two of them. "She thinks you're snobby, prissy, and that you think way too highly of yourself. But that hasn't stopped me from knowing that none of that is true."

Rhiannon blinked, surprised by his words.

"Well, surely she's not too far off…I can come across as a snob sometimes…" she began, only to be interrupted by him.

"You're missing the point. Both of you have these opinions of each other, but I'm really the only one who knows the truth. And the truth is that Blythe is the furthest thing from selfish; she would die for someone she loves. And she has manners, they're just not very refined." He couldn't help but smile a little at the thought, and his entire face relaxed as he shook his head at her. "And you? You're not snobby, in fact you are the most grounded and real person I've ever known. And I know you don't think highly of yourself, because you're constantly criticizing everything you do. So, you see, if you guys gave it a chance, maybe this could all work out."

For a brief, flickering moment, she felt hope glimmer inside her heart. Maybe he was right…maybe things could work out between them.

"And it's so different being with you than it is to hang out with Blythe," Liam said suddenly, laughter in his eyes.

Rhiannon's brow rose skeptically. "What do you mean?"

"With her, it's like riding around in a fire storm, all spontaneity, fun and excitement. That's why we're always getting into trouble, it's all her influence, I swear." He put his hand over his heart and grinned, but then his eyes softened. "But with you, I get to slow down and actually see the world. You notice things, Rhia, that most people don't take the time to see. And you're so smart. I can't believe all the stuff you have crammed into your head. And I don't know why it's taken you so long, but when I hear you laugh, I just lose it."

She didn't know what to say, so she averted her eyes and felt her cheeks flush.

"I should probably go to bed," she said for lack of a better response. She got to her feet, only to have him rise with her.

"I'm sorry, did I say something wrong?" he asked, trying to reach for her hand, only to have her pull away.

"No, you didn't," she replied as she shook out the blanket they had been sitting on and began to fold it, lining up the corners meticulously, needing to do something with her hands.

"Then what is it? Why do you keep pushing me away just when I think you're letting me in?" There was irritation in his voice now, and it chipped away at her resolve.

When she didn't say anything and only continued to pack up their things, he rubbed his face with his hands in frustration.

"Rhia, please talk to me."

Gripping the blanket tightly in her arms, along with the candle and bag of cookies, she turned to face him, fighting to keep the emotion from her face.

"I don't know how to deal with all of this, okay? I've never done anything this crazy before, and I know it all seems so easy to you, but for me it's hard. I've gotten used to being alone and I like it that way. And then you come along and suddenly force yourself into my life, and part of me hates you for it because you make me feel things I've never wanted to feel. All my life I've detached myself from feeling anything because I knew it was easier that way. You don't feel pain when you feel nothing at all. But you've ruined that for me now."

"Why would you rather be alone?" he asked in disbelief. "All I want is to help you, Rhia, not ruin your life."

He walked toward her, his hands reaching out, only to have her step back.

"I don't need your help. I'm fine the way I am," she insisted, staring at him frostily.

"There's a part of you that's perfect in every way, but the person you're showing me right now is far from it. I've seen who you really are, Rhia, and I want to be with her," Liam persisted, feeling helpless and confused under her serious gaze.

She softened, feeling hope sneak its way back into her heart for the second time that night. Was it possible that she could really be with him?

"Maybe," she said quietly, but he knew he'd broken through to her.

"Take as much time as you need to figure this out. I'll always be here, waiting," he assured her, leaning forward to kiss her forehead softly. Without a word she turned and fled, frightened by the look in his eyes. His devotion was just too much for her to handle.

She walked as swiftly as she could without breaking into a full run, more confused than she had ever been in her whole life. She was losing control, losing her grasp on who she was, and Liam insisted that it was good for her. But was it really?

She raced up the stairs to her room, distracted enough to not notice her bedroom door was cracked open until she was right in front of it.

Startled, she hesitated for a brief moment before nudging the door open and staring into her room.

Her mother sat on the edge of the bed, her hands clasped primly in her lap and her legs crossed rigidly. The single lamp on the nightstand lit the room, and her eyes were as cold as ice.

"Where have you been, Rhiannon?" Serendipity asked, her voice laced with velvet and just a tinge of fury.

Rhiannon's mouth fell open, and she found herself with nothing to say. She froze, unable to look her mother in the eye.

With a sigh, Serendipity rose to her feet and approached her daughter, reaching out to examine the blanket, the candle and the bag of cookies.

"A late night rendezvous in the courtyard?" she noted, her sentence more a statement than a question. "I don't know what you were thinking, disobeying your father and me this way. You know you are expressly prohibited from being in the courtyard, unsupervised, at night. It's been that way since the raid eight years ago, so don't tell me you've forgotten."

Rhiannon continued to anxiously stare at her feet.

Crossing her arms over her chest, Serendipity pursed her lips impatiently at her daughter's silence. "Tell me this, Rhiannon. Were you with Brogan tonight? Is that who you've been running off with for the last few weeks?"

Now Rhiannon looked up, her eyes wide as she stared at her mother.

"Oh, don't act surprised that I knew. I can tell when my own child is distracted and not where she should be. Your father has noticed it, too. He says he gave you a project to work on recently and that you've barely done anything with it. What in the world has come over you?"

"I don't know," Rhiannon faltered, shaking her head, remorse eating away at her stomach. "I'm sorry..."

"I want you to refrain from speaking to Brogan except only when it is necessary. Clearly he is a bad influence on you. I will have to inform Balgaire of this so he can punish his son appropriately."

"It's not him, please," Rhiannon begged. She couldn't let Brogan take the fall for this, he didn't do anything wrong. And his father was already unhappy with him, what would this do? "I haven't been seeing Brogan."

"Then who? Rian?"

Taking a deep breath, knowing she was damning them both, Rhiannon whispered his name. "Liam."

"Dear God, Rhiannon." Serendipity's hand flew to her chest as she gaped at her daughter, surprise upon her face. "It was bad enough when I thought you were socializing with the Fury, but with Liam? He's a disgrace! He and that little hellion cause nothing but trouble and Lucian just lets them run rampant with no regard to decency or discipline. Clarity gave up on him a long time ago because she could hardly control him. Your father and I raised you better than this, Rhiannon, and I expect you to put an end to this immediately."

"But–"

"No, Rhiannon. This will end right now and you will stop acting like a child. You are to report to your father or me on your whereabouts at all times. I don't want you leaving the castle without permission, nor will I tolerate you speaking with him anymore outside of class, and then only when I instruct you. Clearly you're going through some kind of a rebellious phase, and I intend to squash it out of you this instant. No daughter of mine would lose focus this way. You are such a disappointment."

"I'm sorry, mother," Rhiannon said again, feeling the recently mended cracks in her heart reopen. In a final act of desperate self-preservation, she steeled herself against her mother's words and disappointment, shutting down the emotions she had let herself feel.

"Haven't I given you everything? Structure, direction, taught you how to be a lady? How dare you defy your father and me like this?"

Even though a small voice inside her head was shouting, screaming at her mother's insane notion that she had ever been a good parent, Rhiannon said nothing. The reasonable part of her acknowledged that her mother had indeed given her structure, direction, and taught her to be a lady. What more could she have ever wanted? Certainly not love, not affection, not one kind word of praise or encouragement…

"It won't happen again," Rhiannon heard herself say as her mind shut down and her heart shuddered closed.

And when her mother left her alone, going as far as to lock Rhiannon's door from the outside, she sat down numbly on the edge of her bed and told herself that this was best.

Her mother was right, it was foolish of her to have ever spent so much time with Liam. And her father was disappointed in her for not giving her full dedication to the project he'd given her. How could she have let herself slip this way, losing who she was just because a couple of boys looked twice at her? No, she wouldn't let herself fall victim to it again, she would be strong and smarter to how things should be.

She wouldn't spend time with Liam any longer. And she would maintain nothing but a casual friendship with Brogan, and not let herself get close. As she had always known, the result of letting herself feel was nothing but pain, and pain was certainly fighting to reach her heart now, no matter how bravely she fought it off.

All her hopes had been so childish…she had known, even as she had felt them, that they were impossible. Hoping and wishing never got a person anywhere, only understanding the harsh realities of life did. And perhaps the harshest reality of all was that she simply did not belong with Liam, nor could she ever be friends with Blythe. She was the outsider looking in, but never belonging.

She had a duty to herself, to her parents, to Thea and to Euphora. That had to be her number one priority. She could never again risk the chance of opening her heart, because all that it had done was nearly destroy everything she had worked for. And really, what choice did she have?

When he saw her the next day, he knew in an instant that she was different. The girl he'd gotten to know so well, the one who smiled and laughed, who was so heartbreakingly beautiful that he could never rid his mind of her face…she had vanished deep within the girl he saw now.

Rhiannon had closed herself off from him, from everyone. She walked around with empty eyes and a mouth that refused to smile. She kept to herself and declined to speak to him, even when he tried to confront her. The only words she'd spoken to him before hurrying away were: *Don't wait for me, Liam. I'll never be ready for you.*

He'd called back to her that he could be patient, that he would never stop waiting for her. But he wasn't sure if she'd even heard him.

And so life continued, just as it did before he experienced the best three weeks of his young life. It was as though it had never happened and had just been a sweet dream that had seemed so real…

And yet every now and again, as the years went by, he'd catch her in a moment, off guard, and see a flash of the girl he loved in her eyes.

Somewhere deep inside her exterior shell, guarded by cool indifference and prickly politeness, was the real Rhiannon, held hostage in her own mind.

He vowed to himself that he would never, ever give up on releasing her.

She was sixteen when she first heard the sound that would ultimately save her soul.

She had been ready to go out into the garden behind the castle, having just gotten permission to pick some wild red roses for the dining table, when she stopped dead in her tracks just before the exit.

Beyond the wood doors that were cracked open, she could hear someone strumming a guitar, rather inexpertly, but they were trying nonetheless. She chanced a peek through the opening, and spotted Liam, sitting with his back to her on the steps leading out to the garden, an acoustic guitar in his hands.

Backing away, intending to come back later for the flowers, she stopped when she heard him begin to sing.

It was a song about a tiny dancer, counting headlights on a highway…

Incredibly moved, she stepped forward and crouched down just inside the doorway, leaning her head back against the cool stone of the wall so she could listen to him.

In that moment, her cold, hardened heart ached and in private she briefly gave herself a moment to grieve over what could have been.

Chapter Nine

July 3rd, 2010
Euphora

She walked, as she always did, with resolute purpose. Her heels clicked along the stone floor of the corridor, echoing hollowly off the walls as she headed to the Greenhouse.

Her mind was sharp as a tack and meticulous, her body tall and slender with delicate feminine curves, dressed in elegant gray slacks and a soft, plum colored blouse. Her dark brown hair that she had always worn long draped down her back and swayed as she walked.

Eyes the color of rich sage flanked by generous lashes focused straight ahead, never wavering from her destination. It was symbolic of her disposition to never dwell on the past, at least not anymore. No, she learned from it, but never did she dwell.

Like her father before her, she wore practical reading glasses when she worked, perched on her straight and narrow nose like a badge of honor.

In her arms she carried her journals and log books, filled with pages upon pages of detailed projections and tracking of plant cycles, animal population density, and earthquake sequences. In the sensible black bag on her shoulder, she had her scientific calculator, three mechanical pencils, an extra eraser, aloe hand lotion, aspirin, a slim tube of clear lip gloss, a nail file, and a tin container filled with sugar free mints.

She was twenty years old.

It was still early and most of those on Euphora would just be settling in for breakfast. But not Rhiannon. She was up and ready to go long before the rest of them even got out of bed.

Her routine steadied her and she took immense pride in it. Rising at dawn, doing basic stretches to wake her muscles, taking a refreshing shower...she'd get ready, carefully put on makeup and classy designer clothes, dry and style her hair. Then she'd head down for a quick breakfast of hot green tea, fresh fruit, and whole wheat toast before heading to the Greenhouse for the day.

In the afternoon, she'd break for a quick yoga session to center her mind and strengthen her conscientiously toned body, then return to work until dinner. After dinner, she would play chess with Brogan or head into the library to read, or perhaps, if she was feeling a bit more social, engage in a discussion of literature with Capri or of human politics with Lucian and her father.

Day in and day out, her life was the same. And she knew without a doubt that it suited her to live this way, thriving on consistency and routine like a dying man in the desert sun yearns for water.

What was the point of living if one did not have structure? She had been taught from a young age that carelessness and frivolity led to nothing but stress and disappointment. And who wanted that?

Yet even with all of her carefully crafted structure and meticulous planning, life still managed to throw curve balls at her once in awhile, the most recent one being Brogan's departure to Richmond to look for Dante.

It worried her to see him go, despite how insistent he was that he could handle himself and that he wasn't in danger. That didn't stop her from trying to convince him to have Rian go in his place, and in fact that suggestion had only upset him. He needed to do this for himself, to prove that he could handle his duty as a Fury. And because she understood that, understood him, she had dropped the subject and let him go without a fuss.

But that certainly did not prevent her from worrying for him. He had been gone for a few days already, and she had heard little about what was happening or when he would return. And everyone else's lack of worrying about him was starting to get on her nerves.

Especially Nyxa. The woman had been attached, quite literally, to Brock for days now, the two of them fixated on each other, not even noticing anyone else around them. It was really quite disturbing, given the circumstances of the whole situation, but that didn't stop them. And it appeared that Nyxa couldn't be bothered to worry about her stepson, who had done nothing but stand by her side and defend her on everything. It was, in Rhiannon's eyes, unforgivable.

It grated on her that Thea had let Nyxa stay on Euphora after the horrific crimes she had committed. The woman had endangered all of their lives, and for what? A chance to get revenge on the one person she despised above all else?

While Rhiannon knew her mother was not perfect, especially now that Serendipity's affair with Brock had been exposed, she still knew her mother didn't deserve Nyxa's retaliation. She felt Nyxa should have known what kind of man Brock was, and she shouldn't have been surprised to find him cheating on her. Rhiannon certainly hadn't been surprised.

She had also correctly predicted that Nyxa would want revenge, and as such had kept a close eye on her. And look at how it turned out–the woman was stark raving mad and deserved to be banished. Of course, part of her knew that such a decision by Thea would destroy Brogan. He looked to Nyxa as the only parent he had left, even though she wasn't even his blood. Rhiannon never wanted Brogan to get hurt, no matter how justifiable the reason.

And how remarkable that Blythe, practically Rhiannon's arch enemy for years, had personally thanked her for uncovering Nyxa's vile plot against Serendipity. It had humbled her more than she cared to admit to see Blythe overcome her pride and simply say thank you. Nothing more, nothing less. But it made her feel incredibly childish to know that she couldn't have done the same if the situation was reversed. Her own grudges were too deeply rooted to allow for such behavior.

Maybe it was the bounty hunter's influence over Blythe that had drastically matured her. Certainly before her month long rendezvous with Jackson Murphy, she had been much more juvenile.

And then she had come home with him, injured and beaten by Dante, and she had proven to be a capable woman and a relentless fighter. Rhiannon had been, despite everything, impressed.

And now the bounty hunter was practically living with them. Oh, her mother had choice words with Thea over *that* decision, but she had been brushed aside with Thea calling her not only prudish, but a hypocrite as well. But even Rhiannon thought it quite unseemly for Blythe to be sharing her room with a man who wasn't even her husband, no matter how much in love they claimed to be. It just wasn't proper.

Not to mention how much the bounty hunter bothered her. Especially with that fresh scar on his face, his strange, drawling accent and those cowboy boots he wore all the time. He didn't pay her much attention, for which she was undoubtedly grateful. Yet when he did look at her, she felt like she was being scrutinized and examined like a fly on a pin. And from the distance he kept and the disapproval in the air she felt whenever he was near, she knew Blythe had divulged all the dirt on why Rhiannon was not a friend, but an enemy.

Well, she didn't want to be his friend anyway, and had no desire to get to know him. He was Blythe's business and not her own.

The person she was responsible for was her father. And the last several weeks had not been kind to him. She watched his gradual decline with unease and a jarring helplessness. Her mother's betrayal had broken his heart, despite how desperately he tried not to show it. But Rhiannon knew...she'd always known when something was wrong with him, even when others didn't have a clue.

Thinking of him, she pushed open the door to the Greenhouse and stepped inside. Morning rays of sunlight drifted through the glass ceiling, dappled and tinted green from the vines of ivy that spread over the glass. For a moment, she marveled at the beauty of it, reminding herself not to take it all for granted.

When she heard the irritated shouting, her eyes flew from the ceiling and focused on her father and her younger sister, Sierra, who were standing by the pond, arguing loudly. Sierra had her hands on her hips and her long waves of honey blonde hair shivered as she whirled around, hearing Rhiannon enter. Her cool blue eyes, the same color as their mother's, narrowed and then rolled in annoyance before she turned back to Rohan.

"I need a new dress, dad! How can you expect me to go to this party wearing something I've already worn? That's just disgusting, no one does that," Sierra said, waving her arms in frustration.

Rhiannon watched her father's right eye twitch as he took a deep breath, clearly upset.

"I don't have time to take you, Sierra, and your mother apparently has a migraine. You're just going to have to wear something you already have."

"*This is stupid!*" Sierra shouted, indignation coloring her pretty face. Looking for leverage, she spun around and eyed her older sister again. Glaring back at her father, she pointed a finger at Rhiannon. "I bet you always let Rhiannon get new dresses when she wanted them!"

Rohan's eyes flicked to his older daughter. Hating himself, but knowing it was the only way to get Sierra out of his hair, he motioned to Rhiannon. "Come here, Rhiannon."

She set her work items down and went over to him.

"I want you to take Sierra to Los Angeles so she can get a new dress for the party tonight."

Dumbfounded, Rhiannon shook her head, staring at him and ignoring her sister's cheer of triumph. "But there's so much to do…I have to finalize the reforestation plans, and collect data on that new species of deer we introduced last year. Not to mention the plate shifts we have planned for today, or the–"

"Stop it. Just stop it," Rohan grunted between clenched teeth, taking a deep breath and rubbing his eyes in aggravation. "Do what I tell you, Rhiannon. I don't have the energy for your excuses right now. Both of you, get out of my sight."

When Rhiannon just stood there, warring between obeying her father and her obligations as an Earth Dryad, he glared at her in a way she had never before seen. "*Now!*"

Startled, she grabbed her notebooks and glasses and fled the room, her little sister in her wake, grinning ear-to-ear. Clearly, Sierra could care less about what was happening to their father, now that she got what she wanted.

"So we're gonna go right now, right? Because I think it's like 9 a.m. in L.A. and that's when the stores open, and I want to get there early in case they have new stock. Plus, we'll need time to go to several places, 'cause I need new shoes, a purse, and jewelry and everything," Sierra rambled on as they walked down the corridor.

Sierra was much shorter than Rhiannon. She had their mother's build, with curves already beginning to show that would make most grown women jealous and have any man with a pulse drooling on his shoes.

Rhiannon, on the other hand, found Sierra to be a pest and nothing more than a sharp thorn in her side.

"I need to put my things away upstairs. I'll meet you in the atrium in a few minutes."

Rhiannon turned away and swept up the stairs to her room, her perfectly normal day ruined. In a sour mood, she tore open her bedroom door and stepped inside, putting her things away in their proper places. She reached for her 'human world' purse, a light and chic Gucci bag the color of warm rose, and deftly transferred the necessary items into it. Her lip gloss, mints, lotion, pen and pad of paper set, her aspirin, and lastly, several hundred dollars of United States currency so they could pay for Sierra's items. Knowing it was too much a hassle to bother her mother, her father, or Thea for the money, Rhiannon used her own private savings that she barely used anyway. Maybe one day Sierra would thank her.

With one last glance around the room to make sure she hadn't forgotten anything, she left the room. She spotted Capri stepping out of her own room, looking light and breezy in khaki shorts and a gauzy white blouse.

With a warm smile, Capri walked forward. "Good morning! Are you going somewhere?"

Feeling the edges of her sour mood fade slightly upon seeing her friend's cheerful, bright smile, Rhiannon forced herself to smile in return. "My father asked me to take Sierra to Los Angeles to get a new dress for tonight."

"Oh, that's right, it's Liam's birthday today!" Capri remembered, smacking her forehead with a bright laugh. "Gosh, you know, I've been so distracted lately, I forgot to get him a gift. Do you think I could come with you?"

She wanted to say no and save her friend the trouble of dealing with Sierra's annoying shopping spree, but Rhiannon didn't have the heart to say no. No one, it seemed, had the heart to say no to Capri.

"If you'd like. Though I must warn you, Sierra is going to drag us to probably fifteen different stores, and insist on trying on every item of clothing in each," Rhiannon warned, leading the way toward the stairs.

"I don't mind. I haven't been shopping with girlfriends in such a long time. This is going to be so much fun!"

Though she wholeheartedly disagreed that what they were about to do was fun, Rhiannon just nodded with a half smile and kept her mouth shut.

By the time they reached the first store on Rodeo drive in Beverly Hills, the initial concept of getting a new dress for Sierra had turned into a full blown girl's day out. Sierra had dragged her closest friend Cilla, Liam's little sister, along for the ride and she was now insisting on getting new clothes also. Rhiannon had a dreadful hunch that she was going to end up footing the bill for that as well, not to mention lunch and snacks to keep the girl's energy up for a day of shopping.

Rhiannon was slowly beginning to feel a headache bloom painfully behind her right eye.

She sat with a politely bored expression on her face outside the dressing rooms in Ralph Lauren, itching to rub the stress point in her neck that was also starting to ache. Capri sat beside her, cheerful and excited to be out.

"So I was thinking of seeing if there's a guitar store around here…Liam's old one is looking a little worse for wear, I think he's had it at least five years or so. I figured I'd get him a new one," Capri said, her smoky eyes lit with vibrant pleasure. "Do you think that's a good gift?"

Rhiannon smiled at the thought, knowing it was exactly the right gift for Liam. "He'll love it, Capri," she said, looking at her friend. "We'll look for one after lunch, okay?"

"Okay." Smiling, Capri covered Rhiannon's hand in her own, squeezing it gently. "Are you alright? You look a little out of sorts today."

"I'm fine," she said automatically, but when Capri continued to watch her with knowing eyes, she knew she was caught. With a heavy sigh, she tried to smile. "It's nothing, really. I just had a lot of work planned for today and being here puts a damper on all of it. But once we get home I'll be able to catch up."

"And you have the party to look forward to tonight," Capri added, sighing happily as she released Rhiannon's hand and sat back against the sofa. "I love the parties we have on Euphora…all the family coming together to celebrate… it's so wonderful."

Reminding herself that Capri had gone years without so much as a decent birthday party, Rhiannon tried to push back her own distaste for them. Sure, it was nice to get everyone together, but it felt as if they were constantly having parties and working less and less. She still took pride in her work and would certainly avoid a party if necessary to finish what she had to do. It was her duty, after all, to be an Earth Dryad, not to party.

She was distracted when she heard a cluster of giggles coming from the stalls of the dressing rooms, only to look up and see Sierra and Cilla both emerge, donned in luxurious knee length dresses.

"So, what do you think?" Sierra asked Rhiannon as she pranced forward, whirling around to showcase the pixie-like ocean blue dress. It had a ruffled skirt and a strapless straight line bodice, and from the looks of it, was genuine silk.

Rhiannon eyed the dress critically. It was too fanciful for her taste but she supposed it suited her capricious, pretty little sister perfectly.

"It's fine," she said mildly, turning her attention to Cilla, who had slipped into a cute coral pink dress with modest lines and a golden weaved belt. The girl smiled at her and tugged at the skirt self consciously.

"Does this one look okay? I wasn't sure, but I really liked the color," Cilla asked, tucking a strand of her curled strawberry blonde hair behind her ear.

Rhiannon nodded politely while Capri gushed. "I think you both look beautiful."

"If those are the dresses you want, then take them off and I'll go pay for them. Then we can find you shoes."

"Don't be so pushy, Rhiannon," Sierra began, her hip cocking out with attitude. "I think we should try on a few more, Cilla, just to be sure."

Cilla grinned in response. "I did see this one green dress that was cute."

"See, we're not finished yet. So you'll just have to wait," Sierra said haughtily, daring her older sister to object.

"Maybe while you girls try on a few more dresses, Rhiannon and I can run down the street and look for a guitar for Liam," Capri suggested, noticing the frustration on her friend's face.

Rhiannon looked away from her snobby sister to meet Capri's eyes. "We really shouldn't leave them alone…Dante is still out there somewhere."

"Oh, you're right." Capri bit her lip thoughtfully. "Well, then why don't you and I browse the store for a bit? I'm sure we can find something for ourselves, too."

With a nod, Rhiannon got to her feet and stared down at Sierra, barely veiled disdain in her eyes. "One more hour, then we're out of here."

Receiving an equal look in return, she swept from the dressing area out into the main store, Capri in her wake. Determined to do nothing more than keep Capri happy, Rhiannon followed her around from display rack to display rack, making appropriate noises of approval and disapproval when her friend held up an item.

When the time was up, Capri had picked a casual autumn dress the color of ripe pumpkin with burgundy floral patterns and a pair of flats to match. Rhiannon, her mind already reeling at the cost of everything, had chosen nothing. Her wardrobe was more than complete already.

Sierra and Cilla went with the original dresses they had tried on, much to Rhiannon's annoyance. But she kept her mouth shut and took the dresses and coordinating shoes up to the register, along with Capri's items, to pay for them all.

Capri insisted on paying her back, but Rhiannon waved off the notion. This was to thank her for coming along on this dreadfully boring trip. Besides, the dress Capri had chosen was much cheaper than the ones the girl's had picked. Sierra's dress alone cost well over a thousand dollars.

They went to lunch at the Blvd, an overpriced sidewalk café just off the Four Seasons Hotel. But it was the closest place for lunch on Rodeo drive, so they didn't have many options. She just ate her thirty dollar Greek salad and tried not to shudder when the bill came.

By the time they made it back to Euphora, it was nearly time for dinner and Rhiannon was exhausted and cranky. Not that Capri hadn't made the trip more enjoyable than it would have been otherwise, she reminded herself, noting that she would need to properly thank her friend later when she had time.

Until then, she had work to do.

She raced upstairs, running on less energy than she'd had that morning. She diligently switched out her bags and grabbed her books and headed down to the Greenhouse.

Sierra and Cilla had disappeared upstairs with their shopping bags to try everything on again, and Capri had gone to her own room to figure out a way to wrap Liam's gift. It was a Gibson steel string acoustic guitar made of Hawaiian koa wood and spruce, stained a rich golden color that faded to black on the edges.

The moment Rhiannon had seen it, she'd known it was perfect for Liam. She had practically forced Capri's decision to purchase it. But Capri was easy going and went along with the suggestion, especially since she figured Rhiannon knew Liam better anyway.

Pushing it from her mind, Rhiannon headed into the Greenhouse with an hour to spare before dinner. If she wasn't able to get everything done before then, which was unlikely, then she would just work through the party. She was sure no one would miss her anyway.

But before she could push open the door, the sound of sobbing stopped her. She hovered inside the doorway, in limbo and unsure what to do.

Peeking in, she spotted her father sitting at his drafting table, his face in his hands and his back shaking with vicious sobs.

For a moment, all she could do was stare at him. All her life he'd been so strong, sturdy and refined. And she only remembered one instance where he had cried around her, and that had been right after Capri had been taken. So to see him now, a broken version of the man she knew, shook her to the core.

Deciding to leave him in peace, she slowly backed away and silently shut the door.

Work would just have to wait.

Chapter Ten

After dinner was finished, everyone rushed upstairs to get ready for the party.

Rhiannon, however, took the opportunity to return to the Greenhouse, this time knowing her father wouldn't be there. He was upstairs with her mother, and other than the emptiness in his eyes and the hollowed look of his face, no one would know he'd been weeping just hours earlier.

Except for his oldest daughter, who still had no idea how to fix whatever it was that was happening to her father.

She sat at her desk in the Greenhouse, lit with dozens of candles that she'd brought with her as there were no other lights there. She placed them around the room so they illuminated it with glowing pools of golden light. Outside the glass walls, she could see the night sky and the stars, along with the moon that glowed full and bright. In the courtyard, fireflies danced in the air, lighting the gardens and the patio dance floor.

As she jotted down important figures in her earthquake projection book, she noticed movement outside the glass walls, through the shadowy protection of the ivy. People were drifting out of the castle, dressed in their best, ready to celebrate.

Not wanting to be distracted, she looked away and rose to her feet, stepping toward the pond. Above it, the globe hung in midair, glowing as though lit from within. Using her hands, she turned the globe until she found the area she was looking for, then proceeded to draw a line down the San Andreas fault. Concentrating, she closed her eyes and filled her mind with the image of the plates, and proceeded to shift them into position, causing a minor 3.0 earthquake to Southern California, where the San Andreas fault lay. Satisfied, she went back to her desk and leaned over her charts, noting the completion of the shift and its new position.

Her hair slipped down from her shoulder and her eyes were focused through her reading glasses as she jotted down figures and notations. So complete was her concentration that she did not hear him enter.

"You always were one to burn the midnight oil."

Startled, she jolted upright and saw Liam standing in the doorway, looking impeccably handsome in steel gray slacks and a royal blue dress shirt with the sleeves rolled up to his elbows. She fought to regain her composure.

"When duty calls, I answer, Liam," she replied, though she suddenly felt weary and tense, the pain in her neck that she had delayed earlier with aspirin creeping back.

"I know." With a grin he stepped toward her. The candles she'd lit shivered in the air, flickering light bouncing off the glass walls and the high vaulted ceiling. "Why don't you come to the party?"

She shook her head, glancing down at her charts and books. "I have a lot of work to do and I'm already behind."

"So make it up tomorrow." He was now standing right in front of her, closer than made her comfortable, to where she had to tilt her chin up to meet his eyes. Determined to hold her ground, she stayed where she was, her back rigid and her hands clasped at her back.

On impulse, he reached out to remove her glasses from her face, setting them on the desk. "It's my birthday, Rhia. You should do me a favor and come dance with me."

His lips curved in his trademark crooked grin and she felt her resolve shudder once. Damn him and that smile.

"I really shouldn't."

"But you will, because you're considerate enough to know it'll mean the world to me." His eyebrows raised as he continued to stare at her knowingly. "C'mon, let's go."

Pursing her lips and feeling she had no other choice, she spun away from him and dutifully shut down the globe and then packed up her books and charts.

"I'll give you one dance, but then I have to come back and work," she said as she straightened up her work area, making sure everything was organized.

Laughing at her, he reached for her hand to pull her away. "Uh huh. Let's go."

They walked toward the atrium in silence, and stopped before the entrance doors. He turned to her and smiled.

"Thank you for the guitar, by the way. Capri said you picked it out."

"Oh." Rhiannon's brow furrowed as she stared at him. "It was her gift for you and her idea. I just told her which guitar I thought you'd like best."

"You were dead on, I love it." He grinned, his hands itching to reach out and touch her. "Let's go dance."

It wasn't until they were on the dance floor that she realized with embarrassment that she was terribly underdressed. She was still in her slacks and blouse, while everyone else had donned elegant gowns and suits. But when she tried to convince him to let her change, he'd simply held her tighter and refused.

Fighting to relax, she let him lead, her right hand placed properly in his left and her other hand on his shoulder with his on her waist. She made sure their bodies didn't touch. This was as close as she was willing to get to him.

The song was slow and bluesy, but it did little to settle her restless nerves. There was still so much to do, and it was hard to concentrate on having fun when she couldn't take her mind off work. Especially since she'd lost nearly the entire workday because of her self-centered sister, and it would probably take her a week to get back on track, a fact which was only stressing her out further. And with her father being in such a state, he wasn't on top of things as he normally was, so that meant she had to pick up even more slack.

"Rhia?"

"Hmm?" She blinked, returning to the present. Liam just smiled at her.

"Where did you go?"

"What do you mean?"

"Just now, you weren't listening, you were someplace else…in your head." He would have given anything to be able to erase the worry lines from her forehead, and to discover whatever secret place it was she had in her mind that she retreated to when she was tense.

"Sorry, I just have a lot on my mind is all."

"Mmm…well, let me distract you." He spun her in a tight circle and brought her back into his arms, their bodies brushing seductively as their eyes met. The instant spark that ignited at the touch sent her mind reeling, despite how frantically she fought it back.

The stunned look in her serious eyes amused and aroused him. He loved it when he could startle her out of herself for even the briefest of moments. It reminded him that she was still in there, somewhere. "I almost forgot to thank you for entertaining Cilla earlier. She loves the dress."

"You're welcome," Rhiannon replied coolly, backing away so they were no longer pressed against each other, determined to maintain her distance from him.

Needing a moment to steady herself, she glanced around at the tables that surrounded the dance floor. She spotted her father sitting with Lucian and Clynn, though he wasn't speaking to them. Instead, he was nursing a single glass of champagne and sitting stiffly in his chair, his hair elegantly combed and his face stoically handsome. But his eyes were troubled and lost looking, the green in them dull and lifeless.

Standing across the way were her mother and the other Muses, and they were entertaining a few men that Rhiannon didn't recognize. Thea and Sebastian were there as well, and they were listening to one of the men speak animatedly.

When Liam noticed Rhiannon staring in their direction, he turned her so she could see them better. "That's Burke Callahan. You remember him, don't you?"

"The Enforcer. Yes, of course I do." She nodded, looking at him. "What's he doing here?"

"You know how it goes." Liam shrugged, grinning. "The Enforcers that want to rise through the ranks always try and mingle socially with the Council, get in good with Thea and Sebastian."

Rhiannon pursed her lips and glanced back over at her mother, who appeared to be openly flirting with Burke, touching his arm and smiling admiringly at him. Before she could turn away in disgust, her mother noticed her and motioned suddenly for her to join them.

"Come here Rhiannon, say hello to Mr. Callahan," Serendipity called over, snapping her fingers in the air imperiously.

With one last glance at Liam, Rhiannon pushed away from him. "I've got to go. Happy birthday, Liam."

"Thanks." He watched her walk away, and wondered if there was something more on her mind than just her work. Then again, figuring out what was on her mind had always been nothing short of a challenge for him. Rhiannon was a closed book, locked with multiple keys and covered in prickly thorns. But, luckily for him, he wasn't one to back down from a challenge, especially one with such great rewards.

When Rhiannon reached her mother, Burke turned around to face her. With a polite smile, she held out her hand.

"Good evening, Mr. Callahan," she greeted.

He smiled broadly and took her hand in his own. "Rhiannon! You have certainly grown into a lovely young woman. Serendipity, why didn't you tell me how beautiful your daughters are?"

"All the better to surprise you, Burke," Serendipity gushed, only to shift her focus and eye Rhiannon up and down critically. Turning back to Burke, she smiled. "If you'll excuse us for a moment."

"Certainly."

While Burke launched into a conversation with Thea, Serendipity clamped her hand around Rhiannon's arm and dragged her swiftly to the side where they could speak without being overheard.

"What are you wearing, Rhiannon?" she asked, her velvet voice tinged with irritation. "This is a formal party. I expect you to go upstairs right now and change."

"I'm not staying, I have to get back to work," Rhiannon informed her frostily.

"Nonsense, who works at this hour?" Serendipity brushed the thought away frivolously with a wave of her hand. "Now, head inside and–"

"Excuse me, ladies." Burke appeared beside them, his smile gallant. He reached out for Rhiannon's hand, smooth charm and all class. "This is the perfect song for dancing, if you'll have me?"

Trying to hide the surprise she felt, Rhiannon politely took his outstretched hand and let him lead her onto the dance floor. Her mother looked immensely pleased, and seemed to forget all about the need for a wardrobe change.

Burke grasped her hand in his own and placed his other on her waist, the proper way an older adult male should dance with a much younger woman. She studied him for lack of anything else to do since she was trapped dancing with him for at least three minutes while the slow, seductive love song played out.

He had aged, certainly, but it had done nothing but enhance his already handsome features. It had been years since she'd seen him, but she knew that he was still heavily involved with the Furies and with Thea. He was one of the lead Enforcers, if not *the* lead Enforcer, second only to the Furies as far as rank and importance.

His chestnut brown hair was weaved with gray and longer than she remembered. His brown eyes were still sharp, but charming nonetheless, set in a face lean and honed at the edges, with near classic movie star good looks. She wondered how much his appearance was a mirage, and if it was hiding something more sinister underneath. He was a ruthlessly exacting Enforcer, one that demons feared and lesser men admired. But the mask he wore was enough to fool anyone to believe he was harmless.

"Your mother tells me you are the best and brightest Dryad on Euphora," he said suddenly, his lips curving in a quick smile.

One of her eyebrows raised in surprise to his statement. "I do my best."

"So humble," he remarked, his eyes boring into hers. "But Thea said the same thing, so you must be very talented. My son, Michael, is a rising star amongst the Enforcers. Do you remember him?"

"Of course." Though the memory was anything but pleasant. Maintaining polite interest, she smiled. "How is he doing?"

"Sick with the flu, unfortunately." He shrugged, chuckling. "He's sorry he couldn't come tonight. He was eager to see all of you again."

She doubted that but she kept her thoughts to herself. "That's good to know that he's doing well as an Enforcer. I recall him wanting to be one from a young age."

"It's his destiny, as it was mine," Burke said proudly, beaming at her. "Soon he'll be promoted and work exclusively with my division. We'll be a father and son team. There's just a few more steps to take before it can all happen."

Something changed in his eyes, his focus intensifying as if she were a prize he desperately wanted to win. Troubled, she broke eye contact with him and noticed her father, sitting alone.

"I'm going to go see if my father needs anything," Rhiannon said suddenly, pulling away from him. "Thank you for the dance, Mr. Callahan."

"Please, call me Burke."

Bowing her head politely, she turned and walked toward her father, slipping into the chair beside him. He looked up from his drink to meet her eyes, and a weak, halfhearted smile graced his lips.

"Hello, Rhiannon," he said quietly, lifting his champagne flute to his mouth and sipping. She watched his hand tremble slightly with the movement.

"How are you?" she asked him, her hands clasped in her lap as she watched him with concerned eyes.

He pondered a moment, staring into the contents of his glass, lost in thought. "I'm fine."

Then he turned to look at her again, setting the glass down on the table. "I should apologize to you. I was rude earlier and you didn't deserve what I said."

"Apology accepted." She tried to smile, wanting to show she had forgiven him. He just took a longer sip of champagne, avoiding her eyes. Talking about emotions and feelings had always been an awkward subject for the two of them, so neither knew how to handle it.

Unsure what else to say, she sat back in her chair and glanced around at the others who were dancing under the glow of thousands of fireflies.

Liam was dancing with Capri, the two of them smiling and laughing with that cheerfulness they both seemed to thrive on. They looked natural together, so much so that when Capri had returned to Euphora, Rhiannon had half expected the two of

them to fall for each other. Certainly, they would have been good together, but instead Capri had found Rian, and Liam had…well, he had served as a brother figure, just as he seemed destined to do.

Blythe had lured her bounty hunter onto the dance floor, and they were dancing slow, wrapped up as close as possible, staring into each other's eyes with such intensity and crazed adoration that it made her uncomfortable to watch. That kind of blatant, exposed passion had never made sense to her, and she supposed it never would.

She spotted Sierra, donned in her ocean blue silk dress, dancing with her arms around Tobias' neck. He had his hands awkwardly placed on her waist, but his eyes were locked on her face. He had been infatuated with her younger sister for as long as she could remember, and ever since Sierra had figured it out, she'd done nothing but toy with the poor boy's heart. She dangled herself out like a carrot to him, and just when he thought he was finally going to get a bite, she'd skip away laughing. It really was vile, but Sierra seemed to find it all highly amusing and entertaining.

At least she had never led Liam on that way, Rhiannon reminded herself contentedly. She'd broken it off clean and precise, with no loose ends that could attempt to tie themselves up again. And ever since that day, any time he had attempted to get close to her again, she'd politely refused him, no matter how hard it was to see the anguish and hurt in his eyes. She'd told him to stop waiting for her, and the fact that he continued to push at her, albeit more softly now, was more his problem than her own.

She'd made her intentions clear. How he chose to act was not within her realm of control. All she could do was govern her own mind and her own carefully locked heart, and see to it that nothing shot through and shattered her meticulously structured life again.

The gardens behind the castle were much different than those in the courtyard. Where the courtyard garden was verdant, neatly trimmed and ostentatiously beautiful, the back gardens were almost forgotten, growing wild and untamed over three acres of land, with white birch trees lining the outside perimeter.

There was a path that wound its way through the tall wild grasses, organically formed by centuries of wandering feet. While most paid no mind to these back gardens, Rhiannon felt a special connection to them, if only because they were essentially forgotten and filled with lost secrets of times past.

Along the path, wild roses bloomed, thorny and beautifully untamed, a sharp contrast to the perfect blooms in Thea's rose garden in the courtyard. And as Rhiannon strolled through the tall grass, an oval shaped wicker basket in her arms, she tenderly picked the roses and tucked them in the basket, intending to use them for a centerpiece for the dining table.

As she snipped a stem, she'd kneel down and lovingly help mend and re-grow what she had taken. Such was her gift, to bestow beauty back to what had been lost.

Thea was in one of her melancholy moods that day, and so she had conjured up misty clouds to hover over all of Euphora. The resulting fog and light drizzle made the back gardens seem even more enchanting and mysterious, and Rhiannon enjoyed the cool feel of light rain on her skin.

The birds and other animals that so joyfully inhabited the courtyard seemed averse to the back gardens, as though they did not feel comfortable there. It only heightened the overall atmosphere with its heavy silence, the only exception the sound of Rhiannon's legs brushing the grass as she walked.

Since Liam's birthday party the evening before, Rhiannon had not stopped thinking of the events that had taken place.

Clearly her mother cared so little about her husband that she would blatantly flirt with yet another man right in front of him. What her motives were, Rhiannon had no idea. Burke Callahan was a happily married man. Though, from the way he'd looked at her while they had danced, she would almost beg to differ.

But what was her mother's motivation to get close to Burke? Surely she wasn't prepared to orchestrate a second affair so soon after her tryst with Brock was exposed and she was disgraced in the eyes of her husband.

It also seemed strange that Burke had asked both her mother and Thea about her character and abilities. Why should he be concerned with her when she hardly knew him, and she was just one of the many people who lived on Euphora? What was it about her that interested him so much?

That was the real question, she supposed. Why were her mother and Burke Callahan getting so close, and why did she have a sneaking suspicion that she was at the center of whatever it was they were doing together?

Suddenly, behind her, she heard the strumming of an acoustic guitar.

When she turned toward the sound, she spotted Liam sitting on the steps, his brand new guitar in his lap and his hand skillfully moving across the strings.

He grinned up at her, his expression playful and a bit sheepish. "I thought I'd play a song for you while you work."

She was about to let him know that she preferred the silence, but before she could say anything he jumped into a song he often played just for her.

She felt a smile tugging at her lips so she turned away so he wouldn't see. She continued walking through the grasses, enjoying his song, even though she resolutely disagreed with its message.

Only the good die young…hmmph. She was convinced that wasn't true. What was wrong with a person dedicating their lives to something more than just themselves? To have a desire to contribute and make a difference in the world, and not live in rash self-interest and self-indulgence? Surely Liam could see that her life had purpose, and that it was purpose that centered her and made her whole. She couldn't imagine how anyone could live without it.

So if being a good, hardworking, dedicated individual meant that her life would be unfulfilled according to this songwriter's standards, then so be it. She wouldn't want to live any other way.

When he was finished, she glanced over her shoulder at him.

"Are you trying to tell me something with that song?" she asked, amused despite herself.

"Maybe." He grinned, rising to his feet. She watched with carefully guarded eyes as he loped lazily across the garden toward her, slinging the guitar over his shoulder so it rested at his back, held by a leather strap. "Though I'll bet you find nothing wrong with being a goody two shoes."

He slung his right arm over her shoulders casually and led the way as they began to walk. She tried to ignore the tingling discomfort she felt from his casual affection.

"There's too much stress involved in breaking rules," she informed him, keeping her eyes ahead and her hands conscientiously clamped around the handle of her basket.

"Hmm...see, I beg to differ," he began, smiling up at the gray and misty sky. "It's liberating to not worry about consequences or rules and just go with what feels right."

Pursing her lips, she found she wholeheartedly disagreed. "But then you don't consider what effect your actions have on others, or on the future. It may feel right to run off to Ireland for a week on a whim, but what about work, and the burden that puts on others who now have to pick up your slack?"

"Is that someplace you'd like to go, Ireland?" he asked, looking at her curiously.

She bristled at the question. "Not necessarily, it was just the first example that popped into my mind."

"It would suit you, that place." His eyes were glued to her, even though she refused to return his stare. "The rolling green hills, dark trees, fields of purple heather and misty fog. Ancient castles filled with even more ancient secrets…"

She thought of the field of barley her father had taken her to that summer long ago, and how much she'd loved it. While Ireland's fields of green may be enchanting, she'd take her fields of gold.

"In case you didn't notice, we have a green field right here, with flowers and fog. And an ancient castle. I have no need for Ireland." She chanced a glance up at him.

He only smiled. "I myself prefer being out at sea. Put me on a sailboat, cruising through the Atlantic to go deep sea diving and I'm in heaven."

She tried to hide the shudder she felt at the very thought. "I don't trust boats, much less one without a motor."

"Why not? It's perfectly safe."

She snorted before she could stop herself, but she didn't quite laugh. His eyes widened at the sound, but she spoke before he could say anything. "Boating accidents occur all the time. Did you know that on average there are nearly five thousand boating accidents in the United States alone each year? And, between seven and eight hundred people die in those accidents."

"Why in the world do you know that?" he asked, amazed at the information she stored away in that avid mind of hers.

She paused, debating whether or not to tell him the truth. Deciding it wouldn't hurt, she explained. "When you and your father went fishing last year and you told me you were planning on renting a boat, I read up on the statistics and passed them along to your mother, just so she was aware of what kind of danger you were getting yourselves into."

"Wait." He stopped mid-step and stared down at her, eyebrows raised. "You're the reason we ended up fishing on the shore instead of in a boat?"

She met his eyes, her expression a bit haughty. "You should be thanking me for saving your life."

"Do you know how much I was looking forward to that boat ride?" He stared at her disbelievingly. "I'd wondered why my mom was so freaked out by us going. In fact, she hasn't let me go out boating since. I should've known..."

She felt a hint of remorse, but her reasoning forced it aside. "She had a right to know what her husband and son were doing."

His face changed, his eyes brightening as he grinned. "You were worried about me, Rhia. I'm humbled."

Caught off guard, she scrambled for something to say. "I would have done the same for any of the Council. Someone has to be responsible."

"Then why didn't you present some kind of death stats chart to my dad when Blythe went sky diving?"

Caught again, she grimaced. "Like any amount of reason has ever stopped her from doing as she pleases."

"Is that such a bad thing?"

"It is when it negatively affects one's life, family, or work."

"Okay, but not everything that's fun is harmful."

"But I would argue that many things that are harmful are fun, or else why would people do them? Such as sky diving, drinking in excess, riding a motorcycle…but in the end, all a person is doing is risking their lives and everything they've worked for or their family has worked for, all for a brief moment of fun. I'm sorry, but I don't see how that one moment is worth it."

He watched her, silently taking in her words. When he spoke, his deep blue eyes filled with a mixture of pity and sorrow.

"For someone so logical, you seem to miss the entire point of living. Life is nothing but risks, and the risks are what make it worth living. There must be things that you want, but are too afraid to take. Maybe it would be good for you to take them, before it's too late."

"I'm not like you, Liam," she said, her eyes betraying none of the uneasiness she felt at his words. "I don't waste time with

unreasonable wants, and certainly nothing that requires I risk everything I am to attain it."

"No," he said dully, his hands gripping her shoulders, bringing an awareness to her eyes that hadn't been there before. He pulled her to him, so his lips could graze her temples and he could breathe in the rich scent of sage in her hair. "You never waste time on anything that doesn't fit into your neatly organized life, Rhia. Not even me."

They'd been through this before, several times over the years. But she had never told him, not once, the reason for her ending what had been between them. She thought that if he knew, he would only fight harder to keep her, thinking that it hadn't been her decision, but her mother's. It was easier this way, to convince both him and herself that she didn't want him, that she didn't need him.

"Liam, you know this can't happen," she said evenly, taking a cautious step back in retreat. His hands fell from her shoulders and he stared at her with dull pain in his eyes.

"Why won't you let me in?"

She just shook her head. He would never understand the reason. How could he? He'd been raised to embrace love, and she'd been raised to conceal it.

"I have work to do," she told him, pushing past him to head back to the castle, her hands clenched tightly around her basket and her pace swift.

He didn't even watch her walk away. That image had been burned into his mind years ago.

Chapter Eleven

She walked briskly down the corridor with the basket still in her hands, needing to be alone.

She wished Liam would just accept her refusal and move on. She wanted him to be happy, and she knew that as long as he was fixated on her, he would never be satisfied. She couldn't give him what he wanted, what he needed–it was impossible.

And whatever it was that had happened between them when they'd been teenagers was nothing more than a fluke. She wasn't that girl anymore. She'd changed, grown and matured beyond silly hopes and dreams that could never come true. And yet, she knew that he remained ageless. He was still the same person he'd always been. Kind, carefree, charming…and she was just cold, detached and reserved.

Distracted and annoyed from dwelling on it, she almost didn't see her mother and Thea leaving the garden room and almost ran into them.

"Oh, I'm sorry," she apologized, bowing her head slightly.

"Goodness, Rhiannon, watch where you're going," Serendipity chided. "You'll mow us all down if you're not careful." Her eyes shot to the basket in Rhiannon's hands. "And what are you doing pruning the roses without gloves? I know you are careless around anything with thorns."

Rhiannon was used to her mother's nagging. "I was careful, mother."

Thea, watching the exchange, couldn't hide the pity she felt. "She's a grown girl, Serendipity, capable of taking care of herself."

Serendipity continued to stare critically at her daughter. "Clearly not. Why is your face flushed, Rhiannon? Do you have a fever?"

She reached out to lay her hand on Rhiannon's forehead, clucking as she did so. "Thea, I told you a rainy day was a bad idea. She went out in the rain without a coat and now she has a fever."

"It's barely raining outside," Rhiannon argued, batting her mother's hand away. "I'm perfectly fine."

"If you're fine, then why is your skin flushed and hot?" her mother demanded.

Thinking of Liam, Rhiannon clenched the basket in her hands tighter. "I was walking too fast, that's all."

Sighing impatiently, Serendipity turned to Thea. "Anyway, he says he should be free to come by in a couple of weeks. Perhaps we'll get together and discuss the details then."

"Perhaps," Thea nodded as Serendipity turned and swept down the corridor, heading to the Muses' tower. Turning to face Rhiannon, Thea smiled. "Can I speak with you for a moment?"

"Of course," Rhiannon obliged, a bit confused but relieved her mother was out of her hair for now. She followed Thea into the garden room and set the basket of roses beside one of the lounge chairs. As she did, Bane loped toward her, grinning wolfishly. She took a seat and ran her hands over his fur, comforted by his presence.

"He's missed you," Thea said as she sat across from Rhiannon, tucking her legs underneath her.

Rhiannon looked up with a polite smile. "I've been so busy lately. Maybe when things quiet down I'll be able to visit more often."

"Mmm, yes," Thea murmured, watching her Earth Dryad carefully, humbled by the girl's seriousness and dedication to her work. She was, by far, the most talented Dryad on Euphora, and Thea had always been proud of her. But she had seen the sacrifices Rhiannon had made to become who she was. She'd virtually missed having a childhood and, under her parents' instruction, devoted everything she had to being an Earth Dryad. Thea couldn't have asked for more dedication than that.

But had it been worth it? She watched the girl now, and saw cool, reserved beauty, a sharp, intelligent mind, and an undoubtedly closed and protected heart. While she understood the desire to be cautious, she would never understand the deeply rooted need for it.

"How is your father doing, Rhiannon?" she asked, noting how the girl stiffened at the question.

Rhiannon knew if there was anyone on Euphora she could be honest with, it was Thea. Therefore she decided to divulge what little she knew.

"He's been depressed, that much I can tell. He won't speak to me about it, but that's not unusual. We never discuss things like that, so I wouldn't even know how to ask him…" Biting her lip worriedly, she felt her brow crease as she met Thea's eyes. "I'm concerned, Thea, really concerned. But I don't know what to do."

"I don't know if there's much any of us can do at this point," Thea sighed, tossing back her dark curls with a frown. "Rohan has always been an introverted soul. He doesn't see the need to display his feelings, but that doesn't mean they aren't in there. It will just take the right person to bring him out of his shell and get him to talk about it."

"Haven't you talked to my mother about this? Surely she should at least be trying to reassure him that what happened with Brock meant nothing," Rhiannon said then, a bit frostily. "After all, she's in the wrong here and he's hurt because of her actions. I have seen her do little to repent."

"Your mother is, shall we say, shallow in her focus," Thea replied, her lips curving. "She doesn't see past the surface to what's happening underneath. Your father forgave her with words and so she assumes all is fine. But he has yet to forgive her with his heart."

"But she must see how much pain he is in!" Rhiannon shot back. Sensing the tension, Bane snuggled against her legs in an attempt to comfort.

"I don't think anyone has noticed, except for you and me, Rhiannon," Thea said softly, her dark eyes sympathetic. "The only reason I can see it is because I've been around long enough to see the cause and effect of such things and so I anticipated his silent suffering. And you can see it because you have always been in tune with him, in a way I don't even think he realizes."

"But I don't know how to talk to him about this. He doesn't let me in."

Thea smiled knowingly. "Frustrating, isn't it?"

Rhiannon's eyes narrowed, wondering she meant.

"In any event, I fear you are the only one who can help him, my dear. If not, he may wallow inside himself for years to come and eventually wither away from it."

The thought of losing him startled her, as she hadn't considered that a possibility. "No, that won't happen. He's going to be fine."

"Only with your help," Thea insisted, watching her closely. "You're all he has."

With a solemn nod, Rhiannon glanced at Bane and stroked her hand through the fur on his head. His golden eyes looked up at her adoringly.

"I should really get back to work," she said, rising to her feet.

"Oh, before you go," Thea began, tilting her head up to watch Rhiannon with curious eyes. "Are you currently involved with anyone…romantically?"

Confused, Rhiannon lifted her basket off the floor and held it close. It bothered her that the question had brought Liam's face to her mind. "No, not at all. Why?"

For a brief moment, Thea didn't say anything. Rhiannon had the distinct feeling that Mother Earth knew more than what she was letting on. "Alright. You'll see, in time."

Understanding she was dismissed, Rhiannon bowed her head and left the room, shutting the door behind her.

Rhiannon busied herself in the kitchen.

Since she was thirteen, she'd been coming to the kitchen to help the fairies prepare meals, mostly in secret. At first it had been just a place to go to essentially hide away for a few hours, especially when things were too much for her to handle. She always knew she could come here and lose herself in what she considered a fun and safe hobby: cooking.

Not to mention over the years she'd developed an impressive herb and vegetable garden in the tiny greenhouse just off the side of the kitchen. Eventually, her secret had been unearthed, but her father and Thea had managed to convince her mother that it was important for her to have a hobby and at least her hobby was educational and productive. Serendipity had finally given in when she'd sampled one of Rhiannon's tomatoes and deemed it 'suitable.'

And, busying herself with creating new recipes and assisting the fairies in cooking gave her a sense of satisfaction she rarely felt elsewhere, other than with her Dryad work. Even though the fairies couldn't speak to her, they knew her and appreciated her, which was more than she had ever received from her coolly detached parents. It was a comfort in itself to go to the kitchen and know that she was welcome there.

It was late in the afternoon, and the fairies were cleaning the castle, leaving the kitchen peaceful and quiet. It was a good sized and well lit space, with red brick walls covered with cabinets on three sides, and big bay windows and a small greenhouse attached to the fourth. The cabinets were a rich, golden birch wood while the counters were made of butcher block. The kitchen housed a fridge, freezer, double oven, a gas cook top and an oversized cooper farmhouse sink.

A large walk in pantry off to the side housed not only a sizeable wine cellar, but an entire stockpile of dry goods such as flour, sugar and all the staples one could need. Everything from the bread they ate to the coffee they drank was all made from scratch. Sometimes Rhiannon wondered if anyone realized the time and effort the fairies and she put into the dishes that were served to them. It seemed to her that if one day the fairies didn't do their job and the food didn't magically appear on the table, then most of the Council would simply starve with no clue how to feed themselves.

She, at least, had made sure to understand what most of the others quite simply forgot to even think about. It was simply her way.

Kneeling beside her tomato plants in the small greenhouse, she carefully pruned and enhanced the stalks, gently lifting leaves to examine her ripening creations. Lifting one of the plumper tomatoes in her hand, she closed her eyes and let her power course through her palm and into the tomato, assessing its maturity and vitamin content. Satisfied, she placed it in a basket at her side, and moved on to another plant.

She wore her gardening slacks, casual linen the color of khaki, and a short sleeved white blouse that she miraculously managed to keep dirt free. Her dark hair was piled on top of her head in a loose bun, with a few pieces escaping to fall near her face. She brushed at one of them impatiently with the back of her hand as she lifted branches and examined what had grown.

A noise caught her attention and she tilted her head to look up, a surprised smile blooming over her face.

"Brogan," she said, rising to her feet.

He was standing just outside the doorway looking whole and unscathed, to her immense relief. His tall figure that was always too thin was covered in his black Fury uniform, though he looked disheveled and exhausted, as though the last several days had been hell for him. His eyes were hollow with dark shadows, but his smile was genuine.

"Hi, Rhiannon," he greeted, his soft, poet's voice courser than usual. He cleared his throat, embarrassed by the sound of it.

Because he looked as if he needed it, and she knew she certainly did, she stepped forward and hugged him. It wasn't easy for her to show affection this way, but with everything that had been going on since he left, she realized just how much she'd missed his calm, comforting presence. With him, she always knew what to expect and what to say. Brogan was the very definition of consistency.

"I was worried," she said, pulling away to examine his appearance with concerned eyes. "How did it go?"

He shrugged, trying to look as if he didn't care but instead he only managed to show his frustration. "Dante's long gone, unfortunately. I tried to track him down, but the trail got cold."

"Is that why you were gone so long? No one would tell me anything," she asked.

"I tried to be as thorough as I could. I visited the alley, his now empty apartment, the stores he went to on a daily basis…no one has seen or heard from him. He must have fled the night he attacked us. It's going to take more investigating to find where he's gone."

"Did you tell Thea?"

"I just came from there. Rian thinks it's best that we keep an eye out, but lay back for awhile, let him come to us, so to speak.

But Jax and Blythe are antsy. They want blood, ya know?" He smiled, as if it were a joke between them.

"Blythe has always been impatient," Rhiannon mused, smiling back at him. "How is that going, by the way? Being on speaking terms with her?"

He shrugged again, knowing it was a tough subject between them. "It's fine. Nova and I…well, we just wanted to make things easier for Nyxa, and since she and Blythe are trying to mend things, we figured it would help if we did our part."

"That's nice of you," Rhiannon told him, though Brogan could hear the disdain in her voice.

"Are you worried I'll start spending more time with her than I do with you?" he asked, a bit timidly, hoping not to offend her. He knew she had a tendency to close down if confronted with too many questions about her thoughts and feelings, and usually it was easier to avoid those topics. But he had been friends with her for so many years, and he knew better than most how she felt in regards to Blythe.

"If you wanted to spend time with her, I wouldn't hold it against you," she assured him, though she turned and started busying herself with repotting a basil plant on the counter in the greenhouse.

"I don't think I could spend longer than five minutes with her. She's too high strung for me." He chuckled, resting against the doorjamb as he watched her. "I can't help but feel uncomfortable around her most of the time. With you, it's never been that way. I've always felt relaxed with you."

"Likewise." She smiled, looking at him.

Despite everything that had happened over the years, he appeared relatively unchanged by the tragedies he'd been through. He had a resilience she admired more than she could say. He'd lost his father in the most brutal of fashions, had found out all of the horrible deeds his father had committed, and yet he still carried on with unshakable strength. She wondered if anyone else had any idea just how strong he was as a person, and how wise and caring a soul he had. It seemed sometimes that she was the only one who noticed. He was, much as the fairies were, forgotten by most of those on Euphora.

"Do you want to help me pick some tomatoes for dinner tonight?" she asked impulsively, no longer feeling like being alone.

"Sure." He smiled and brushed at his curly dark hair, pushing it out of his face. "It feels good to be home. I missed you."

"I missed you too, Brogan," she replied, feeling at ease for the first time in days.

A few weeks later, she had a bad, and very unwelcomed, case of déjà vu.

She had left the breakfast hall and was on her way to work one uneventful morning, only to notice two men walking briskly through the atrium, heading straight toward her.

She paused mid-step, her eyes honing in on none other than Burke Callahan, and a younger man she could only assume was his son, Michael.

"Rhiannon!" Burke greeted, a bright smile on his face. "How lucky we are to run into you this fine morning."

He approached and offered his hand. She took it, her lips curving politely even as her eyebrow lifted in annoyance the moment he raised her hand and lightly kissed her fingers. Gallantry from a man did little to impress her, especially because it was often a cover for hidden motives. And she could tell from a mile away that Burke Callahan had an ulterior motive…she could sense that mirage again, that mask that portrayed friendliness when she was certain he would offer no such thing if you crossed him.

"Good morning, Burke," she responded as he released her hand, which she made a mental note to scrub clean. She turned to his son, who looked remarkably the same as he had the last time she'd seen him nearly twelve years before.

"You remember my son, Michael," Burke beamed proudly, as though showcasing his thin son as a magnificent piece of art.

Rhiannon shook Michael's hand politely, noting the disdain and indifference in his eyes. Interestingly, he looked very little like his father and he certainly had none of his charm.

Michael was barely as tall as she was, his body slight and his hands soft. His pale skin looked as though he avoided the sun at all costs. In fact, by the look of his scrawny, unused arms, he avoided manual labor at all costs, as well. Just what it was he did as an Enforcer, she couldn't be sure.

He had the same sandy blonde hair, combed over to the side with meticulous care, not a strand out of place. His face had honed over the years, but his brown eyes had the same arrogance in them that she remembered too well from when they were kids. His mouth was curled into a sneer edged with boredom and annoyance.

"Nice to see you again," Rhiannon said courteously, though it was a bold faced lie. Nothing about him was nice and never had been.

"This place hasn't changed," Michael drawled, glancing around with bored eyes. When he stared back at her, he looked her up and down with equal boredom. "Nor have the people."

"Yes, well, our lives are rather unexciting compared to yours, I'm sure, being an Enforcer and all," she replied, tilting her head up and displaying equal disdain.

"Nonsense!" Burke chimed in, patting his son on the back and chuckling. Michael glared at his father but Burke didn't notice. "Surely we see more action, but we all know the world wouldn't be able to function without all of you."

"Nor without the fine work the Enforcers do," Rhiannon nodded, meeting Burke's eyes. "If you'll excuse me, I have work to do."

She swept past them without bothering to look at Michael, who she sincerely hoped never to see again. How in the world Thea and the Furies allowed that scrawny, arrogant prince to be an Enforcer was mind boggling to her. There was just no way he pulled his own weight. In fact, she was certain that all he did was boss others around while they did the hard work, and he just sat back and took all the credit.

She wondered, yet again, if he even wanted to be an Enforcer or if he was just doing this because his father was forcing him. If so, sooner or later he was going to get himself killed, because there was just no way he could handle himself around a demon in a one-on-one fight.

Deciding he wasn't worth her time and energy, she pushed thoughts of him out of her mind and instead focused on her tasks for the day.

She entered the Greenhouse, mentally going through her *to do* list, her notebooks in one arm and her other reaching for her glasses in her purse. She glanced up as she found them and spotted her father sitting at his drafting table, staring at a blank sheet of vellum, his hands clenched into fists on his knees. She stopped and watched him, wondering if he was okay.

Hanging up her bag and setting down her books on her desk, she approached him, clutching her glasses in her hands to steady herself.

"Good morning," she tried, hoping not to startle him. But he didn't even flinch, or move; instead he remained still, his eyes staring at nothing.

Tentatively, she moved into his line of vision, and slowly reached out her hand to touch his shoulder. Biting her lip, she brushed her hand over the cashmere of his classic, steel gray sweater, and he shivered slightly under her touch.

"Is everything alright?" she tried again and this time she saw a shimmer of light flicker over his face, and a flash of agony so brief she almost didn't notice it. But it was there, and as swiftly as it had come, it was replaced by an expression so empty he appeared dead.

His eyes shot up to meet hers, the green in them dulled. It alarmed her to see his vitality, his strength, sucked out of him this way.

"What are you doing here?" he croaked, his voice hoarse as though he hadn't had water in days.

Startled, she blinked and stared at her watch. "It's seven, I always come to work at seven," she reminded him, wondering if he had lost his mind.

His eyes narrowed, and he scowled as he stared around him. "It's seven already?"

She nodded and then realized he was wearing the same clothes he had worn at dinner the night before.

"Were you in here all night?" she asked, dumbfounded.

"I must have lost track of time." He cleared his throat and rubbed his face, looking tousled and agitated.

Concerned, she gripped his arm and pulled him to his feet. "Go to bed, get some sleep. I'll take care of everything today."

He suddenly looked at her with a kind of weary wonder, as though he was seeing her for the first time.

To her bewilderment, his eyes filled as he watched her silently and fear punched viciously through her chest.

"What's wrong?" she asked, more frightened by the desolation in his eyes than she could say.

He shook his head. "Nothing. I'm fine, Rhiannon."

With that, he turned away from her and left the room, leaving her standing alone, feeling lost and confused.

How was she supposed to interpret any of this or deal with it? She was used to order, structure and finite actions, tidy feelings and predictable words from her father. To see him virtually self-destructing right before her, and to quite literally have no clue what to do about it, was killing her. And despite what Thea had told her, she just wasn't sure she was up to the job of rescuing him from himself.

Because it was easier, she pushed away the uncertainty, and the fear and the pain, mentally disposing of them with greedy haste. Later. Later she would deal with it, when she could figure out what to say and how to say it.

And if the thought crept in that maybe it was something inherently wrong with her, not him, that was keeping her from understanding how to help, then she simply disposed of that, too.

Because it was easier, she pushed away the uncertainty, and the fear and the pain, mentally disposing of them with greedy haste. Later. Later she would deal with it, when she could figure out what to say and how to say it.

And if the thought crept in that maybe it was something inherently wrong with her, not him, that was keeping her from understanding how to help, then she simply disposed of that, too.

Chapter Twelve

As if things weren't already stressful enough, Michael and Burke had been graciously invited to stay the night by Serendipity and Thea, which Rhiannon had been unaware of until she strolled into the dining hall and spotted them seated directly beside where her parents usually sat. They were the first ones there, save for her mother, who was busy chatting up Burke with engrossed veracity. It made her sick to see the adoring way Serendipity fawned over Burke, like he was a hero or something. It was downright shameful for her to act that way as a married woman, especially one who had so recently been caught in an affair.

Though Rhiannon was beginning to seriously doubt if her mother really cared for her father at all, especially given her blatant refusal to see just how depressed he was. The memory of her earlier encounter with him that morning shuddered into her mind, and she had to shake it away as she took her seat.

She noticed Michael glance at her, and once again look her up and down, as if deciding for himself whether or not he considered her to be attractive. Disturbed, she nodded in his direction, but did not smile.

She took a sip of wine as the fairies finished conjuring up the meal. She watched them, finding comfort in this one, timeless tradition that reminded her that some of her structure was still in place. The golden lighted fairies, as small as fireflies, soared over the table with rapid speed, hundreds of them, using their special kind of magic to transport what was in the kitchen to the table.

Many of the dishes they brought were ones Rhiannon had created, though she wondered if the other inhabitants of Euphora even realized it. But she didn't require any credit; she didn't do it for them. She enjoyed her hobby of cooking and creating new recipes, exploring different kinds of produce, always altering and perfecting. As a result, the tomatoes in the sauce over the chicken parmesan were exceptionally high in lycopene, more than standard tomatoes, and they grew larger and ripened at a quicker pace for faster consumption.

The fresh rosemary that graced the roasted chicken had a sweeter, more robust aroma, thanks to her meticulous attention to detail while the plant was just a seed. And she was certain no one would even realize that the very wine they were drinking had started as grapes from vines she'd grown years earlier, when she'd tried her hand at being a vintner, just for fun.

She saw her father enter the room and felt relief wash over her. He looked much better than he had earlier. Sleep and a shower had done wonders for his appearance. He walked around the table, passing Burke without a word, and took a seat between Serendipity and Rhiannon.

"Did you sleep well?" Rhiannon asked, a small smile curving her lips.

"Yes," Rohan said simply, nodding to her cordially as he sat straight and rigid, unable to look at his wife, who hadn't even acknowledged his presence.

Though his hair was combed neatly, his handsome face scrubbed and fixed with an expression of stern politeness, Rhiannon saw his hand tremble as he reached for his wine glass. Seeing it devastated her.

He was pretending everything was fine, that he was better… but it was still there, in his eyes, in his hands…that empty, hollow despair that it seemed only she could see.

Deciding she still had no words of comfort to say to him, she turned away, fighting back the distinct feeling of inadequacy that seeped into her system. Did she have no heart at all, that she didn't have it in her to help him? Was it her complete and utter lack of understanding emotions that made it impossible for her to know what to say? She'd long ago promised herself she wouldn't feel anything that wasn't tidy and predictable…but had it gotten to the point that not feeling something was keeping her from saving him?

That very thought worried her almost more than his condition had.

Others began to file in, greeting Burke with either polite indifference or cheerful smiles. Rhiannon was taking another sip of her wine when she heard Blythe's telltale husky laugh.

She came into the room, looking bright, vibrant and happy, hand-in-hand with Jax, both of them smiling ear-to-ear. The happiness radiating from them, not to mention the sparks, seemed to resonate and fill the entire room. It made Rhiannon incredibly uneasy.

Both of them stopped when they noticed Burke and Michael sitting at the table, and in an almost comical fashion, they both gaped.

"Hey, Mikey." Blythe recovered with a grin, brushing back her vivid red curls with her free hand. "Long time no see."

Michael sneered even as his lips attempted to curl into a smile. "Michael," he corrected, his brown eyes sharp with dislike.

"Oh, my bad." She laughed as she jabbed Jax in the side. "Say hello, cowboy. Don't be rude."

"Hello, Callahan," Jax drawled, eyeing Michael with a hardened, sarcastic smile.

"What the hell are you doing here, Murphy?" Michael demanded, glaring at Jax.

"I live here," Jax replied, his arm winding around Blythe's tiny figure possessively.

"Ah." Michael's eyes trailed back to Blythe and he smiled cruelly. "Must be nice to shack up with one of the Council. Free meals, a place to sleep…someone to sleep with…"

Jax just laughed. "I can't complain." He tilted his head down to kiss Blythe, who lushly obliged him, just as eager to irritate Michael as he was.

Rolling his eyes, Michael lifted the nearly empty glass of wine in front of him and downed what was left. Rhiannon could hardly hide the amusement she felt seeing him turn red with both jealousy and indignation. Clearly he had known Jax from when Jax was an Enforcer years before, and, just as clearly, the dislike between them was mutual.

As Blythe and Jax took their seats, Lucian and Clynn came in, along with Brogan and a few others, all of whom greeted Burke kindly. Liam wandered in as well, and when he spotted Michael, the smile that spread over his face took Rhiannon by surprise.

"Hey Michael," he greeted, reaching over the table to shake hands. Michael rose to his feet, only because he knew his father expected it, and shook Liam's hand.

"Liam." He nodded, though he made sure to keep his head tilted up in arrogance, a show of superiority. Rhiannon wondered if he felt intimidated by Liam and this was his way of combating it.

Liam sat between his father and Blythe, directly across the table from Michael. He greeted Burke with a gracious grin, then sat back nonchalantly in his seat, wine glass in hand, watching Michael as if he was the most entertaining person alive. Clearly this was an attempt to irritate him because Michael was just as determined to keep eye contact with Liam; each of them participating in a male staring contest, laced with dare and obvious challenge. Liam was still willing to protect his home, and Michael was arrogant and foolish enough to challenge him.

When Capri and Rian came in, hand-in-hand, Rian nodded to their guests in greeting and pulled out Capri's chair so she could sit. She sat and thanked him with a kiss as he sat beside her.

"Capri, this is Burke Callahan, and his son Michael. They are both Enforcers," Rian told her, motioning across the table. Burke glanced up and nodded to her courteously, before resuming his conversation with Serendipity.

Michael turned from Liam and eyed Capri strangely. "Aren't you the girl who got kidnapped?" he asked.

Capri blushed, but acknowledged him with a nod. "Yes, fifteen years ago."

"My father said they found you living in the real world, with my kind," he continued, his eyes narrowing as he studied her.

"I was living in an orphanage in Virginia, until Liam found me back in March." Capri smiled politely, still embarrassed to talk about her past.

Michael snorted. "How embarrassing that no one adopted you the entire time you lived there."

Rhiannon stared at him incredulously, not believing his blatant lack of civility. How dare he say such an awful thing?

She was about to give him a piece of her mind, but when she glanced over at Capri's shocked face and then saw the fury in Rian's eyes, she knew she wasn't alone in feeling insulted for her.

"You're out of line, Callahan," Rian said slowly, his eyes hard and dangerous.

"What? All I said was that it was embarrassing for her." Michael scoffed, chuckling to himself. "Some people are way too sensitive."

"And others are much too insensitive," Rian added, his hand protectively holding Capri's beneath the table.

Rhiannon had a feeling this was going to be a long night.

Though she would have preferred nothing more than to go upstairs and crawl into bed with a good book, her mother insisted she stay and talk to Michael. Which was, as she would soon discover, an incredibly grating task.

They were standing together beside the grand piano in the parlor, sipping wine and forcing conversation. He seemed as annoyed with the idea of talking with her as she was with him, sheer boredom written across his face. Either that or he just always looked that way, which wouldn't surprise her one bit.

"Did you enjoy dinner?" Rhiannon asked, trying to be polite.

He sighed, visibly uninterested. "It was alright. At home we have our own chef, Luis. I have yet to taste food that is better than his, so I admit I'm spoiled when I visit other places." He chuckled to himself with a smirk, and she had to summon all the power within her not to roll her eyes. Had she ever met someone with such arrogance?

"And the wine? Is it to your liking?" She took a sip herself, and eyed him over the rim.

He sampled another taste, rolling it on his tongue before answering her. "This is quite exceptional. Hint of cherry, kind of a..." he swirled the glass and sniffed, shifting his gaze to her as he did so, "woodsy aroma, bit of vanilla mixed in…yes, quite exceptional. You'll have to give me the name of the winery."

"There is no winery." Rhiannon replied, a hint of pride in her voice. "I made this wine here."

"Hmm." He stared down at the wine. "My father said you were talented, but I didn't realize your talents stretched into wine making."

"It was a hobby of mine for a few years. I don't have much time for it now," she told him, brushing away the thought. "So tell me about life as an Enforcer."

"There isn't much to tell," he muttered, irritated. "My father tells me to jump and I ask how high."

Her brows creased together as she stared at him, realizing that this was probably the most candid thing he'd said to her all night. "Are you saying you don't want to be an Enforcer?"

He shrugged, taking another sip of wine and glancing over her shoulder where his father was entertaining the Muses. His eyes tightened at the sight. "What I want is respect."

She turned and followed his gaze, only to find herself also annoyed by what she saw. Her mother, cozying up to Burke once again. She didn't even see her father, who had probably gone up to bed without anyone even noticing.

"Your father speaks very highly of you. Surely that is a sign of his respect?" she offered, turning back to him.

"I'm his project, nothing more." Michael scowled, meeting her eyes. "But that doesn't matter. I'll earn my own respect soon enough. Until then, I'll play his little game like an obedient puppy."

One of Rhiannon's brows shot up at his words.

"What kind of game could he possibly be playing with you, Michael?" she asked, curious and dismayed at the same time. Unfortunately, the way he felt seemed to mirror her own sentiments regarding her parents. Hadn't her entire life been a project for them? Molding her into the perfect Dryad, the perfect woman, never giving her a choice to be anything other than what they wanted?

"You'll find out soon enough, Rhiannon." Michael chuckled, downing his glass of wine with a disturbing smirk. "Your mother's quite an industrious, devious bitch."

Shock flashed across her face as she gaped at him, unsure what to say. Before she could do more than digest his words,

Liam appeared at her side and wrapped one arm protectively over her shoulders.

"Hey Michael," Liam greeted easily with a grin, looking casual and cool as always. Yet there was a warning in his eyes, subtle, but distinct none the less.

Michael's smirk vanished as he eyed Liam with intense dislike. "Come to monopolize the ladies like always, Liam?"

"What can I say, it's a gift." Liam laughed, his hand subtly squeezing Rhiannon's shoulder to get her attention.

She had been so startled by Michael's words and realized that she had no clue what he had meant. Only one thing seemed to stick out…was it true that his father and her mother were planning something together?

"Rhiannon, can I speak with you a moment?" Serendipity said suddenly as she glided toward them, pulling at Rhiannon's arm. Liam released her, surprised by the force her mother used to jerk her away.

She pulled her daughter to the corner and turned on her, clearly upset and irritated. "How dare you let Liam paw all over you while Michael is here? How is he supposed to feel welcome and comfortable if you don't give him your full attention?"

"First off, mother," Rhiannon began, eyebrows raised. "I resent the insinuation that I was letting Liam 'paw all over me' when all he did was put his arm around my shoulders in a purely friendly manner. And secondly, I was being more than gracious to Michael as a guest. And he certainly doesn't look like he requires my full attention."

She motioned back to where Michael and Liam were having a heated match of wits, with Blythe and Jax joining in. Serendipity pursed her mouth in disapproval. "Such blatant disrespect. Lucian needs to get a handle on that son of his. Poor Michael is being harassed to no end."

Feeling a headache coming on, Rhiannon rubbed at her temple and closed her eyes, not even sure she wanted to get into the many reasons why her mother's opinions were horribly unfounded and incorrect. For God's sake, both Liam and Michael were acting immature, it was certainly not one sided.

"It appears as though Michael can handle himself," Rhiannon said.

"He needs your support, Rhiannon. He's trying to get his bearings and fit in here, and you won't even stand up for him!"

"Don't be a hypocrite, mother. Father needs your support, yet you seem incapable of offering it," Rhiannon snapped, the words coming out before she could stop herself.

Shock flashed across her mother's face, swiftly followed by anger. Her eyes froze like ice, and her voice lowered to a dangerously quiet murmur.

"How *dare* you speak that way to me?" she countered, her cold blue eyes narrowing to dangerous slits. "If you had any heart at all, you'd see that I have repented for my mistake and how terrible I feel for what I've done to your father. But clearly you feel nothing but contempt for me in that black heart of yours."

"Any contempt I feel is with myself, for not knowing how to deal with his pain. Can't you see he's hurting?" Rhiannon asked, even though she knew it was useless. Her mother would never see, because she simply chose not to.

"Your father is fine, Rhiannon. You need to stop worrying about him and focus on our guest. Michael specifically wanted to talk to you, no one else. You need to give him the respect he deserves."

"I don't care about Michael, mother," Rhiannon said crossly as she rubbed at her temple, which was now pulsing with pain.

Serendipity's eyes widened in surprise and she looked horrified, as if Rhiannon had told her the sky was actually red, not blue.

"You don't care? You don't care that he came all this way just to see you again and that Burke was nice enough to bring him? He wants to get to know you and you don't care?" She looked down her nose at her daughter, disgust clear in her eyes. "When did you become so cold, Rhiannon?"

I'm cold because you've made me this way! Rhiannon thought, her head reeling with the injustice of it all. How could her mother not see that? Any warmth she'd ever wanted, her mother had refused to give or allow her to have. Her entire life had been nothing but cold.

And for her mother, the ice queen herself, to accuse her of being cold, and then wonder where it came from? Good God, she must be blind…

"I don't feel well, I'm going to bed," Rhiannon managed, fighting to maintain her composure. "Goodnight, mother."

Before Serendipity could retort, she left the room, brushing past Liam and the others, retreating so she could get her bearings.

She raced out into the corridor, the moonlight cascading through the stained glass windows and the torches lit with vivid orange fire. Her heels clicked against the stone floor, her mother's words resounding like a giant bell in her head.

*If you had any heart at all…*God, was it really her own fault she couldn't understand what was happening around her? Why she couldn't help her father? Had her years of building this wall to protect herself from pain and emotions closed her in, separating her from everyone else?

"Rhia!"

When she heard Liam's voice call out to her, her chest clenched and she nearly stumbled from the ache she felt from hearing his voice. He, the one person who had given her warmth…which she had refused, time and time again, because there was something deep inside her that feared and abhorred it, even as she craved it…

She considered ignoring him and continuing upstairs to her room, but her years of carefully ingrained manners had her turning around to face him.

He jogged to her, concern in his eyes. She took a deep breath to try and calm herself, unsure if she could handle a conversation with him right now. Everything about him made her feel worse and reminded her of what she had given up all those years ago.

"Are you okay? I saw you arguing with your mom and then you bolted. I wasn't sure..." He paused, his eyes honing in on her face, and the brief flash of pain he saw in her eyes. "What did she say to you?"

"She said she thought I was being rude to Michael. Nothing else." She told him, eyeing him frostily, her mask carefully back in place. "Please leave me alone, Liam. I just want to go to bed."

"No, that's not what she said, because that wouldn't have bothered you one bit. But something did, Rhia, I can tell. Tell me what it is so I can help." Knowing she wouldn't let him touch her, he tucked his hands in his pockets to squash his desire.

Rhiannon watched him for a moment, suddenly feeling very cold, miserable and dried up, just as her mother suggested she was. God, was it normal to want nothing more than to hide from all of it, to run away so she didn't have to think about the regret?

"I don't need you to rescue me every time you think I'm upset. I'm perfectly fine. Goodnight." She whirled around, needing to put as much distance between herself and him as possible.

"One day, Rhia," he called out to her, his voice echoing off the stone walls of the corridor. "One day you'll open up to me again."

"I can't. I don't know how," she whispered to herself as she pulled open the door that led up to the bedrooms, avoiding looking back at him at all costs.

She raced up the stairs, and all she could think was that she was quite sure she was incapable of giving him anything warmer than ice.

She was cold and empty. Just like her mother had said.

In her dreams, she was a child once more.

She was perched on a graceful rope swing inside a brilliantly gilded bird cage, with a garden bursting with stunning flowers and lush green plants inside with her. The ground at her feet was grassy and pristine, and reminded her of the courtyard. But she wasn't in the courtyard; she was inside this strange cage, surrounded by thick gold bars that glimmered in white light that seemed to come from the nothingness outside.

Beyond the walls of her cage, her parents watched her, pressed up against the bars like visitors at a zoo. She stared at them inquisitively, admiring their elegant clothing and beautiful faces. Her perfect parents, she was so lucky to come from them…

And yet, there was disgust in their eyes. She looked around, wondering if they saw something behind her that they found unseemly. But there was nothing, only flowers. Surely they didn't hate the flowers…

And then it hit her. They were staring at *her* with revulsion and disappointment, and when she turned back to face them, she wanted to ask them what she had done wrong. Why weren't they proud of her? But the words didn't come… couldn't form on her tongue, no matter how hard she screamed them in her mind.

She felt it then, the hollow ache blooming in her chest, and she glanced down with wide, terrified eyes.

There was a huge, gaping black hole, singed around the edges through her dress as though it had been burned. Where her heart should be, there was nothing but ash.

Her breathing came fast and shallow as she tried to come up with some logical reason why her heart was missing. Who had taken it? Where was it now?

That was when the cold settled in, and everything around her faded to darkness. Her bones rattled in her body as she trembled, aching with an icy chill…

And without her heart to pump warm blood through her body, she felt her skin shrivel up to nothing but cold flesh.

When she awoke, gasping for breath and clutching her chest, feeling that hollow ache as if it were as real as her own hands, she felt her eyes burn. But the tears wouldn't fall, couldn't fall. She had never known how to cry.

Instead she held her knees to her chest and rocked back and forth, the blankets pooled around her and the moonlight shimmering through the gauzy curtains at her window.

She knew exactly what had happened to her heart, and accepting the truth only made the ache more real. Her mother had ripped it from her chest the moment she'd condemned her for being with Liam all those years ago, and had cruelly convinced her it was for her own good.

But how could not having the capacity to feel anything, let alone love, be good for anyone, let alone her?

And now it was too late.

She couldn't help her father. She couldn't love Liam. And she certainly couldn't cry. For how can one cry, if one does not know how to feel?

Chapter Thirteen

The next morning, she tried very hard to justify her dream to herself. And so far, every argument she had only fell to pieces miserably, which agitated her even more.

She attempted to convince herself that all was not lost. Certainly she had spent the years of her life so far shutting out emotion and feeling, but that didn't have to be seen as a bad thing. Why, if anything, she was more focused and more driven than she would be if she'd let emotions cloud her thinking.

That was why she was the most successful and the most talented of all the Dryads, and quite possibly all those in her generation on Euphora. She didn't waste time dallying with emotions and complicated feelings. No, she accomplished things, and expanded her mind and learned new skills with her time. There had to be something said for such conviction, such devotion to her duty and her destiny as a Dryad. And one day, when the time came, she'd probably settle down with an Enforcer, most likely of her mother's choosing, and have a child to carry on the Earth Dryad powers. And that would be that. No messy emotions, no unattainable dreams and no wasted time.

But even with all the arguing and fighting to convince herself that everything was fine, that her life was just as she wanted it, some tiny part of her nagged from the empty hollows inside, begging for release from this prison of sanctity and purpose.

Freedom, it screamed. *I want my freedom…*

And as she sat at the dining table, numbly eating her breakfast, listening to Burke talk with her mother, and Michael discuss something with Brogan, she felt a tingling on the back of her neck and looked up to see Liam enter the room. He looked fresh and relaxed as always, and that tiny part of her strained toward him. She was quite certain it showed in her eyes as he looked at her. *You're the only one who can free me…*

When his lips slowly curved into a warm smile, she felt her heart beat fast and steady, fighting back against the emptiness. She allowed herself the briefest of moments to feel the sensation, before turning away to sip her tea.

It wouldn't do to lead him on, she knew. If anything, she wasn't cruel.

Her father sat down beside her, looking much as she felt–empty. She wondered if he felt as though his heart had been ripped from him, and if that was why he had been walking around like a zombie for several weeks. Was that the answer, the understanding she'd been looking for?

No. She still had no clue how to talk to him, how to bring it up. She didn't have the courage, the ability to push past her fear of rejection from him, her fear that her intervention might only push him deeper into his hole. She needed more time…

Later, she stood alone in the Greenhouse, the globe in front of her and her mind focused intently on her work. She was tending to a recent burn area in Australia, urging re-growth and decontamination of the soil. Her hands hovered over the affected area, and her eyes were closed as she created fresh seeds beneath the surface, seeing in her mind as they took root and began to grow. Without her assistance, the area would quite possibly never re-grow. Yet it was crucial for the ecosystem to thrive and start anew; for the forest to begin fresh growth with plants she'd helped make even more dynamic and useful for the environment and the animals that lived there. Her gift was to restore and improve the Earth, as it cycled through its ever changing eternal life.

She heard a noise and turned, her hands still hovering over the globe. Michael was standing in the doorway, his hands in the pockets of his expertly tailored black slacks. He looked, as usual, bored and annoyed.

"What are you doing here?" Rhiannon asked, pulling her hands away from the globe and crossing her arms as she faced him.

"My father suggested I come see what kind of work you do." He shrugged, stepping into the room and glancing around, looking unimpressed.

She watched in irritation as he stepped toward her father's boards and sneered at all the charts, figures and drawings of new plants they were creating.

"So I know your element is Earth, but what is it exactly that you do?" he asked, wandering toward the globe, peering at it with a skeptical look on his face.

Letting out a huff of breath, she attempted to be polite, despite how much his arrogance irritated her.

"As an Earth Dryad, it is my duty to regulate plate shifts in the Earth's crust, maintaining balance at all times so that everything continues to function properly. I also monitor and influence flora growth throughout the planet, ensuring that the various ecosystems are flourishing and continually improving. The Earth is a forever constantly changing organism and as Dryads we maintain every part of it. Without me, plant and animal life would not be able to sustain itself. Without water, my creations would perish, and the Earth would dry up. Without air, water would have no means to travel and spread throughout the planet.

And without fire, nothing would ever have the chance to start anew and re-grow, better and improved. We are all just part of maintaining the delicate balance of our planet, and no one of us is more valuable or more important than the rest."

Michael walked around the globe, eyeing it. He turned his attention back to her. "Show me."

"Alright." She went to one of the worktables where a round ceramic pot sat, filled with fresh soil. She motioned for him to come watch, and as he stopped beside her, she held her hands a few inches over the soil.

Closing her eyes, she summoned her power and felt it shimmer from within her, then spread to her arms and then down to her palms, where she felt it leave her and go into the soil. She imagined a seed growing, one of her latest creations, and guided it through development, seeing in her mind's eye the green stalks emerging from the seed, and pushing up through the soil, seeking air and light. She imagined the leaves sprouting from the stem, and buds growing, spreading skywards to bloom into soft, yellow flowers. Opening her eyes, she glanced down at her creation, pleased. And when she turned to Michael, his eyes were bulging and he looked more than a little petrified.

"It just…came out of nothing," he stammered, eyeing her with a mixture of revulsion and horror. "How does it work?"

"I created a seed within the soil and expedited its growth so you could see it. That's all," she explained, concerned by the look in his eyes.

"You really are a freak," he told her, backing instinctively away from her, shaking his head. "None of this makes any goddamn sense."

Anger flashed in her eyes as she rounded on him, crossing her arms over her chest again.

"You asked to see how it was done, Michael. Don't act surprised when I show you."

"It isn't normal…" he muttered, eyeing her with disgust now. "My mother was right to warn me about this place, but my father wouldn't listen. He's so hell bent on coming here, on being with you people. But it's just not natural, it's not right."

"Not natural?" Rhiannon's eyes narrowed as she glared at him. "What I am is as much a part of this planet as the soil itself. I would argue that you, Michael, are the unnatural one out of the two of us."

"I should have listened to her. She was right about all of you. You're nothing but freaks; you shouldn't exist. It goes against all common scientific knowledge."

"Your mother sounds like quite an ignorant woman," Rhiannon spat, feeling her rarely used temper rise. "Maybe it's better for all of us if you just go back to her and never return."

"Trust me, I wish for nothing else but that," Michael muttered, looking bitter and distracted. "I hate this place."

With an exasperated sigh, Rhiannon threw up her hands and rolled her eyes. "Then leave. No one is forcing you to stay."

Knowing if she didn't get away that she might very well strangle him, she swept past him and left the room, indignation coursing through her. What an egotistical, insufferable child he was...

Storming through the corridor, she threw open the door to the kitchen and shut it behind her, needing something to do with her hands to distract herself. She went straight to the greenhouse and began grabbing different pots from the shelf and arranging them on the counter, deciding she would grow more sage for the turkey they had planned for dinner.

Almost manically, she began shoveling fresh soil from a giant drum into the pots, spilling more on the floor than she was managing to get into the pot itself. Scowling, she slammed the pot on the counter and began rummaging through the cabinets, searching for a broom to sweep it up.

She finally found it, and whirled around to face the mess, only to knock one of the pots over with the broom handle, causing it to crash to the floor. With a low growl through clenched teeth, she inhaled deeply and closed her eyes, trying to calm down.

Her hair was falling in her face, and her eyes were hard as steel as she opened them and began fervently sweeping up the fallen soil, her breath coming out in raspy gasps and her hands trembling with barely controlled anger.

Liam entered the kitchen and was taken aback to find her in this state, quite clearly crumbling to pieces. He almost blinked at what was surely a mirage. Rhiannon didn't fall apart like this…

"Rhia?" he called out, stepping toward her.

She glanced up at him, startled out of her manic rage, her lips parting with surprise. She watched him stare down at the ground, and at her hands that were clenched so tightly around the broom handle that her knuckles were white. Good God, what was happening to her?

Carefully, she set the broom aside and backed away until she was pressed up against the counter behind her. Closing her eyes, she inhaled deep and slow, feeling embarrassment creep up to flush her face.

"What are you doing here, Liam?" she managed, not wanting to look at him.

"I came in to get a snack…" he murmured, still dumbfounded by the scene he'd just witnessed. "Jesus, Rhia, what's going on?"

"Michael," she muttered, her lips curling into a snarl before she could stop herself.

"Can't stand him either, huh?" Liam asked, relieved that it wasn't something more serious. He stepped toward her, dodging bits and pieces of ceramic from the broken pot on the floor.

She opened her eyes, only to see he was right in front of her, staring down with amusement in his deep blue eyes, warmth radiating from him in glorious waves. The part of her that yearned rose up in desperation and screamed, begging for him to free her. The reasonable side of her shuddered in near submission.

"Am I cold?" she whispered suddenly, not even knowing where the words came from. She saw the surprise flash over his face, and his smile fade as he shook his head.

"Of course not," he replied, the urge to reach out and hold her threatening to consume him. She had always been the most beautiful creature he'd ever laid eyes upon, and seeing her like this, with clear sadness in those serious green eyes, destroyed his control in one vicious swipe.

She recognized with startled relief that her heart was indeed beating in her chest. It was pumping life through her, this very moment, and it was all sparked by the very sight of him. It had always been him, and only him, who could make her heart pound and her pulse jump. And all her life she had ignored it. But just then, the freedom-seeking lost soul inside of her jumped up and seized the chance awakened by the weakness in her resolve.

Pressing one hand to her heart, comforted by the rapid, pulsating beat, she reached out hesitantly with her other hand to touch his chest, eager to feel his own heart. She focused on her hand as she tenderly extended her fingers, palm spread, over his shirt. Her eyes felt hot and heavy as she reveled in the sensation of another heart, beating in time with her own.

Impossibly shaken, she clenched her hand over his shirt, holding him there, knowing if he moved she would crumble. Her knees felt weak as she looked into his shocked and mystified eyes, and when his hands came up to touch her, she didn't object.

Cupping her face, he moved in, hovering just over her mouth, closing his eyes to wrangle back the beast raging in him. The urge to take her, the desire, had always been lying in wait. And the utter submission in her beckoned it forth with surprising strength.

But she needed tenderness, that much he knew. And he wanted nothing more than to give it to her.

He said her name as his lips found hers, and he lost himself in the feel of her body pressed against his, in the scent of her, everything he'd ever wanted.

Rhiannon shuddered once and gave in, the little soul inside of her shouting with exalted joy. *I have a heart! It does feel!*

And the feel of him, the tall, lean body and lightly calloused hands, his black curls of hair and warm, sunkissed skin…it took her back to when she was thirteen, and the sweet, sweet memory of it staggered her. It was just the same…

But no, it wasn't the same. It would never be the same, because she wasn't the same. He was, certainly, but she had changed in ways that were irreversible. Whatever she thought she felt now was only a fallacy, sparked on by a brief moment of weakness and temper. It wasn't real…it couldn't be. How could she handle it if it was?

Pushing him back, she turned her head, breaking the kiss. She didn't want to look at him, not after what she had just done. Oh, she was horrible. She'd let him in, led him on, when she couldn't possibly be what he wanted her to be.

"I'm sorry Liam," she managed, the hollow ache returning to her chest as she forced back the part of her that had rejoiced. She wasn't that, couldn't be. It was too messy, too confusing, too much for her to handle…

"What are you sorry about?" Liam asked, even though he knew. As swiftly as she had given in, she was closing up again. "Damnit, don't be sorry about this."

"I have to be. It was a mistake. I was feeling weak and vulnerable, and I used you. But nothing's changed."

"You were her again, Rhia. For a moment, you were the girl I remember, the girl I want. This proves she's still in there somewhere, like I've always known. Release her, damnit, and let yourself be free." Agitated, he stuffed his hands in his pockets, annoyed that she wouldn't even look at him.

"I can't," she whispered, despising herself. "And I won't."

Frustrated, he started to leave, only to whirl around and point a finger at her. She glanced up, her face unreadable. "This isn't over."

With that, he left the room, leaving her to dwell in the dull silence and come to terms with what had happened between them, yet again.

Over the next week, she avoided him as best she could. It wasn't an easy task, as he insisted on suddenly showing up nearly everywhere she went, whether it was in the back gardens pruning roses, in the courtyard eating lunch with Capri, or in the kitchen working on a new recipe. She couldn't seem to get away from him, and all it was doing was making it harder for them both. Him, because of the constant, frosty rejections. And her, because just looking at him quickened her pulse and weakened her knees. It was a sensation she would rather live without.

Since their argument in the Greenhouse, Rhiannon hadn't seen Michael, which relieved her enormously. The last thing she needed was another forced conversation with that pompous dunderhead. And since her mother had been hopelessly busy doing God knows what, she hadn't been pestering her oldest daughter with questions or demands regarding the Callahans, which suited Rhiannon just fine. She sincerely hoped the Callahans would stay away from Euphora for good and leave her in peace.

Though peace was quite an understatement. Her father was still lost in himself and seemed to be getting worse as the weeks wore on. She'd begun to feel more and more helpless. Though he spoke to her and worked alongside her, it was as though a light had gone out inside of him. He never smiled, his voice was much too flat, his temper too easily provoked, and he was constantly leaving her to be alone. What he did when he was gone, she could only imagine.

One day she'd gotten exasperated with him during one of his comatose daydreams as he sat in front of one of the ceramic pots and grew a shrub with spreading vines that began to overtake the entire work area. By the time she'd found him, the plant had spread and wrapped around his legs, crept up his arms, and nearly devoured the desks and chairs around him. And when she'd snapped him out of it, he'd stared around him in disbelief, and had the gall to accuse her of growing the wildly spreading plant.

She had corrected him, ripped the plant from his legs and arms and demanded to know what he'd been doing, what had been going through his mind. He'd just stared at her, dumbfounded and aged looking, and had no answer. The lost look in his eyes had broken her heart, and the only thing she could do was sit on the ground beside him and hold his hand. It seemed to provide some comfort, but it certainly wasn't enough.

And it was times like that when she was reminded of her dream, and how her father had looked at her in disgust because she had no heart.

That night, they sat together in the parlor, both lost in their own thoughts. She figured the others probably looked at the two of them, both sitting on the sofa with rigidly straight backs and vacant expressions, and thought them to be dull, boring people. Little did they know that they weren't dull, they just lacked the ability to show emotion, and quite possibly the capacity to even feel it. It made them pitiable, she thought, but not boring.

Her father suddenly rose to his feet and the movement shook her out of her own thoughts. Around them, the other members of the Council talked and joked with each other, and their happiness seemed to contrast so sharply with her and her father's misery that she resented every last one of them. Staring at her father, she watched him step over to the bar against the wall, where the snifters of brandy and other liquors were displayed in beautiful mahogany and glass cabinetry. He poured himself more brandy, and was about to head back to the sofa when Brock sauntered over, looking drunk and more than a little mean, his lips curled in a cruel grin.

"How much brandy're you drinkin' these days, Rohan?" Brock chuckled darkly, eyeing his long time enemy with arrogant challenge. "Would hate to see you waste the woman I gave you."

Rhiannon's eyes widened as she stared from Brock to her father, who froze in place and turned to glare at his arch nemesis with vivid loathing. It was the most emotion she'd seen on his face in weeks.

"You mean the woman who chose me over you, who you couldn't resist trying to take back?" Rohan charged, standing tall and proudly tilting his head to stare down his nose at Brock.

They were both tall men, but where Rohan was slender and elegant in his crisp dress shirt and slacks, Brock was burly and mean in jeans and a blood red t-shirt. The contrast between the two men had never been more apparent.

Brock stepped toward Rohan, pointing a finger at him accusingly. "She wanted me more and you know it."

Rohan sneered, refusing to rise to the bait. "Then why did she choose me?"

"Because she's a woman and she let you charm her away. But she came back. They always come back to me," Brock growled, his voice rising.

No one had been paying attention until that moment. The entire parlor went instantly silent and Rhiannon was now no longer the only one staring at the two men with alarm in her eyes. Serendipity rose to her feet, edging forward as if to intervene, but even she looked troubled as to which of the two men she should defend.

Seeing the color rise in her father's face, seeing his hand that held the glass of brandy tremble, she knew he was on the verge of a fight with Brock. And since she knew it was a fight that had been a long time coming, she saw no other choice but to intervene. Now was not a good time, not when this particular subject was destroying him…she knew without a doubt that in a physical fight, he stood no chance against Brock. The other man was meaner, bigger and would fight much dirtier than her father would.

Rising to her feet, she stepped to her father and gripped his arm, pulling at him.

"Come sit down, ignore him," she said quietly to her father, though he wouldn't stop looking at Brock, deep rooted hostility in his eyes.

Brock barked out a loud laugh, his head falling back with it. "C'mon, Rohan, don't let your kid push you around. Be a man and let's settle this once and for all."

Rhiannon glared at Brock, feeling her face flush with temper and embarrassment. "He is twice the man you are. You shouldn't forget that."

"Woah, woah, woah," Blythe piped in, rising up to stand with her father, fists on her hips as she stared angrily at Rhiannon. "Twice the man? He's weak and pathetic enough to push around a girl half his size, or did you forget *that* little incident?"

Rhiannon grimaced, the memory of her father practically attacking Blythe just a few months earlier flashing in her mind. "At least he's a good husband and a good father, which is much more than can be said for him," she spat, nodding at Brock, who flushed red with anger.

"Hey, don't put this bad father shit on him, he was unfairly punished for a crime he didn't even commit," Blythe growled, stepping toward Rhiannon with her temper sparking. "And unlike you, princess, I missed out on having a dad for fifteen years because *your* dad and Balgaire were jealous."

Tilting her head up just slightly, Rhiannon glared down her nose at Blythe in disgust. "Jealous? Of what? A drunk, a gambler, a failure as a Dryad? Oh, but you have the same arrogance he does, don't you? You think everyone should be just like you."

"*Screw you!*" Blythe shouted, preparing to launch herself at Rhiannon full force. But Jax grabbed her arms and held her back, wrestling with her until the red cleared from her eyes. But even as he did, he glared at Rhiannon with such derision she actually shuddered.

"Hey, ice queen, wipe that snotty look off your face and take a look in the mirror for once. You should be so lucky to be even *half* the woman Blythe is. Get off your high horse and maybe then you'll see that you're just conceited, miserable, and cold to the goddamn bone."

Rhiannon felt the breath leave her lungs as she stared at him, seeing for the first time just what is was that made him such a feared man by demons and humans alike. He could be ruthlessly cruel.

"You're out of line, Jax," Liam cut in, no longer able to stand by and let this happen. He walked to Rhiannon and stood at her side, wrapping an arm around her as he glared at the man who he'd thus far considered a friend. "Apologize to her."

"Why?" Jax stared disbelievingly at Liam, his arm tucked around Blythe, who was still spitting mad. "If she can't take it, then she shouldn't dish it out."

"Because we're all adults here, and yet you're acting like children. Apologize," Liam ordered.

"Don't say sorry for speaking the truth, cowboy," Blythe spat, staring at Liam as she shook her head. "Clearly, Liam would rather defend the bitch than see reason."

"Blythe!" Lucian gaped, his eyes darting from his son to the girl who was practically his daughter. Liam only scowled at her.

"Rhia doesn't deserve the way you treat her, Blythe. I've always told you that."

Rhiannon looked at him, her eyes wide with wonder. He would still defend her, after everything she'd done to him? What had she done to deserve such devotion?

Unable to take any more of the fighting, she quietly pulled her father away as Liam and Jax continued to argue, other members of Euphora joining in the fight, including her mother and Nyxa, who were now face-to-face, practically clawing at each other. Obviously, tonight was a night to release pent up frustrations all around.

She led her father into the corridor and continued to pull him along toward their rooms.

He didn't object, nor did he say a word to her. Apparently, he was just as shaken by the fight as she had been, and the fact that it had started between him and Brock. Did it surprise him to see the divide that their hatred for each other caused, even still?

And did it surprise her to see Liam standing so valiantly at her side, despite everything between them?

Yes. Yes, it did.

Chapter Fourteen

She sat at her bedroom window in darkness, staring out at the moonlit courtyard, lost in thought.

Her father was safely in his own room down the hall, hopefully sleeping by now. She wished that she could sleep, then maybe all her inner demons would leave her alone.

She was wrong to fight back at Blythe, that much she knew. Blythe had always been a powder keg, ready to explode at the first sign of retaliatory fire. And, really, all she'd done was try and defend her father. Hadn't Rhiannon been doing the same?

But she'd fought back nonetheless, because despite years and years of portraying nothing more than cool indifference and a barely veiled dislike, the truth was, she couldn't stand Blythe. She couldn't stand anything about her, and though she refused to admit it, part of her knew it all had to do with Liam. Blythe had, unwittingly of course, stolen Liam from her all those years before. She'd monopolized his attention, and taken away any hope Rhiannon had of competing for him. And so, accepting her jealousy, Rhiannon had simply turned from both of them and shut them out. It had been easier that way.

But with Capri coming home, it had seemed as though things might be mended. Maybe she really was the missing link that could pull them all back together, the glue that could bond what had long ago been shattered. And yet, it seemed as though progress was slow, and fickle at best. And after tonight...God, she knew this was a huge setback. With all the baggage their fathers carried with each other, it would be hard to ever forge an amiable bond, much less a friendship. How could she or Blythe escape the sins their fathers had committed all those years before?

She was afraid that they couldn't and that they wouldn't. They were both too proud, too defensive, and much too eager to blame each other. It was their biggest and most dire fault. And all it was doing was tearing the family apart.

What was it going to take for them to break free of the past and start fresh, when even their fathers couldn't put aside their animosity for each other?

No...it was a feud that would most likely never end. And all would suffer because of it.

She heard a soft knocking on her door and jolted at the sound of it. Thinking it was probably her mother, ready to scold her for making a scene, Rhiannon padded to the door and opened it.

When she saw Liam, the hallway torch lights glowing behind him, she nearly shut the door in his face. But how could she do that to him, no matter how desperately she didn't want to speak with him at that moment, when he had defended her so boldly before? He deserved at least some graciousness on her part.

"Can I come in?" he asked, leaning against the door frame and eyeing her solemnly.

She nodded, backing up so he could enter her dark room.

"We're you asleep?" he asked, even as he noticed her bed was neatly made.

"No, I was just...thinking," she told him, stepping to her nightstand to turn on the light before sitting on the bed and staring at him. "I'm sorry for dragging you into that fight…I was being immature, I don't know what came over me."

"All of you are guilty of being immature tonight." He chuckled, sitting beside her and watching her knowingly. "Some more than others."

Rhiannon sighed, feeling mentally drained and exhausted. "I hate fighting, Liam, but I just got so angry seeing Brock provoking my father that way. He's been in such a bad place lately, and this was the last thing he needed."

"Is he alright? Where is he now?" Liam asked.

"Sleeping. And to be honest, I don't really know if he'll ever be alright again. I can't figure out how to help him." She stared down at her hands clenched in her lap, and felt all of the helplessness and fear boil over and consume her. "He's going to wither away because of my inaction."

"Why didn't you tell me any of this was happening? Maybe my dad can talk to him, do an intervention or something." He tried to smile, hoping to cheer her up. He hated seeing her look so worried and tense.

She shook her head. "I don't know."

"Well, we'll give it a shot, okay? We'll figure this out, I promise."

"Always the optimist." She smirked, though it was more callous than amused. "How do you manage to be so cheerful all the time when there's so much turmoil around us?"

"Because even though there is turmoil, there's beauty too, Rhia," he told her, aching to reach out and touch her. "I know you see it, whenever you're in the back gardens with the wild roses, or in the kitchen with all the vegetables you slave over… and when you lose yourself in one of your favorite books. So don't tell me the whole world is a dark and evil place, when you know yourself it isn't true."

She watched him for a moment, taking in his kind eyes, his handsome face…what had she ever done to deserve someone like him in her life?

"What Jax said about me tonight was true, Liam," she said softly, shaking her head before he could object. "No, you know it is. I know it is, too, and that's okay. It's because it was the truth that his words hurt as badly as they did. You shouldn't have put yourself between Blythe and me that way…you chose the wrong side."

"The hell with that," Liam retorted, eyeing her disbelievingly. "You've always had this critical opinion of yourself, Rhia, and I just don't understand it. Why do you focus so much on your faults? You have much more to offer than that."

"As a Dryad, I have a lot to offer." She straightened proudly. "I'm an excellent Earth Dryad, I know that. But as a daughter, as a friend? I'm mediocre, at best."

"Are you kidding me?" he managed, his eyebrows raised. "You know how often my mom looked at you and wished you were her daughter instead of me being her son? I was a pretty ill-behaved kid, and my mom couldn't handle me, so she backed off and left me to my dad. But you were the picture perfect child, all of us knew that. You did the best in school, you were obedient and well mannered. And as a friend? I've seen you with Brogan, with Capri…you help those who don't have anybody else. You care for those that others have pushed aside and forgotten. Including the damn fairies. It blows me away that you never stopped thanking them, or helping them, when no one else even bothered. It says something about you that you take the time and are considerate enough to care."

"But I've never been good to you, Liam," she managed, unbearably moved by his defense of her, but miserable nonetheless. "I don't understand why you won't give up on me."

He stared at her, his head shaking in disbelief. "How could you not see it, Rhia?"

"See what?" she managed, her throat tightening at the look in his eyes. God, it was like being thirteen all over again…he was so much the same…

"See that I've been in love with you my entire life."

"Why?" she shuddered, unable to stop that tiny piece of herself from leaping up to dance with pure, unbridled joy at his words. The rest of her shunned in retreat, fearing the words like the plague. No…how could she possibly run from him now? Now that the truth was out…

"Because you're you, there isn't really much more to it." He watched her, gauging her reaction. "Is it such a horrible thing, me loving you?"

Even before she could fully consider his question, her head was shaking, her heart rising within her to bloom warm and heavy in her once hollowed chest. Only he could do this, bring emotion to her when she had never felt it before. It was his gift, and maybe his destiny, to free her.

And, when she considered everything that had happened, not only with her father, but with her mother and with Blythe… maybe it was time she tried something different. Maybe it was time to see if trying to embrace emotions, if opening herself up to feel, could actually save not only her father, but herself, from impending gloom. It would be another experiment and hopefully this time it would not fail. She wasn't sure she could bear it if it did.

"Liam…I don't deserve you," she said softly, her lips barely parting to speak the words, but he heard her loud and clear. Tentatively, she reached out and touched his face, holding her hand there, enjoying the desire that bloomed in his eyes. Eyes she knew as well as her own; eyes that she'd been looking into since the day she was born.

And when she leaned forward, curving into him to touch her lips to his, she felt her body and her mind let go. The feeling was pure bliss; it was freedom.

His arms came around her, pulling her closer, his mouth diving deeper to take what she was offering. He'd waited so long to have her come to him this way, and now that she was…he wasn't sure he could safely maintain his control. The feel of her yielding to him, the sound of her breath catching as he touched her…it was pure magic.

After all, they were earth and water, elements that could not exist without each other. He knew it was the water in his blood that drew him to her, time and time again, and demanded he have her, and her alone. She, the embodiment of Earth, was the reason for his existence. What was the purpose of water if not to sustain the Earth? And what was the purpose of Earth if not to take all water had to offer, and survive?

Her hands gripped his shirt as his mouth trailed down her neck to graze along her collar bone, sending shivers down her back that had her gasping for air and whispering his name, desperate to feel. Her heart pounded in her chest, full and red hot, filling her with more warmth than she had ever felt before. If she'd known it would be this way, would anything have changed? But, then again, maybe this was that one impossible want that she had denied herself all her life; the want Liam had told her she needed to take before it was too late.

All she could do was thank God he still wanted her, after all the time she'd wasted.

When his hands trailed down to rest on her hips, he started to pull away, choking back the need coursing through him, knowing he couldn't rush her...rush this. Rhiannon wouldn't want haste. She'd want care and caution, a chance to think things over and make a sound decision. He could never forgive himself if he didn't give her that opportunity.

"What is it?" she asked, backing away to look in his eyes, fearing for one brief moment that he'd changed his mind, that he'd decided he didn't love her anymore, and that he didn't want her…

"I need to know if you want me to stop, Rhia, before this goes further," he managed, gripping her waist to keep himself steady.

She just stared at him, the answer in her eyes. Having no words, she simply shook her head and pulled him down with her, crushing her lips to his as they hit the bed.

At dawn, she awoke to the sound of birds and to the feel of Liam's breath on her neck. She lay there, still and silent, and stared out her open window for what felt like ages. Golden sunlight streamed in, glittering on dust as it fell over the floor, spilling out on her bed and glowing warm on her skin. She closed her eyes and breathed deep, basking in this moment of peace and blissful quiet.

She felt Liam shift, nuzzling his face into her neck as his arm pulled her closer to him so she was pressed against his body. This simple act of affection, something so normal to anyone else, touched her deeply. No one had ever held her, not like this. But Liam was unlike anyone else she had ever known. And being with him…it had filled the gap within her soul that had been hollow all her life. Water had, once again, given her hope, given her a sense of freedom.

Curious, she lightly touched his hand, trailing her fingers over his skin. He loved her…how was that even possible? But she knew Liam would never lie to her, so it must be true. Did she love him? She had no idea what it felt like to love…but perhaps this fullness in her heart, this deep, inner yearning for him was love. Still unsure, she pushed the thought away. One thing at a time, Rhiannon, she thought with a sigh, knowing she shouldn't rush it.

His hand suddenly turned to hold her own, and she felt him kiss the back of her neck.

"Morning," he greeted, his voice husky and deep with sleep. She welcomed the shivers that coursed down her spine at the feel of his lips and the sound of his voice.

"Good morning," she replied, closing her eyes, unsure what to do. There was work to be done, as always, and she really needed to shower and get to it…but lying here, in his arms, was a sensation she was reluctant to give up just yet.

But, as was her way, the minute she started thinking about work, she could no longer enjoy lying in bed idly.

Sitting up, she pulled the sheets to cover her chest and stared down at him, lazily stretched out beside her, a relaxed smile on his face.

"So beautiful," he said quietly, reaching out to touch her hair, his eyes trailing down her bare back as he did.

With a snort, she pulled the sheet with her and slipped out of bed, wrapping it around her to make sure she was covered. Modesty, even though quite useless at this point, was still deeply ingrained in her. She looked at him again, this time with a playful grin.

"If you leave now, your father might not catch you. I know he wakes you up every morning…" She glanced at the clock over her dresser. "About two minutes from now."

"Shit." Liam laughed as he stumbled out of her bed, taking the remaining blankets with him and almost tripping over them. She clapped her hand to her mouth, stopping the laughter bubbling in her throat at the sight of him, her other arm clutching the sheet around her body. He scrambled to tug on his jeans and shirt, and swiftly grabbed his shoes off the floor. Rushing to her, he pulled her against him with his free arm and kissed her fully, the move shocking the humor out of her. Would she ever get used to such impulsive affection?

Breaking away, he grinned down at her. "I love you, Rhia."

"I know," she managed, fighting back the swelling in her chest at his words. He gave her one last, lingering kiss before hastily leaving the room. When the door shut behind him, she stood where she was, marveling at her own daring.

On impulse, she wandered to the mirror over her dressing table, inspecting her face, wondering if she looked as different as she felt. Maybe her cheeks were a bit flusher, glowing with an odd sense of happiness she certainly hadn't felt in ages. And her eyes seemed brighter, more alive, the sage in them less dull than it had been before. It was incredible for her to see the results of her experiment thus far…to feel warmth replacing the coldness in her chest, and her heart beating with newfound purpose. Her goal now was to keep her heart open, and hope it gave her the courage to save her father. Already that hope was filling her, bit by glorious bit, until she almost raced down to find him that very moment. She'd wasted so much time already, and never had she felt as incredibly free as she did now.

She was almost there, almost entirely freed. God, how easy it was once she allowed it, once she broke through her own barriers with a brazen axe and fierce determination. And on the other side had been Liam, calmly waiting with his hand stretched out, reaching for her. She was closer than she ever had been, that much she knew. And as long as she stayed strong and didn't cower from the dangers she knew were inherent with having an open heart, then perhaps sooner than later, she would be free.

Riding on the memory of him, on the awareness that he loved her, she took a shower and got ready, her lips curving into a genuine smile as she left her room.

With her logbooks tucked neatly in her arms and her bag slung over her shoulder, she headed down the steps and out into the corridor, hoping to catch a quick breakfast before meeting with her father in the Greenhouse. But before she reached the dining hall, she spotted Thea and her mother standing just outside the doors, watching her. Thea looked tense and aware, while Serendipity looked eager and impatient.

"Rhiannon, there you are." Serendipity glided toward her, her smile serene and dignified. "Thea and I need to speak with you, right this moment."

Disliking the gleam in her mother's eyes, Rhiannon stopped and turned to Thea, her expression carefully guarded. "What is this regarding? I have a lot of work to get to after breakfast."

"It won't take long." Thea tilted her head, watching Rhiannon very closely, as usual giving the impression that she knew way more than Rhiannon was comfortable with.

Knowing she had no other choice, Rhiannon nodded and followed the two women to the garden room, anxiously chewing her bottom lip. What could her mother want now?

Serendipity shut the door and hastily beckoned Rhiannon to sit down on one of the sofas.

She took a seat, setting her books beside her and folding her hands together in her lap, forcing a look of polite indifference on her face.

Serendipity and Thea sat together on the opposite sofa, facing Rhiannon. With a lustrous smile, Serendipity spoke first.

"I am pleased to tell you that I have, just this morning, completed the arrangements for your marriage. I received word just an hour ago that our agreement was accepted, and I have thus confirmed our compliance on your behalf."

Rhiannon blinked, unsure she had heard her mother correctly. "Marriage?"

"Yes, to a fine, upstanding Enforcer. It is the perfect match, if I do say so myself." Serendipity preened, sending a satisfied smile to Thea before turning back to Rhiannon.

Thea, however, was not smiling. She was watching Rhiannon, gauging the girl's reaction. And what she saw thus far displeased her enormously. The panic that flashed briefly in Rhiannon's eyes, and the way her hands clenched together tightly in her lap had not gone unnoticed.

"But...this is all so fast, you didn't even tell me you were doing this," Rhiannon stammered, a disbelieving numbness spreading throughout her chest. No, not now, not when everything was slowly but surely going just right...

"Rhiannon, I expect you to be appreciative of all the time and effort I have put into securing this husband for you. I have spent several weeks putting aside other projects and even your sister's needs to ensure that you are taken care of."

Dully, Rhiannon glanced over at Thea, who had remained silent and observant. "Who is he?"

Thea inclined her head, knowing that the girl was not going to be satisfied with the answer. "Michael Callahan."

"But he hates me," Rhiannon managed, shaking her head and staring back at her mother. "I can't marry him."

"You can and you will," Serendipity huffed, waving away the words impatiently. "This is not open for discussion, Rhiannon. It is traditional that parents make the final decision on who their children marry, and your father and I have both agreed that you shall marry Michael."

"Does Michael know this? Because I am certain he will refuse."

"Michael has known for awhile now. Burke has assured him that marrying you will not only be an important and crucial career move for him, but that he will get to live here and bear the next Earth Dryad heir. It is quite an honor for a human to be considered for such a responsibility, but Michael is fully prepared to do so." Serendipity crossed her legs casually, smirking at her daughter. "I've made you into a lady, Rhiannon. Now accept this last token from me; it is the last thing I can give to you as your mother."

"Father agrees with this?" Rhiannon asked quietly, feeling the walls closing in on her, imprisoning her once again in a cage.

"Rohan is thrilled. You are of marriageable age and he wants nothing more than for you to marry a respectable young man and produce an heir."

"Do I have a choice?" she murmured, her voice cracking as her hands trembled in her lap. Her eyes held her mother's, but instead of sympathy, she only saw coldness.

"What is there to choose, Rhiannon? Michael is the son of the most respected Enforcer we have. He is as good of a match as I can secure for you. There is nothing better."

It occurred to her, rather painfully, that her mother would never allow her to be with Liam. In order to marry him, she would have to go against her parents, shaming herself to them. They saw Liam as an immature dreamer, capable of nothing good in this life. And even if she tried with everything she had to convince them that they were wrong about him, they wouldn't listen. They never listened to her, and they had certainly never given her a choice before. What made her think they would in regards to her future husband?

She had, unwittingly it appeared, dug herself into a painfully deep and muddy hole. What choice did she have, other than to accept her mother's rope and climb to safety, all the while covered in muddy guilt and shame? Liam would be left in that hole, left behind to wallow in one last, vicious rejection. But what else could be done?

"Well, now that you are informed of the arrangement, we can begin planning the wedding. Two months should do, don't you think, Thea?"

"A fall wedding. It will be lovely," Thea replied, not looking away from Rhiannon. "Serendipity, can you give Rhiannon and me a chance to speak alone for a moment?"

Serendipity looked momentarily confused, but rose to her feet nonetheless. "Certainly."

With that, she swept from the room, shutting the door with a soft click at her back.

Rhiannon was staring at her hands, wondering what she had done to herself. A few weeks earlier and this would have been nothing more than a mild inconvenience. But now…with Liam's scent still with her, the feel of his hands and the look in his eyes when he told her he loved her…everything had changed, so swiftly and suddenly that she wasn't even sure she had a good grasp on it all yet.

"Rhiannon, I want you to look me in the eye and answer me very honestly," Thea said, rising to her feet and crouching down in front of Rhiannon, resting her hands on the girl's knees.

Rhiannon lifted her eyes, meeting Thea's, knowing her face betrayed everything.

"Is there someone else, dear? Do you love someone else?" Thea asked gently, though from the look in her eyes she already knew the answer.

The urge to scream it, to confess to everything, was struggling for purchase within her, fighting to get out. But reason bashed it on the head and her face cleared, masking what was roiling inside of her.

She shook her head, all the while damning herself for the very act. "No."

Thea let out a huff of breath, the urge to shake the girl senseless coming over her. "Why do you do this to him?"

"Excuse me?" Rhiannon's eyes widened as her hands clenched tighter together in her lap.

"Something has changed, I can see it in your eyes, girl. You are not the same as you were weeks ago when we last spoke about this. My best guess would be that you have finally let yourself be happy and now you are prepared to throw it all away. Why?"

"I don't have a choice," Rhiannon insisted, rising to her feet now, resentment coursing through her. "I've never had a choice."

Thea pressed a hand to her temple, frustration mounting inside her as she rose to her feet as well. "It is not my place to regulate the parenting techniques of members of the Council, nor is it my place to interfere with you now. Arranged marriages have been commonplace on Euphora for centuries, and for many of those who did it, the marriage was successful. But I can see it in your eyes that you are not prepared to do this, Rhiannon, and though I cannot tell Serendipity what action to take with her own child, I think you should tell her you love another, and perhaps she and your father will be swayed to approve that marriage instead."

"She won't be swayed, Thea, not in favor of him," Rhiannon shook her head wearily. "It's done. I will marry Michael Callahan in two months time."

"And destroy my Water Dryad in the process?" Thea charged, eyeing Rhiannon bitterly. "Everyone can see the way he looks at you, the way you look at him. Perhaps that is why your mother is forcing this marriage on you so suddenly. Even she could sense you yielding to him these last few months, since Capri returned, and she wanted to stop it before it was too late."

Rhiannon nodded solemnly, knowing Thea was probably right. "That sounds like something she would do."

"I hope you'll change your mind, Rhiannon." Thea turned away, unable to look at her any longer.

"What good will changing my mind do? I don't have a choice. It's either obey or disobey, Thea, and I think you know the side I've always been forced to take. If this is what my father wants for me, I can't refuse him. Especially not now, not when he's suffering."

For a moment, neither spoke, the silence heavy in the air between them. Then Thea sighed, and without turning around, uttered words that stung like an arrow to the heart.

"Prepare for the backlash, Rhiannon. It will be brutal."

Sensing the dismissal in Thea's voice, Rhiannon grabbed her books and left the room, feeling numb and unbearably cold. She was right; there was sure to be an uproar over this.

What would she say to Liam when she saw him? How could she possibly convince him this was for the best?

It was going to be a hard task to convince him or anyone else, when she was so unsure of it herself.

Chapter Fifteen

She skipped breakfast, not feeling remotely hungry, and headed straight to the Greenhouse. Her father was there, but she couldn't bring up the topic with him, feeling all her earlier confidence slipping away. Instead, she worked in silence, as did he, and the hours ticked by, minute by painful minute.

When it was time for dinner, her chest felt hollow and clenched painfully, fear and panic rising within her. Would anyone know yet? Had her mother gone around, boasting of the good news? Or would she have to be the one to tell them?

Trembling, she grabbed her books and her bag, and headed out before her father, hoping to clean up before dinner. But the minute she stepped out of the Greenhouse, she spotted them in the corridor, crowded near the dining hall.

Capri, Rian, Brogan and Liam stood by the doors, and the four of them glanced over when they saw her. Like lightning, they all raced forward to meet her.

Here was the backlash.

"Rhiannon! We just heard about Michael…is it true?" Capri asked, reaching Rhiannon first, worry and distress clouding her pretty face.

Rian and Brogan hung back, but Liam rushed forward and stared at her, shaking his head.

"What is going on, Rhia?"

She couldn't look at him, so she looked to Capri instead. "My mother has arranged for me to marry Michael."

"But you told her you don't want to, right? Because they can't just force you to marry someone, that's ridiculous," Capri urged, glancing around at the others for support. "Right?"

Rian met her eyes and frowned, hoping he could make her understand. "Arranged marriages are not uncommon on Euphora, Capri, though I must say I disagree with them. It has been a general practice for centuries that parents have the final say on who their children decide to marry, sometimes with the parents going as far as to select for them. Now that the arrangement has been made, Rhiannon's hands are virtually tied, as far as tradition goes."

"Well, I say to hell with the tradition," Capri said heatedly in response, turning back angrily to Rhiannon. "There has to be a way out of this. Maybe if you talk with Thea?"

Rhiannon was quiet for a moment, looking into her kind friend's eyes, knowing her answer was going to upset all of them. She just shook her head, fighting to keep her expression free of the pain she was feeling inside.

"There's nothing Thea can do. I'm going to marry him," she said simply, fighting to put the sound of assurance into her voice.

"This is bullshit!" Liam exploded suddenly, nudging a startled Capri out of the way and gripping Rhiannon's shoulders tightly in his hands, his face inches from hers, desperation and anger clear in his eyes. She couldn't help but look at him now and her breath caught in her throat as her resolve wavered. When he spoke again, his voice was dangerously low and laced with torment. "Did last night mean nothing, Rhia? You would be so cold to me, after that?"

She felt a shudder run through her, and knew he felt it, knew he saw the weakness in her eyes and the pain shock her system. God, an open heart was terribly painful, so horrifically agonizing…

But she couldn't back down. She had to push him away; there was no other alternative.

"I don't have a choice, Liam. It's done."

"You have a choice to fight. Stand up to them, Rhia, tell them this isn't what you want."

Thinking of her father and what her refusal might do to him had her shaking her head. The added stress alone from her mother's wrath might finally break him, and she couldn't allow that to happen. Until she knew for certain he wanted this marriage as much as her mother did, she couldn't risk hurting him.

Liam stared at her silently for a moment, his eyes searching hers. She tried to force the pain from her expression, the doubt and uncertainty. But he could see right through her.

"If you won't fight, then I will. I won't lose you, not like this." With that, he released her and stormed off down the corridor. The moment he was gone, Rhiannon let out a shuddering breath and wrapped her arms around herself, feeling her chest constrict painfully.

She felt Capri's arms go around her and pull her in for a tight hug. Rian and Brogan both approached, Rian placing his hand on Capri's shoulder as Brogan softly touched Rhiannon's.

"Rian and I can try and scare Michael away, make him call off the wedding," Brogan joked, trying to smile, hoping it might make her feel better. He knew, perhaps more than the others on Euphora, just how she felt. His own father had been in complete control of his life as well and he would have never had the nerve to stand up to him.

Rhiannon let out a strangled laugh, her throat tightening even as she pulled away from Capri and fought to compose herself. Eyeing the three of them, she forced herself to smile. "Thank you, but that won't be necessary. It's best for everyone involved if I go through with the marriage as planned."

Capri shook her head, tears brimming in her eyes.

"Do you really believe that this is what's best for Liam? You're breaking his heart," she managed, a single tear slipping down her cheek.

Rian put his arm around her and pulled her close, angered to see her hurting over this. But he knew there was little that could be done unless Rhiannon chose to go against her own parents.

Forcing back the guilt she felt at knowing she was making Capri cry, Rhiannon straightened and fought to maintain her composure. "What's best is for Liam to forget about me."

With a polite nod, she pushed past the three of them, knowing they all solemnly watched her as she left.

If she thought things couldn't get any worse then she was gravely mistaken. Not only did they get worse, they damn near erupted into chaotic madness the likes of which she could never have predicted.

Dinner was, per Thea's strict orders, strained and civil. Liam wasn't there; but no one commented on that fact. Clearly it was obvious why he would want to avoid seeing anyone. At least Rhiannon knew he would be spared the violence that was to come, for the moment everyone was released to the parlor for the evening, all hell literally broke loose.

Blythe rounded on her first.

"What the hell is wrong with you?" she spat, glaring up at Rhiannon with fire in her eyes. "Wait, don't answer that. I know exactly what's wrong with you. You're a selfish, scheming, snobby bitch who enjoys toying with my brother's heart like a cat with a goddamn mouse."

"I didn't toy with him," Rhiannon replied defensively, though part of her knew Blythe was right. She should have never let Liam in, should have never given in to the temptation to feel, the temptation to be free…

"Oh, excuse me, but I consider screwing his brains out one night and then dumping him the next day to marry someone else to be toying with him. Don't you agree?"

"Blythe!" Rhiannon gaped, staring around to be sure no one heard. But a few of them were staring apprehensively, and she felt her face flush with embarrassment and fury. "That is none of your business."

"I love him and care about him, so yeah, I'd say it's my business when he tells me he loves you and you pull this shit on him," Blythe charged, jabbing a finger into Rhiannon's chest furiously. "I don't care what it takes, but you fix this and make him happy or God help me I'll kill you. I never liked you anyway, so it won't weigh much on my conscience."

"How *dare* you threaten my daughter!" Serendipity swept to Rhiannon's side, glaring down her nose at Blythe with intense dislike. "I suppose civility means nothing to you, you little heathen. You see fit to threaten anyone who gets in your way."

"Excuse me?" Blythe's eyes widened with shock and fury as she rounded on Serendipity, her hands clenched at her sides as if she was seriously considering clocking the older woman. "Don't even talk to me about civility. You're the one who cheated on your husband!"

Serendipity's face paled, but she didn't lose her composure nor her anger. "How dare you…"

Lucian, seeing the exchange, stepped in and grabbed Blythe, holding her back. Jax followed suit, standing beside Blythe protectively.

"Apologize for that hateful comment, Serendipity. It was quite unnecessary," Lucian requested, his eyes cold.

"She threatened to kill Rhiannon, Lucian, that is nothing short of barbaric," Serendipity huffed, glaring at the two of them.

"Surely you can see that she doesn't mean it, she is only upset that Liam is hurting, as am I." Lucian reasoned, restraining Blythe with one hand firmly on her shoulder.

This time Serendipity laughed, and the cold sound of it had Rhiannon staring at her mother with startled eyes. "If he was under some kind of delusion that he had any hope of marrying Rhiannon, then he is nothing short of a fool. Rhiannon can do much better than Liam and we both know that, Lucian."

Lucian's mouth fell open at Serendipity's crassness and he let go of Blythe as he started toward Serendipity himself. "That is my son you're talking about, Serendipity, and I will defend him. He is a good boy, an excellent son, and any woman should be proud to be the object of his affection."

"Certainly he is a nice boy, Lucian. All I am saying is that he is not right for my daughter," Serendipity corrected, one eyebrow raised condescendingly.

"Perhaps your daughter is not good enough for my son," Lucian shot back, anger flushing his normally calm and placid face. Even Blythe was staring up at him, a mixture of pride and shock in her eyes.

"Is there a problem here, Lucian?" Rohan said, suddenly appearing at his wife's side and putting an arm around her supportively. He eyed Lucian with disdain, which took the other man by surprise.

"Your wife seems to take some kind of sick pleasure in the fact that your daughter has broken my son's heart," Lucian managed, his hands shaking with fury. This time, Blythe had to hold him back, though she wanted nothing more than to pounce on Rhiannon's snobby parents herself.

Rohan, looking indifferent, shrugged. "This is far from our concern. The arrangements have been made; Liam will just have to get over it. He's young and resilient. Don't worry yourself, old friend." Reaching over, he patted Lucian on the back with a nod, and then led both his wife and Rhiannon from the parlor.

Rhiannon, unable to help herself, turned around to see Lucian standing there, looking furious and helpless, with Blythe stoically at his side, glaring directly back at her. Behind them, the rest of Euphora watched with a mixture of dark curiosity and disapproving disgust.

Clearly, no one was on their side now.

Her father led them upstairs to their rooms, but when they stopped in front of Rhiannon's, he urged Serendipity along.

"I need to speak with Rhiannon," he said, opening the door to his daughter's room and beckoning her inside. Serendipity brushed him off and strode away, unconcerned.

Rhiannon, feeling numb from the assault that had just occurred on her and her parents, sat on her bed and stared up at her father.

It suddenly occurred to her that he was…different. He held himself straighter, seemed more composed and more alive than he had in weeks. Was this arranged marriage really bringing him out of his semi-comatose depression?

Standing with his arms crossed over his chest, he faced her and tried to smile. It was more than she had gotten from him in longer than she could remember.

"I'm sorry this marriage business has been sprung on you like this, Rhiannon," he began, starting to pace, clearly searching for words to say. "I myself did not find out until yesterday. Apparently your mother saw fit not to disclose the reason she was repeatedly speaking with Burke Callahan, thinking I may spoil the surprise for you. To think I was worried about him…" He paused mid-step, frowning. "In any event, I am pleased with Michael. He seems like a nice young man with ambition and class. Your mother assures me he will be a lead Enforcer in the near future."

Trying to smile again, he sat down beside her, meeting her eyes. "He is a good choice for you, Rhiannon. It would please me for you to marry him."

When Rhiannon said nothing, lost for words, he continued. "Now I know Liam has had some kind of crush on you for a long time, but since you've never returned his affections I've come to the conclusion that you don't feel the same way."

Guilt and shame crept into her at his words. If only she knew how to tell him, if only she knew it wouldn't just make things worse…

"This arrangement has made your mother very happy and in turn has made me happy. I've been…out of sorts lately and I apologize for that. But this has given me new hope for the future."

He reached out and, in a rare sign of affection, wrapped his arm around her shoulders and kissed the top of her head. "I'm proud of you, Rhiannon."

At his words, she felt the last and final nail slam into the coffin, sealing her fate. How could she ever have the heart to tell him she didn't want this marriage now? When he'd been awakened, enlightened in a way that she thought she would never see again. And it was all a result of this arranged marriage…

She knew she didn't have it in her to back down from it, not now, not ever. She couldn't risk his life, not for her own selfish gains. No…she would give in and marry Michael and her father would survive.

When he left her alone minutes later, she stayed where she was on the side of her bed, slowly but surely accepting her fate. She wasn't certain if she should be thrilled that her father had awoken from his deep, drugging depression, or if she should be devastated that she would have to tie her life to some arrogant imbecile who thought she was a freak.

But, perhaps it wouldn't be all bad…her life would most likely continue as it had for years, and surely she could convince Michael to stay down in Washington, D.C., and they would come together one time and one time only, to produce an heir, and then that would be it.

But God, even her practical and cynical nature revolted at the thought of a completely loveless marriage. Especially when she'd come so close to knowing love…to experiencing how breathtaking it was to look into another's eyes and see the desire in them. To see the love, something she had never before known, staring right back at her, pleading for her to accept without fear.

And how sad was it that she had always been terrified of love. Receiving it, and giving it.

Upon hearing a knock on her door, she stared blankly at it for a moment, pulling herself back to reality. Rising to her feet, she opened the door, only to have an electric jolt pierce through her. She should have expected this…

"I need to speak to you," Liam said evenly, looking disheveled and broody. She bit her lip and stepped aside, letting him in. Shutting the door, she turned to face him, hoping she could retain whatever strength of purpose she had just gained from the conversation with her father.

Without hesitation, he rounded on her and cupped her face in his hands, crushing her mouth with his, shocking the very breath from her. She stood, her knees buckling weakly, her hands grasping at his shirt as her mind spun wildly. The urgency, the desperation, the need pulsing from him and into her sent shockwaves coursing madly through her system.

He poured all of his emotion into the kiss, needing to know if she felt anything for him. And from the way she gave, from the way her body curved to his and her skin shivered under his hands, he knew he had her.

Breaking the kiss, he pushed her away from him, looking angry and feral as he glared at her. So shocked was she to see it that she crumbled to the bed, her knees too weak to support her. She fought to keep a look of quiet indifference on her face, knowing she needed her wall firmly in place now more than ever.

"I know you want me, Rhia," he said, his chest heaving, hurt mixing with the fury in his eyes. "So why are you going along with this ridiculous marriage?"

Remembering her father, Rhiannon stared back at him coldly. "Sex is not love, Liam. Wanting you is purely physical and yes I'm guilty of that. But that is all I wanted from you."

"Bullshit," he growled, pacing. She held her breath as she watched him, her chest too tight to breathe. "I know you don't want to marry him. I know how much you despise him. So why go along with this?"

"It is a smart match," she began, only to be cut off when he groaned and grabbed his hair exasperatedly.

"Damnit, no it's not!" He stared at her again in disbelief. "You know as well as I do that he's an asshole. Look, I want to fight for you, but I need to know that you're on my side."

Knowing in her heart that the only way to push him away was to hurt him, and hurt him as badly as she could, she fixed a disdainful look on her face and stared at him indifferently.

"I don't love you, Liam. I never have and I never will," she said evenly, her voice colder than ice. "I only used you last night to scratch an itch, nothing more. I don't want you and I certainly don't want to marry you. I want to marry Michael. My mother has assured me that he is of proper pedigree and that he will soon be a lead Enforcer like his father. You, however, are a disgrace to the Dryad name, too lazy to do the most trivial of work, and your father has raised both you and Blythe to be careless and arrogant. Why would I want the father of my children to be someone like you, when I could have my children raised by a prominent Enforcer? How many times do I have to reject you before you understand that I don't want you?"

For a moment he said nothing, he only looked at her with disgust in his eyes.

"That's a pretty speech, Rhia," he said softly, shaking his head at her. "Did your mother tell you to say all that to me?"

The derision in his voice snuck under her shield of indifference and stabbed her viciously, but on the surface she merely lifted an eyebrow. "It's the truth."

"Do you think I'm too stupid to understand what you're doing? You're trying to push me away so you don't have to deal with all this messiness I'm dumping into your perfectly structured life. You think it's just easier all around to marry Michael to please your parents, damned what happens to anyone else. Well, I'm not falling for it and I'm not giving up on you. Taking the easier road is not always the best choice. We have to fight for what we want in this world, and I want you more than I have ever wanted anything."

Frustrated and emotional, he grabbed her by the elbows and pulled her to her feet, wrapping his arms around her, needing to breathe in her scent, to feel her body against his own.

"I can't turn off my love for you like a switch, Rhia. It doesn't work that way."

Her eyes burned hot and heavy as she clenched them tight, burrowing her face against his neck, feeling ashamed and worthless and miserable all at once.

"I'm sorry," she murmured, the pain in her chest excruciating as her heart broke for him. Because, in the end, she knew nothing had changed. She was still going to have to marry Michael. "I can't be with you, Liam."

"Why not?" he asked, pulling her away so he could look into her eyes. "Tell me why I'm not good enough for you."

Shaking her head, she took a deep, shuddering breath and stared at him, her cool, reserved mask gone, showcasing her true pain. Perhaps it was seeing it that made him relax, made him lead her to the bed and hold her in his arms.

"Tell me what's really going on, Rhia," he murmured, kissing her forehead and rocking her.

Leaning against him, basking in the comfort he gave her, she sighed and tried to figure out how to explain it all.

"My father was just here. Liam, he's so happy…you wouldn't believe the contrast to what he was just yesterday. This whole marriage thing has brought him out of his misery; he says it's given him hope for the future. It's made him himself again."

Tilting her head up, she met his eyes. "If I say no, if I choose to go against them, there's no telling what will happen to him. I could lose him for good, and…" her voice cracked, the very thought of it tearing her apart. Liam rubbed his hand up her arm, more than a little shocked to see her nearly in tears. Not his serious, composed Rhia…she never cried. Forcing back the pain, she continued. "I have to go through with it, for him. I'm sorry, but I hope you understand."

He inhaled deeply, pressing a lingering kiss to her forehead. "You always were the least selfish person I've ever known," he chuckled, despite the empty feeling in his heart. But when he spoke again, his voice was softer, and there was misery behind it. "Was this why you decided you couldn't be with me when we were younger, too?"

She nodded slowly, feeling perhaps now it was time to tell him the truth. "I was naïve, Liam, and weak. My mother convinced me that I was disappointing both her and my father because I was so distracted and that you were to blame. I believed that for a very long time and I'm sorry for it."

"So am I." He pulled her against him and held her, knowing there was little to be done about any of it now.

They sat in silence for a long moment, the only sound the soft beating of their hearts. It amazed her that a broken heart could still beat…even after the wreckage.

"This is going to sound ridiculously foolish," she began, nuzzling into his chest, feeling embarrassed but somehow strangely relieved. "But I wish we could run away, Liam. I wish we could run away and be together, without all of this."

"What happened to little Miss Practicality?" he laughed, even though he would have given anything to make that wish come true. It was the first time he had ever heard her wish for anything. "I've got enough wild and crazy dreams for the both of us, Rhia. I need you to stay focused so I don't lose my head."

"Right," she sighed, closing her eyes. "You know, my mother could hardly judge me if I kept you as my lover. I'd just tell her I'm following her example."

"Okay, now you're scaring me," he chuckled, pushing her away to inspect her. He pursed his lips as he tilted her face side-to-side, causing a light laugh to escape from her throat. The sound of it delighted the hell out of him. With a grin, he kissed the tip of her nose. "That's it, the Rhia I know and love has gone mad. Now, darling, I know that Michael is terribly boring in bed, but you mustn't fear. I am more than willing to steal you away from him, anytime, day or night."

Laughing again, she fell back against the bed and felt a kind of delirious, exhilarating release. God, it felt good to laugh. How had she gone so long without it?

And what was it about this moment, this horrific, troubling moment where her fate was assuredly bleak and miserable that gave her a reason to laugh?

But she knew the answer when Liam lay beside her, turning toward her with his head resting in his hand as he stared down at her, his grin fading to a kind of sad smile.

Hadn't he always helped her through the worst of times? That was just who he was…

"What do we do now?" she asked, watching him and wondering how she would ever do without his touch now that she had felt it.

"I don't know," he murmured, reaching out to caress her cheek. She stared into his eyes, and felt her pulse jump and her heart begin to race. How was it he could do this to her, make her feel real and beautiful and alive all at once?

Riding on the moment, she curved toward him, rising up on her elbow to press her lips to his, her free hand running through his dark hair.

"One last time," she whispered, pushing him back against the bed and climbing over him, her mouth cruising over his face. "Before it's too late."

Chapter Sixteen

"This is ridiculous," Michael huffed, looking pompous and resentful as he stood in his black designer slacks and crisp, white dress shirt, feeling more than a little ambushed.

"What's ridiculous is your attitude, Mikey," Blythe shot back, standing right in his face without hesitation or fear. "Just what is it that makes you such a douchebag, huh? Did your father shove a stick up your ass when you were born?"

Michael flushed angrily, but his chin tilted with undaunted superiority. "That is my fiancé and you are keeping me from her."

"Yeah because we're gonna do all we can to make sure this wedding bullshit doesn't happen." She jabbed a finger into his chest, temper flaring.

They stood in the parlor, Blythe and the others acting as a barrier between Michael and Rhiannon, who was sitting with her head in her hands on one of the sofas, Liam and Capri flanking her.

Rian, Brogan and Jax joined with Blythe, blocking Michael from getting any closer to Rhiannon. It was, if anything, a show of their complete and utter dislike for Michael, and their deeply ingrained instinct to protect their own.

Liam had explained to Blythe and the others why Rhiannon felt she had to go through with the marriage. But all they said in response was that they would just have to get Michael to back out, and then the blame would be on him, not Rhiannon. Surely Rohan and Serendipity would not fault Rhiannon for Michael deciding not to go through with the marriage…or so they believed.

Rhiannon knew better, but there was little she could do to control their actions. And watching it, knowing all of this would only make the situation worse, was giving her a massive migraine.

Liam rubbed her back gently in a sign of support, but his eyes were hard as stone and focused directly on Michael.

Capri had her hand on Rhiannon's knee, more concerned with her friend at that moment than with Michael.

"Are you feeling okay?" she asked quietly, her smoky gray eyes filled with worry.

Rhiannon took a deep breath and pulled her hands away from her face, wincing at the pulsating pain behind her eyes. "It's just a headache, it will pass."

"I can get you some aspirin, will that help?" Capri brushed back Rhiannon's hair, exposing her face so she could see her better.

Shaking her head, Rhiannon tried to smile. "I'll be fine. It's just that all of this is wearing on me. I feel helpless, Capri."

"I know." Tears brimming in her eyes, Capri reached out and hugged Rhiannon close, her own heart filled with sorrow and uncertainty over her friend's situation. She understood completely the desire to please a parent…hadn't she gone through the same worries with her own father? But she had chosen to go against his wishes and be with Rian, despite what her father had felt… Rhiannon, it seemed, wasn't going to pursue that same path. But Rohan was in a much more dire position than Clynn had been.

The sudden, elevated shouting had them both pulling apart and staring at the others apprehensively.

"This show of support is cute and all, really, but this does not concern any of you," Michael was saying, looking exasperated and furious. "I don't really understand what all the fuss is about. Why do you care if she gets married? Jesus, it's just a business arrangement, a contract, it's not like I'm taking her away from any of you. She'll still live here."

"We don't feel that this is best for Rhiannon," Brogan replied, eyeing Michael distrustfully.

"Well, it's not up to you, is it?" Michael challenged, getting in Brogan's face, though the Fury was much taller than he was. Rian stepped forward, his hands snaking between Michael and Brogan to push them apart. He would, at all costs, prevent a brawl from taking place.

"It may not be up to us, but it doesn't mean we don't care," Rian put in, staring coldly at Michael as he stepped back, Brogan at his side.

"Burke is a good man, but I think I speak for those of us who have known you for quite some time that you're pretty much good for nothing," Jax drawled, his hands tucked into the pockets of his jeans as he grinned cruelly at Michael. "Or do you disagree with me?"

"You're one to talk, Murphy." Michael scowled, his eyes narrowing in challenge. "I heard you let Dante slip right through your fingers. If it had been me, I would have killed the son of a bitch."

"Doubtful," Jax snickered, eyebrows raised. "But then again, we have yet to see how you handle a demon one-on-one. Maybe we should go find one and lock you two in a room and see who comes out alive."

"Ooh, I like that idea." Blythe nodded, grinning lushly. "I bet he'd be crying for his daddy within two seconds."

Michael flushed again, his hands clenched at his sides as he glared at all of them, furious at once again being taunted by a bunch of freaks. He was better than this, better than them…how dare they condescend to him this way. But, in a few weeks time they'd all be eating their words. He'd show them just how strong and intelligent he was. Then he would have the last laugh.

"You know what I think this is all about?" Michael asked suddenly, looking from face to face until his eyes landed on Rhiannon's and held. "I think all of you want her, and she's now going to be mine." He paused, grinning wickedly as he began to pace, staring at each of the men in turn. "In fact, did she let you into her bed to buy your protection? Certainly four men wouldn't so devoutly protect a woman they weren't screwing on a regular basis. Maybe I should tell my father that he's marrying me to a whore."

Rhiannon's eyes widened in shock. How dare he even think of such a vile, disgusting thing…

Before anyone could do more than blink, Liam shot to his feet and lunged at Michael, growling with pure hatred.

"*I'll kill you!*" he snarled, even as Rian and Jax fought to hold him back.

Michael took a cautionary step in retreat, alarmed by the madness in Liam's eyes. Clearly there was more to this situation than he had realized.

"Threats will get you nowhere with me, I won't be frightened off like some weak animal," Michael managed, trying to put the confidence back in his voice. "You can't keep her from me forever."

With that, he swept from the room, hiding his trembling hands in his pockets.

Liam's teeth were bared and his chest was heaving with hate and frustration. Rian and Jax eyed him uneasily as they loosened their hold on him.

"You alright there, son?" Jax asked, patting Liam on the back.

"That sick, twisted, lying son of a–" Liam began, only to be cut off by Rhiannon's sharp, strangled cry.

"*Damnit, stop it, all of you!*" she roared, jumping to her feet, her head pounding with brutal, startling pain. Yet the worst of it was pushed aside by the irritation and righteous anger pulsing through her system.

They all gaped at her, stupefied. None of them had ever seen an outburst from her like this. But at that moment, all hell broke loose inside of her and something wild, rabid and free reared up to speak her mind, loud and clear.

"I'm sick of all this fighting and I want it to stop," she ordered, fighting to be reasonable despite the assault on her system. "While I appreciate your concern for my wellbeing, though certainly most of you are doing this for Liam, not for me, I don't see how bickering is going to change anything. What's done is done, I've made my decision to go through with this, and nothing any of you can say or do will stop it from happening. So everyone just needs to get over it, and move on. Am I making myself clear?"

She glared around at all of them, noting the shock, and in Brogan's and Capri's case, the hurt in their eyes. But what did that matter, when she couldn't, and wouldn't, change her mind? Her father's life came before her friends' feelings. That was just how it was. And she wouldn't, not for one flickering moment, be sorry for it.

When she glanced over at Liam, he looked ashamed more than anything and she felt a flash of guilt course through her.

Pressing her hands to her eyes, feeling her headache pulsing like a jackhammer against her skull, she shook her head and stared back up at them again.

"Forgive me," she muttered before fleeing the room, needing peace more than anything at the moment. They watched her go, still too stunned to do more than stare.

However, as if by chance, she ran into her mother in the corridor, looking pristine and beautiful as always.

"Rhiannon! Come, let's talk." She grabbed Rhiannon's arm without waiting for an answer and led her toward the courtyard. Feeling numb and knowing she didn't have the energy to argue, Rhiannon followed, praying this would be quick.

Serendipity led the way to a bench shaded by a giant willow tree and took a seat, imperiously crossing her legs and folding her hands in her lap.

Rhiannon sat beside her, clutching her head as it pounded mercilessly.

"Sit up straight, Rhiannon, don't slouch," Serendipity chided, eyeing her daughter critically. Rhiannon did as she was told, letting her hands fall into her lap as she turned to face her mother. "Good. Now, Burke and I have discussed hosting the wedding here, of course, in the courtyard, in two months time. We will need to get you fitted for a gown, but other than that I will take care of everything else. I want this to be the biggest event of the year, so I'll expect you to be on your best behavior. I'm thinking it might be best, given the circumstances, to encourage Lucian and his children to go on a vacation or some such thing on that day, just to keep things civil. God knows how rowdy they can get, and I wouldn't want Burke's family and friends to be insulted by their poor judgment and manners."

"You're not going to let Liam be there?" Rhiannon managed, feeling her heart sink. She hadn't realized until that moment just how badly she was going to need him on that dreadful day.

"No, and I don't think that bounty hunter should be there, either. I don't much care for him, so he will have to go too." Serendipity pursed her lips with a tiny, impatient sigh. "Now, we will, of course, want to host an engagement party as soon as possible. Burke has assured me he will be bringing along a few good suitors for Sierra. It would be lovely to get an arrangement in place for her as well for the future."

Rhiannon eyed her mother in disbelief. "You're doing this to Sierra, as well?"

"Obviously, Rhiannon," Serendipity replied, eyebrows raised. "Why wouldn't I? Besides, it irritates me the way Tobias hangs on her. She can do better than that boy."

"What in God's name is wrong with you, mother?" Suddenly furious, Rhiannon got to her feet and glared down at her mother,

her hands shaking and her head spinning with a mixture of pain and disbelief. "Do you even realize how controlling you are?"

"Sit down, Rhiannon, you're making a scene." Serendipity frowned, glancing around to be sure no one was walking by.

"No, I'll stay standing." Crossing her arms over her chest, Rhiannon tilted her chin up, preserving whatever ounce of pride she had left. "Why does it matter so much to you who Sierra and I marry? God, she's only fifteen, give her the chance you never gave me to be young and in love."

"Love, Rhiannon? Please." Serendipity smirked, tossing back her luxurious blonde curls dispassionately. "Marriage is a contract and should be taken seriously. If all of us got married on a whim to the first man we thought ourselves in love with, why, we'd hardly get anywhere in life. Look at Brock, Rhiannon, and how much better off I am with your father. Brock is a sorry excuse of a drunk and a gambler, and while I'll admit he had me under his spell for quite some time, I have wised up and moved past that. I only want my daughters to do the same."

"You have never once regretted not marrying him? When you yourself claim to have loved him?" Rhiannon asked.

Serendipity sighed. "My father opened my eyes to what Brock was, and I am eternally grateful for it. He pushed me toward Rohan, and honestly, it was a much better match. Your father may be a tad bland at times, Rhiannon, but he is a much more respectable and proper husband than Brock ever could have been."

"And Michael? You think he will be a respectable and proper husband?" Rhiannon spat, feeling her temper rise heatedly. "Because every time he opens his mouth I want to throttle that scrawny neck of his and shut him up for good."

"Good Lord," Serendipity gasped, her eyes bulging as she clasped her hands to her chest in shock. "How dare you say such a terrible thing?"

"Because it's the truth, mother," Rhiannon sighed, trying to calm down, reminding herself why she was going through this foolish marriage in the first place. "But because it makes father happy, I will go through with marrying him. But only for that reason. Don't for one minute delude yourself into believing that I want this for myself."

"What you want is of no consequence, Rhiannon. It is up to your father and I who you and your sister marry, and you have no say in the matter."

"Then I feel sorry for her," Rhiannon said softly, feeling her temper fizzle, replaced by bitter regret. "You should really take a step back and look at what your critical, controlling style of parenting did to me, and wonder if you still have time to spare Sierra the same fate. You've made me into you, but maybe that was your goal all along. And what's worse is that for the longest time I wanted nothing more than to be you…to be beautiful, elegant, well read…but you aren't just those things, mother, and as a result neither am I. You wondered before when I had become so cold? It started with you, because you're inherently cold yourself, and distant, and selfish. You never saw just how badly I needed you to hold me, to show me any small amount of affection to prove you loved me. But maybe you didn't show it because you don't love me, you only see me as an obligation, an acquiescent doll for you to dress and bend at your will. And here I am, bending one last time, but know that it's not for you. It's for my father, who has suffered so much because of you and the only thing that has brought him back from the hole you shoved him in has been this marriage, so I'll be damned if I take it away from him."

For a moment, Serendipity was silent. She only stared directly at her daughter, her eyes betraying nothing. If she felt any small amount of remorse or guilt, it didn't show on her face.

"You are my obligation, as is your sister. I have given both of you a solid foundation and guided structure for you to live by, and I resent the implication that I have been in any way selfish. Look at your life, look at how intelligent and successful you are! Look at the man you're going to marry, and how prominent and well bred he is! All of that is because of me and your father, and if you can't see that then perhaps you have let the others blind you to reality. Emotions are messy, trust me when I tell you that. You are much better off not getting tangled up with them."

"You would have me not even feel love?" Rhiannon whispered, wondering why she even said it. Her mother's answering cool gaze said everything.

"Love is for fools, Rhiannon. Don't forget it."

A movement by the castle doors caught both their attentions, and they glanced over to see Burke and Michael walking down the cobblestone pathway.

"Smile and be polite. I taught you better manners than to cry in public." Serendipity rose to her feet, checked her hair and fixed a delighted smile on her face, all traces of coldness and hostility gone. It was, as Rhiannon knew from personal experience, a neat trick.

"I wasn't crying," Rhiannon murmured, turning to face Burke and Michael as they approached.

"Ladies," Burke greeted, grinning ear-to-ear as he held out a hand for Serendipity's, lushly kissing it when she obliged. He reached for Rhiannon's as well, and she could barely hide her grimace as he pressed his lips to her fingers. "I am pleased with our arrangement and I look forward to joining our two families."

"As do I, Burke." Serendipity preened before turning to Michael and frowning with an appropriately concerned look. "Dear, are you feeling alright? You look a bit piqued."

Michael shrugged, his eyes narrowing in on Rhiannon. "No ma'am, I'm fine."

Rhiannon stared right back at him, noting that he still looked flustered from the confrontation in the parlor. Clearly, the boys had him running scared, after all.

"Well, why don't you and Rhiannon have a seat and talk for a bit while your father and I go for a walk?" Serendipity suggested, motioning to the bench she had just been sitting on.

"What a wonderful idea," Burke put in, patting his son on the back. Michael flinched at the movement and scowled. "You kids get to know each other. We'll be back in a few."

With that, he held out his arm graciously for Serendipity and the two of them strolled away.

Rolling his eyes, Michael sat down and splayed out on the bench, stretching out his legs casually and spreading out his arms over the backrest, looking haughty and bored.

Annoyed and still suffering from the migraine, Rhiannon perched on the very edge of the seat and folded her hands in her lap. It had already been a trying day for her, and she had a feeling that if she engaged in a conversation with Michael that it was only going to get worse.

But Michael had turned his head and was watching her closely, his eyes scanning up and down, taking in her clothes, the way she wore her long dark hair, her ivory skin and soft hands. She really was beautiful, he knew as much. Maybe he preferred blondes, but he'd settle for the classy, green eyed brunette.

"I'm sorry for calling you a whore earlier," he told her unceremoniously, causing her to turn her head slightly to face him, her eyebrows raised.

"It was uncalled for," she said after a moment, her lips pursed as she eyed him curiously, wondering if he really was sorry.

"I was backed into a corner, quite unfairly, by your entourage in there." He sneered as he looked away, the memory of it coinciding with most of his memories of Euphora. "I let my temper get the best of me, at your expense."

"I am humbled to hear you lower yourself enough to apologize to me, Michael." She smirked, watching him more closely now. "Though I suppose even you have a heart in there somewhere."

He rolled his eyes, but smiled a little anyway as he turned to her. "Look, I don't want this any more than you do, but the powers that be are forcing us together. But it might not be all that bad. We're both going to have to make sacrifices and compromises, but in the end, I feel this marriage can be successful."

"If you don't want this, then why did you agree to go through with it?"

Michael looked away from her, staring out at the expansive gardens. "My mother. I'm doing this for her."

Her eyebrows raised in honest surprise at his words.

"I thought your mother despised Euphora?"

"She does, but she knows what my father gave up to marry her, and she doesn't want the same thing to happen to me."

Rhiannon shifted, moving closer to him on the bench, curious now. "I don't understand, Michael."

He sighed deeply, clearly not used to discussing his private life. But when he turned to look at her, she saw that there was more to him than what met the eye. There was deeply rooted pain somewhere inside of him, the kind that she knew all too well came from years and years of suffering in near silence.

"My mother was thirty-three when she met my father. At the time, he was only twenty four, and just starting out as an Enforcer. She worked as a secretary within the department part-time just to have something to do, but she didn't need the money. You see, my mother's family is very wealthy, old money, very prominent in politics and in business in America. And my father, being the kind of man he is, was drawn to that kind of prestige. He's always wanted to be powerful, to be significant, to go down in history as this great man who accomplished great things. And for awhile, it seemed as though marrying my mother would be a great way to supplement his budding career as an Enforcer.

"But when he was introduced to this place, and to you people, he was captivated by it. He understood that he could further his career and his reputation even more by finding a way to marry into the Council. He even went as far as to court one of the Fates, and he might have married her if my mother hadn't broken down when he told her his intentions. She begged him not to leave her, told him she was pregnant with me, and so he pushed aside his aspirations to do the right thing. She knows as well as I do that he has always regretted it, which is why he is now living vicariously through me. He wants me to live the life he didn't get to have. And as a result, my mother and I have both come to despise this place because we know he wishes he'd chosen this life instead of us. So we demonize all of you, because it's easier than accepting the truth."

"I'm sorry," Rhiannon murmured, though she knew it didn't change anything. But it did help her to know his story, to know the truth behind why Michael was who he was. And, despite everything, a part of her felt sorry for him.

"So why are you going through with this, if you don't want to?" he asked suddenly.

"Oddly enough, for a slightly similar reason." Her lips curved in a slow, considering smile. "I'm doing it for my father."

With an acknowledging nod, Michael turned away from her. He stared back out at the courtyard, lost in his own thoughts. She wondered if he was thinking, as she was at that moment, just how interesting it was that the two of them were committing to marriage not for themselves, but for the one parent each of them actually cared for. Because it was clear to her that Michael did not care in the least for his father, and she knew herself that she cared not for her mother. It was probably the only thing they had in common, though Rhiannon supposed there were worse traits they could share.

Following his gaze, she sat back against the bench, content to sit in silence now that whatever was between them was aired out. It was like the final lock clicking shut. She didn't have to wonder any longer if some miracle would occur that would put an end to this arrangement their parents had crafted. No, now all she could do was sit back, and place her fate calmly into the hands of others.

Chapter Seventeen

Though she knew it was foolish and incredibly dangerous, she couldn't stay away from Liam. He was on her mind all hours of the day, even in her dreams, penetrating her thoughts when he wasn't around and jolting her to life when he was.

It was in desperation that she tried to get as much out of what little time they had left. She spent her days searching for him in the gardens, following the bluesy sound of his guitar. Sitting beside him in the parlor after dinner, just to be next to him. Inviting him into her bedroom in the dead of night, where no one could be any the wiser…

And every time they parted ways, though it was never for long, it felt like deep, embedded fractures tearing her heart to pieces. The heart that he had brought out in her; the heart that would cease to exist the moment she pledged herself to another. And that was it, really–marrying Michael would be the end of her. Her father would survive, but the best thing in her life would come to an end.

But it was worth it, that much she knew. It was worth the sacrifice to know her father would stay as he was now, content, sharp and alive.

And as the days passed, she came to accept the fact that Michael would be her husband…at least in those moments when Liam wasn't around. When he was, her mind couldn't concentrate on more than the deep blue of his eyes, the quick flash of his crooked grin, or the sound of his voice pledging his love for her, despite how little it seemed to matter now.

She could see it in his eyes that he hated being helpless to do more than sit back and let her walk out of his life as quickly as she had walked into it. His moods had been like a chaotic whirlwind; one minute he was smiling and hugging her and the next he was pacing the floor, running his hands through his hair, his brow creased in anxiety and distress. Other times she'd catch him playing something fast and upbeat on his guitar, strumming along with a bright grin and his usual careless, free attitude. Then, minutes later, he'd switch to some somber ballad, his voice filled with anguish as it rang out through the back gardens, haunting her with the sincerity of his emotions. It was in those moments that she realized he was mourning her as if she were dead, and really that's what she would be once this was through.

Sure, he'd still see her on a regular basis and they could be friends. But even she felt that friendship would never sate her in regards to Liam. It had for years, but going back to the way things were was proving to be much harder than it had been to establish distance in the first place. Now they had history together; dark, passionate secrets that time could never erase.

But time would move on and they would find some way to cope with the hand they were dealt. She could be resilient and she had faith that, eventually, Liam would move on and find someone new. She couldn't ask for better for him than that.

The morning of her engagement party came with swift and unexpected speed. She supposed that most girls would be filled with anticipation, excitement, joy…she just felt a numbing acceptance. She rose early, unable to sleep, her mind and body restless. She had the urge to go for a walk, to be alone in the quiet of the meadow and forest surrounding the castle.

Her strict routine had been shot for weeks as her life was turned upside down faster than she could keep up. And yet, there was a part of her that was glad the routine was pushed aside, that she had found whatever tiny speck of freedom that existed and had snatched it up greedily, just in time to embrace the effects before she completed the task at hand.

And so she walked, clad in a long, cotton dress the color of the deep sea that flowed around her legs, caressing her skin as she strolled down the cobblestone walkway. In her arms she carried a wicker basket, hoping to pick some of the wildflowers in the meadow, maybe for a centerpiece or for her own pleasure in her room. Her mother despised wildflowers, so it was unlikely they'd fair long if she placed them in plain sight of the guests coming later that evening. Pristine, perfect roses in shades of pink and red were what her mother preferred, and her discerning and overly critical eye could spot a flaw with a bloom from a mile away.

But Rhiannon loved wildflowers, she always had. Just like the wild roses in the back gardens, the wildflowers in the meadow were the essence of freedom. And maybe that was just it…she was drawn to the Earth's interpretation of freedom. Surely, there was nothing more free than a wildflower, flying on the wind as a seed, carelessly burrowing wherever fate chose to plant it, and bursting to life without restrictions. It was beautiful, and stunning, that freedom. She only wished she possessed more of it herself.

Because thinking of her freedom had her thinking of Liam, her lips curved slightly as she began to hum one of his favorite songs. It was a song of her namesake, with lyrics about a woman taken by the sky.

As she approached the wrought iron entrance gates, she heard a rustling of birds overhead and glanced up in time to see them flutter from the tree and dart away, almost as if they were skittish and agitated. Her brow creased as she watched them go, but she heard no sounds other than her own which would have disturbed them. It was still very early, barely even six in the morning, and no one would be awake. The silence hung heavy in the air around her now that the birds had fled the area. The strangeness of the still air, coupled with an odd feeling of dread had chills shimmering down her spine. Something was off, something was different…

She glanced around, half expecting to see someone jump out of the shadows at her, only to see nothing moving and to hear nothing except her own beating heart. Even the gardens were still, all the creatures that dwelled there either asleep, or cowering in fear.

She debated whether or not to just go back into the castle. Surely she could pick flowers another time, later perhaps, when the others were up and about. She just had this terrible, all encompassing feeling of trepidation cloaking her like a dark shroud, and she couldn't seem to shake it.

Just as she was about to turn and go inside, she spotted something in the meadow that caught her eye. It was black, laying in the tall grasses amongst all the wildflowers.

Eyes sharpening, she tentatively approached the gate, attempting to stare through the wrought iron bars to get a better look at the object. It wasn't moving, but it was hard to tell not only what it was, but how large it was due to the grasses covering it from view.

Again, she deliberated whether she should just ignore it and go inside, but her curiosity got the better of her. It was probably just someone's jacket that had been dropped yesterday and had been carelessly forgotten. And once she confirmed that was all it was, then she could pick her flowers as planned. Surely there was no need to be afraid…she wasn't in danger, not here, not on Euphora…

With a deep, steadying breath, she laid her palm against the wrought iron gate, causing it to melt away at her touch. Clutching the wicker basket tight in her hands, she began to walk along the path through the grasses toward the mysterious object.

It was about halfway between the gate and the giant oak tree, several yards away, so she took her time, glancing in all directions, listening for any sound and searching for any sign of movement. If this was some kind of trap, she was prepared to run. And if it wasn't…then she'd feel foolish, but that was the least of her worries.

As she got closer, she eyed the object apprehensively, biting her tongue as her heart beat furiously in her chest in both fear and uncertainty. Was that hair?

Pausing mid-step, she struggled to see around the grasses, unsure she was seeing what she thought she was seeing. Certainly this wasn't a body…

But then she saw the hand, laying pale white against the rich brown soil, and her heart leapt from her chest into her throat, lodging itself there, choking her breath and preventing any sound from escaping.

She was screaming inside her head to run–run fast and far and away from this nightmare. Certainly it wasn't real, but if it was…

Still something had her stepping forward again, and again... until she was a few feet from the form, which was now in plain view. What she saw made the basket fall from her hands as they clamped over her mouth in horror and shock.

The body lay face up, dressed in a black Enforcer's uniform and drenched in blood that pooled into the soil. Sandy hair fell back from a chalk white face, and the still and empty brown eyes stared up at the sky, seeing nothing.

It was obvious the blood had come from the vicious gash slit across the throat…blood that no longer flowed; blood that had gone cold in the night.

Tears sprang hot into her eyes as she gasped out a breath, her hands still pressed against her mouth, as if it may keep her from screaming.

But she knew that screams couldn't save him.

Michael was dead, and she cursed the part of her deep inside that wept with ashamed, delirious relief.

The next few minutes were a blur. She remembered running, remembered nearly tripping over the skirt of her dress as she flew through the atrium. She had brief flashes of seeing Blythe on her way to enjoy her morning run and collapsing into the other girl's arms. Blythe had been alarmed, but thankfully she had believed her when she somehow explained what she had found. She didn't even remember what she had said, had blocked out the words in a haze. But Blythe had understood and rushed with her to get Thea and Sebastian, who in turn went immediately out into the meadow.

Rhiannon had led the way, but she hardly remembered offering to do so. It seemed as though her feet just carried her back to that spot, drawn to the destruction and demise of the man who would have been her husband.

Within an hour, everyone knew.

Sebastian had ordered most of them to stay inside the castle, away from what was now considered a crime scene. It was surreal, Rhiannon thought, as she stood just outside the gates of Euphora, clutching her arms around her chest. The idea of someone being murdered…here, just outside her home? Surely they had seen bloodshed and battle there, but not cold-blooded murder in the dead of the night with no explanation.

Who in the world would want to kill Michael? Perhaps he had made enemies in his life, maybe in his time as an Enforcer… but then why kill him here?

In the meadow, Rian and Brogan surveyed the scene, checking for traces of demon or of human…unfortunately though, it appeared as though too much time had passed and whatever trace was gone. So they searched instead for the murder weapon, stepping tentatively through the grass.

Rhiannon watched them with dull eyes, trying to figure all the possibilities. But nothing seemed logical…there just didn't seem to be any reason she could come up with for Michael to have been the target of assassination. And though she knew he was not well liked, surely no one had killed him for being arrogant.

She heard a sound behind her and saw Liam approaching, his eyes clouded with worry and apprehension. She watched as he came closer, held his eyes as he thrust his arms around her and pulled her against him, burying his face in her hair. She held on, closing her eyes, blocking out everything but the feel of him against her. Her hands clung to his shirt as she pressed her face to his neck, comforted by the feel of his warm pulse. He, thank God, was still alive. If it had been Liam out there in that field… but no, she didn't even want to think about it.

"I'm sorry, Rhia," he murmured, pulling away to look into her eyes, cupping her face in his hands. "I'm sorry you had to find him this way."

"I'm sorry, too." She looked away, feeling the shame and guilt rise in her as she remembered her first lucid feeling upon finding Michael…the wave of relief. For that, she was truly sorry.

Pushing away from Liam, she spotted her mother and father racing forward, having apparently slipped past Sebastian. Serendipity looked furious and mortified, and Rohan just looked dumbfounded.

"Rhiannon," Serendipity spat as she rushed toward her daughter. She glared once at Liam before turning to Rhiannon. "Thea has contacted Burke. He should be here any moment."

"Are you alright, Rhiannon?" Rohan asked, watching her closely, examining her, gauging her emotions.

"This isn't about me," Rhiannon replied, straightening up as she faced both of her parents. Beside her, Liam braced like a fighter poised to spar. "If I hadn't found him, Blythe most likely would have. It's pure coincidence that I happened to stumble upon the body first, so don't try and make this about me. Burke is going to be understandably upset and we need to focus on finding out what happened to his son."

Serendipity's eyes narrowed, then shot to stare at Liam. "I'm sure we will get answers, soon enough."

They all turned at the sight of a bright gold light, signaling Burke's arrival to Euphora.

Rhiannon watched, chest clenched with sympathy, as Burke rushed forward to where the Furies were standing beside the body. He collapsed to his knees and stared with dull shock at what was left of his son. Rian and Brogan stood at his side, ready to console him as best they could.

"This is just disastrous," Serendipity was muttering, shaking her head as she stared at Burke, her eyes cold and dry.

Rohan patted her on the back, thinking she was upset, as he watched Burke mourn his son. Reaching out with his other arm, he wrapped it around Rhiannon and pulled her close.

Unused to the gesture, she was momentarily confused, only to realize he intended to comfort her. Strangely pleased by it despite the circumstances, she leaned into him and glanced over at Liam, who turned to meet her eyes.

He tried to smile, but there was a dark, restless anxiety in him that resonated through the air.

Thea and Sebastian emerged from the castle, having heard that Burke had arrived. They walked swiftly, with purpose and righteous anger over what had happened, the two of them emanating pure power. Rhiannon watched them, mystified by the sheer energy sparking in the air. Certainly they would not be resting until this murder was solved.

They swept past where she stood with her parents and Liam, and went straight to Burke. He got to his feet and stood straight and tall, his grief fading and fury replacing it. Even though they were several yards away, Rhiannon heard him loud and clear the moment he spoke.

"*Who did this?*" he bellowed, his voice echoing through the meadow. Thea was saying something to him that Rhiannon couldn't hear, but it was clear that it did nothing to soothe him.

He glanced over Thea's shoulder and spotted Rhiannon and her parents standing by the gates, and without hesitation he bolted forward, charging through the meadow like an enraged bull. Rhiannon braced against her father, pulling out of his grasp just in case Burke decided to throw a punch. God knew what any man was capable of after losing his son…

"Burke, I don't even know what to say…" Serendipity rushed forward to meet him, her hands on his shoulder to comfort, but he only swatted her away without a second glance.

His eyes had honed in on Rhiannon and he rushed toward her, murder in his eyes. Both Rohan and Liam started to pull her back, to step in front of her, but Burke suddenly reached out and gripped Rhiannon's throat, roughly dragging her to him in one vicious swipe. Her feet dangled above the ground as he held her inches from his face, looking quite capable of strangling the very life out of her.

"*This was because of you, wasn't it?*" Burke roared, squeezing the very breath from her throat. She struggled against him, her hands over his, desperately trying to pull them away. But the anguished rage in his eyes terrified her more than anything she had ever witnessed.

"Let her go!" Liam shouted, lunging at Burke, only to stop short as Burke pulled the pistol from his holster and pointed it at Liam's chest.

"Stay the hell away from me, boy," Burke growled, pointing the gun at Rohan when he started to move toward Rhiannon. "This is her doing, I know it is."

"Burke, what's going on?" Thea and Sebastian raced forward, looking alarmed and confused. Burke just rounded on them, his hand still clamped around Rhiannon's throat, but loosening just enough for her to gasp in snippets of air. "This whore is responsible for my son's murder."

"What? How?" Thea demanded, eyeing Rhiannon, fear in her eyes. "Damnit, let her go, Burke, you're hurting her. And put away your gun."

Rhiannon felt her body weakening from little oxygen, and knew her neck would be bruised. But perhaps she deserved this; perhaps she had earned this miniscule punishment for even one moment feeling relieved over Michael's death.

Burke's chest was heaving with fury, but he wasn't insane. Taking a deep, cleansing breath to clear the red from his vision, he released Rhiannon, pushing her away from him as he slid the gun into the holster at his waist.

Rhiannon stumbled as her knees gave out, clutching her throat and gasping. Without a second's hesitation, Liam rushed forward and grabbed her, pulling her out of Burke's reach. He stopped just inside the gate, letting her sit on the cobblestones so she could catch her breath. He instinctively shielded her, his heart pounding with fear and indignation.

Rohan was at her side in an instant, pale white with shock and fear. "Rhiannon, dear God," he murmured, unsure if he should even touch her. He met Liam's eyes helplessly.

"I'll take care of her. Make sure the bastard doesn't try this again," Liam said between clenched teeth, fighting to push aside his own fury over what Burke had done so he could help her.

Nodding, Rohan glanced back down at Rhiannon, who was clutching Liam's shirt to steady herself, her face burrowed against him as her breathing began to finally settle. Following the younger man's advice, Rohan rose to his feet and went straight to where Burke was now arguing heatedly with Thea and Sebastian, and where Serendipity was standing, wide eyed and tearful.

"What are you saying, Burke? That one of my own did this?" Thea demanded, her eyes filled with anger at the thought. Sebastian had his hand on her shoulder supportively, but even he looked incensed.

"There is no other explanation, Thea," Burke snarled, his hands clenched into fists at his side as he glared out at the field where the Furies were wrapping up his son's body in cloth. "Those two, and Murphy, and that one, back there." He shifted around and pointed in Liam's direction, eyes flashing with cold understanding. "They were all trying to force him out to prevent our arrangement. One of them must have killed Michael to keep him away from your whore daughter."

"*What?*" Rohan managed, looking shell shocked and deeply offended. "How dare you make such a claim? Maybe it was your son's own doing that got him killed. Don't unfairly accuse them without any proof!"

"My son's word is enough proof for me." Burke got in Rohan's face, glaring at him. "And he told me those heathens assaulted him, and that they seemed to have some kind of allegiance to your daughter."

"So that makes them murderers?" Thea cried, not believing what she was hearing. "Burke, you are out of line!"

"No, he's not!" Serendipity said suddenly, wide eyed and skittish as she looked back and forth from her husband and Burke, Thea and Sebastian. "Burke confirmed with me the actions those men took against Michael just last week. And I can speak on behalf of Rhiannon that she did not want this marriage, and it would not surprise me if she convinced one of those men to make Michael go away, whatever the cost."

"Serendipity!" Rohan gaped at her, alarmed. "How could you think for one second that Rhiannon did this?"

"Because I'm not blind to what she is, Rohan, unlike you," Serendipity replied coldly, staring at her husband. "I am inclined to believe that Michael's death has to do with our arrangement, and therefore the killer was likely acting on Rhiannon's behalf, whether she ordered the killing or not. But the responsibility still lies on her shoulders."

Thea and Sebastian were staring at Serendipity in shock, and Burke was nodding his head fervently, gulping down Serendipity's cold explanation like water.

"See, it all makes sense. I want to speak with these four men immediately. One of them did it and I'm going to find out which one." Burke turned to Thea, as if daring her to object. Instead, she took a deep breath and eyed him as coolly as she could muster under the circumstances. Someone had to be reasonable, after all.

"Alright, Burke, you may question them. But I will be present and if you lay one hand on them in haste I will have your badge. Have I made myself clear?"

"Yes," he grunted, hands clenching again at his sides.

"Good. Sebastian, gather Rian, Brogan, Jax and Liam and meet me and Burke in the garden room. So help me God, we're going to settle this in a civil manner."

She stood in the field of golden barley with the wind swirling all around her, sending her dark hair flying into the fading blue sky. Doubt and fear and uncertainty plagued her, raising questions she had never dreamed she'd have the occasion to ask.

Michael was dead, murdered…had one of them...Liam, Brogan, Rian or Jax wielded the knife? Had one of them taken it upon themselves to rid her of this burden, once and for all?

Burke was interrogating them all at that very moment… asking each of them in turn that same question. She hadn't had it in her to watch, had needed time to clear her head, to prepare for what could only be an onslaught of more destruction, doubt and vile anger back home. For she knew, as well as she knew her own name, that Burke would not rest until he found out who had killed his son. And it was very likely that once he did know, he might very well take it upon himself to provide swift, effective justice.

Feeling her throat tighten at the thought, she wrapped her arms around herself and took a deep, steadying breath. If it had been Liam…but no, he couldn't…

And then she remembered his last words to Michael, and a dizzying jolt of horror shot through her system, stunning the breath from her.

I'll kill you!

Good God…what had he done?

Chapter Eighteen

When she came home, her father took her aside before the others could get to her. They went for a walk out into the forest, heading out toward the cliff's edge and the bench that was there, ready and waiting.

Rhiannon sat down warily, unsure what is was her father wanted to say to her. But for a few moments, he simply sat beside her in silence, gathering his thoughts and staring out at the ocean. When he did speak, he sounded a little ashamed, and very uncertain.

"Rhiannon, I brought you out here because I wanted to ask you something, in private," he began, his hands folded in his lap and his back ramrod straight. He kept his eyes on the horizon, knowing if he looked at her he might lose what it was he was trying to say. "Is it true that you didn't want to marry Michael?"

Rhiannon sighed, the guilt rising within her. "Yes."

He only nodded, having his assumptions confirmed. "So you were going along with it solely because you knew it pleased your mother and I?"

"Yes," she admitted, her hands clenching together in her lap uncomfortably.

"You always have been an obedient child." His lips curved sadly, his eyes softening. "I'm sorry you were put in this situation, Rhiannon. I assumed this would be what you wanted; a good, successful husband to start a family with. But this past week I've noticed something very strange and I'll admit it's worried me greatly." He tilted his head to look at her, taking in his quietly serious daughter with fresh, opened eyes. "There's someone else that you want, isn't there?"

Rhiannon's eyes widened slightly, but she kept the rest of her face carefully blank. "No, there's no one."

"You're lying to me." He chuckled, shaking his head. "Obedient enough to marry the man I tell you to, but so quick to lie to me about this. Why?"

Because she could feel her hands shaking, she kept them firmly together and willed her body to stay still. She didn't want to lie to him, it was just that she had been lying about this particular subject for so long that it seemed odd to admit it to even herself, let alone to him. But from the look in his eyes, he wasn't going to let her go without the truth.

"You know, I never told you this, and I don't know if Lucian ever said anything about it…but do you know what the first word you ever spoke was?" There was a light in his eyes now, and she held on to it, captivated.

Shaking her head, she stared at him, wondering what it was about this moment or this conversation that had him opening up to her more than he ever had in her entire life.

"Your first word was his name, Rhiannon." Rohan smiled at her, the memory sweet to him. "You said 'Liam,' clear as day. And something about that has stuck with me all these years, even today, with everything that's happened."

Rhiannon blinked, startled at the revelation that her first word had been Liam's name and just how odd that was. Surely it was more normal for a baby to say 'mama' or 'dada' or something more traditional…why had she picked his name?

But maybe that was just it. Maybe this was a sign that she had been meant for him, all along.

"I've seen how you look at him, how he looks at you. I'm not blind, Rhiannon." He chuckled again, looking out to the sea with a sigh. "I don't know what is happening right now between the two of you, but I know in my heart that you're not responsible for this. It remains to be seen if Liam is, though I find it hard to believe. But I want you to know that I'm going to stand by you. I owe it to you, after all the times I neglected to see you, or hear you. It's time I opened my eyes."

She gaped at him, startled. "What brought all this on?"

A shadow passed over his face, his eyes darkening with bitterness. "What your mother so carelessly said today alarmed me. That she would be so quick to assume her own daughter capable of this horrific act shows who she really is. I've been a fool for so long, Rhiannon, groveling at her feet, and for what? So she could tarnish our marriage, abuse my love for her? So she could turn me into her puppet, hurting my own friends to please her inflated sense of superiority over them? No, I won't have it anymore, and I hope you have it in you to forgive me for all the years I chose her over you. God knows I don't deserve it."

Humbled and utterly speechless, Rhiannon reached out for his hand, holding it in her own.

At last…he was free. Now, hopefully, it was her turn.

Freedom, it seemed, had alluded her once again. Because she was quite certain that being holed up in a room, all but chained to a chair and suffering through a harsh and near violent interrogation was not considered freedom. No; it was a cage, a prison, and her mother and Burke had become her guards and her captors.

"We've talked to your...friends, Rhiannon, and they all claim they are innocent," Serendipity said, pacing before her daughter, staring down her nose skeptically. "However, only two of them have relatively solid alibis, given by their girlfriends, which I am inclined to believe only because they were the least likely suspects to begin with."

Rian and Jax, Rhiannon thought with a small sigh of relief. At least her mother and Burke would leave them be, for now.

"But Liam and Brogan have no alibis," Burke grunted, stepping toward Rhiannon and glaring down at her, his face that had been so charismatic and friendly before now hardened and sharper than a steel blade. This was the true face behind his gallant, gregarious mask...the one she'd always known was lurking inches under the surface, ready to lash out when provoked. This was the man who conquered demons, the man who garnered unwavering respect from fellow Enforcers and the people of Euphora. This was the man who would spare no expense, and spare no means to find justice for his only son. His legacy, wasted.

Rhiannon shivered once, not wanting him to see just how terrified he made her. She remembered quite vividly what it had felt like to have Burke nearly choke the life out of her just hours earlier. And the bruises that were gradually blooming on her skin, in the shape of his fingers that had pressed brutally into her throat, were a wicked reminder of what he was capable of. She knew, without a doubt, that she was right to be scared of him.

"Which one of them did it? *Answer me!*" Burke roared, gripping her shoulders and shaking her, causing her head to whip back and spin with dizzying fear.

"Neither of them," she gasped, trying to keep her expression neutral and her breathing even. She had to maintain control, at all costs.

"*Liar!*" Burke pushed away from her, clenching his fists, the urge to strike her flooding fast and eager through his system. But

Thea would have his head if he laid a hand on her in that manner again. "If it wasn't Liam or Brogan, then who was it?"

"I don't know." Rhiannon met his eyes, cold and determined, and repeated herself. "*I don't know.*"

Burke shook his head, looking disgusted. "You know, girl, you sure are calm and collected for someone whose boyfriends are being accused of murder." He began to pace around her chair, circling her as a new thought occurred to him. "Tell me, why did you decide to go for a walk outside the castle this morning? We've talked to everyone, and no one has ever seen you break from your usual routine to go for a walk so early in the morning before. Did you go out there because you knew what you'd find, and you wanted to be the one to break the news of what you had done?"

"*What?*" Rhiannon stammered, her mouth falling open in shock at his words.

"That's right." Burke stopped mid-step and leaned toward her, a gleam of triumph in his eyes. "You had the most to gain from killing my son, so you took it upon yourself to do the deed, didn't you? You lured Michael onto Euphora last night, and you slit his throat the minute he arrived."

Serendipity made a small gasping noise, her hand pressed against her lips, her eyes wide. "Rhiannon, how could you?"

"I didn't do this!" Rhiannon insisted, shaking her head in disbelief. "I don't even own a knife!"

"Perhaps now you don't." Burke tilted his head, eyes narrowing maliciously. "If I remember right, you do a lot of work in the kitchens; there are plenty of knives down there. Where did you go this afternoon? Somewhere to stash the murder weapon?"

"No!"

"So what, then? Were you considering running away, but then chickened out and came back?"

Rhiannon let out a shuddering, dubious breath, unsure this could really be happening. They really believed her capable of slitting a man's throat? Of letting the blame fall on men who'd stood up for her, men who, in Brogan's case, considered her a friend, and in Liam's case, loved her? Not even she could stoop so low…

"Why would I kill Michael?" she asked, meeting Burke's eyes and then her mother's. "I may not have wanted to marry him, but I was going to go through with it because it made my father happy."

"Rhiannon, you told me just the other day that you wanted to strangle Michael," Serendipity said accusingly, her eyes narrowed in suspicion. "And now you want us to believe that you are not capable of murder, when you yourself expressed an explicit desire to commit it?"

At a loss for words, Rhiannon merely shook her head, feeling utterly trapped. Her own mother believed her guilty…

Thea burst into the room, having just met with the Furies to discuss the lack of evidence found in the meadow. She glided toward the three of them, noting the pale shock on Rhiannon's face, and the accusatory stares coming from Serendipity and Burke.

"Have you finished your interrogation, Burke?" Thea asked, looking disgusted with both of them.

Burke turned to look at Mother Earth, and all of the respect he'd had for her was clearly gone. He knew she would stand up for his son's murderer, simply because members of the Council were virtually untouchable in the eyes of the law. Hadn't Brock gotten away, time and time again, with purchasing demon weapons illegally? She would not let him arrest Rhiannon, not without tangible proof.

"Yes, Thea. We're done." He stood up straight, using all the control he could muster to not exact his revenge then and there. In time, hopefully very soon, he would see that Rhiannon paid for what she had done, because he was now convinced without a doubt that she had killed his son.

Without a word, Rhiannon went straight to her room, hoping for some time alone to figure out how in the world she was going to prove to her mother and to Burke that she was not a killer. The fact that this had turned on her was mind boggling enough. She had never so much as killed a bug, much less a human being! And to see the way her mother worked Burke up into a frenzy, feeding the madness in his grief stricken and vengeful mind, turning this on her own daughter without even a second thought.

It was disgusting. Downright disgusting.

Pushing open her bedroom door, she stopped mid-step as her eyes landed on Liam, who was laying unceremoniously on her bed.

"What are you doing here?" she asked him, carefully shutting the door behind her so no one could walk by and see him there.

He shot her a dark look. "I thought I was welcome to your bed now, Rhia."

Her eyes narrowed and she crossed her arms over her chest, unsure what he was getting at. "Being welcome in my bed has gotten you into a lot of trouble. I figured you'd be inclined to stay away."

"Bullshit." He grunted, sitting up and glaring at her. "They can speculate all they want, but they're wrong."

"You didn't kill him, Liam?" she asked in a murmured whisper, unsure why the words came to her. But she knew it had to be asked, especially since she herself was now a prime suspect…

"God, Rhia, no, I didn't." Liam got to his feet, approaching her with frustration and anger in his eyes. "I'm not stupid enough to think killing him would solve anything, which it obviously hasn't."

"Then if it wasn't you, who was it?" she asked, matching his anger with her own frustration.

"Rian and Jax have no stake in this, no motive. And I imagine if either of them wanted someone dead, they wouldn't be stupid enough to leave the body lying in plain sight," Liam reasoned, running his hands through his hair. "So that just leaves Brogan."

"No." Rhiannon shook her head fervently, upset to even be speaking of it. "He wouldn't do this."

"He has motive, Rhia," Liam began, watching her with narrowed eyes. "He's liked you forever and he wouldn't want to see you married off to some prick like Michael. Plus he has access to weapons; weapons he knows how to use. He's a born and bred soldier, Rhia, that's what the Furies do. He knows how to kill. And maybe he left the body there to make a statement."

"How dare you," she managed, angry heat rising up to color her face as she jabbed at his chest with her index finger. "You're no better than they are if you start accusing people without even knowing them! Brogan is a good person, kindhearted and caring, more than you could ever know. He's my friend, my dearest friend, really, and I won't stand by and let you think for one minute that he would do something this vile in my honor."

He reached out and gripped her wrists, holding her in place, his eyes boring into hers. "If it were Brogan doing the accusing right now, would you defend me so passionately, Rhia? Or do you reserve this fevered devotion for him alone?"

"Screw you!" she spat, struggling against his grip to release herself. When he let go, she glared at him, her hair falling over her face and her chest heaving with indignation. "You chose a horrible time to suddenly get jealous about Brogan, Liam."

"I'm just considering all the angles," he told her, tucking his hands in the pockets of his jeans, his eyes hard as stone.

"Fine, you want to consider all the angles? Then consider the idea that maybe *I* did it. Because that's what Burke and my mother think, and you seem so ready to jump on the accusatory band wagon."

Liam's mouth fell open and his brow creased with disbelief. "Are you serious?"

"Would I lie about that?" she managed, feeling her anger fizzle at the look of horror in his eyes. "Burke accused me because I wouldn't name one of you as the murderer, and then my mother brought up how I told her the other day that sometimes I wanted to strangle Michael to get him to shut up. That was enough to convince them that I'm a killer."

"Damnit," Liam cursed, mostly without feeling now as he sat back down on the bed, his head in his hands. "What a nightmare."

She stayed by the door, unsure what move to make next. All she knew was it was probably best for Liam to disassociate himself from her, at least for now. It was the only way she could protect him and the others.

"I think you should go," she told him, fighting to keep her voice level, controlled and distant.

"What? Why?" He glanced up at her, confusion and hurt in his eyes.

"It's best if I handle this alone. It's my burden to bear." She watched the anger flash over his face and felt sorry for it. But she couldn't let him, or any of the others, fall victim to Burke and her mother's madness. Let them focus all their attention on her and away from the others. Eventually the truth would come out and she would be exonerated. But until then, she wouldn't let the others face any more of Burke's wrath. It just wasn't fair, not when Michael had been her burden, not theirs.

"You would push me away, now, when you're accused of goddamn *murder*?" Liam shot to his feet, incensed. "I thought we were past all of this?"

"Time will tell just what happens between us, Liam. Until then, I want you to lie low. Don't give them any reason to suspect you any more than they do now."

"I won't just stand by and let you take the fall for this all on your own. Who do you think I am?"

She was silent for a moment, considering his words, knowing exactly who he was. She had always known, hadn't she? "You're a hero, Liam. But I'm telling you right now that I don't need you to be mine."

"Unbelievable," he muttered, shaking his head at her, the sting of betrayal haunting his eyes. She felt her heart shudder at the sight of it, and shrink into hollow darkness as he spoke again. "It must be lonely up there on that pedestal, Rhia."

With that, he pushed past her and left the room, slamming the door behind him. She stayed where she was, unable to do more than let out a shaky, unsteady breath.

It was lonely, she thought. But at least she would be the only one to fall when the time came.

Thousands of miles away, he took a shot of whiskey in some dank, run down bar and silently thanked the Devil for inventing gossip. What better way could a man get all the latest news on his familiars and his enemies than by mingling with those whose tongues wagged the most? It was disgustingly easy, not to mention extraordinarily entertaining.

Especially since he had learned quite a few interesting bits of information in his short hour long probing session, having only been back stateside a couple of hours. Already he'd heard word that the lead Enforcer's son had been murdered and that a few members of the Council were at the top of the suspect list.

How thrilling it was to watch the empire crumble upon itself, he thought with a cold, wicked grin. There might not be much left for him to destroy after all, if this Enforcer was as ruthless as he had heard. According to the demons he'd talked to, Burke Callahan was not known for showing any mercy to those he captured.

He could only imagine the horrors Callahan would subject to those accused of murdering his only son. Just thinking about it made him giddy with sick excitement.

It felt good to be home, now that he knew they were no longer looking for him. They had plenty of problems of their own and the timing could not have been better.

Soon he'd have them under his thumb where they belonged, once and for all. They'd pay, every last one of them, until nothing was left of Euphora except dust.

If he'd learned one thing from his travels, it was that there was evil in every corner of this world that could be harnessed and used against those who foolishly thought themselves untouchable. From the deep, uncharted jungles of the Amazon to the primeval, crumbling castles of eastern Europe, evil lurked and lay in wait for someone to release it.

Dante was more than willing to oblige.

Burke took his son's body back home to be autopsied by experts in the department. Because of his unprompted and rough interrogations of four members of the Council and an ex-Enforcer, he was not surprisingly given the cold shoulder by nearly everyone on Euphora. His only ally, it seemed, was Serendipity. And few could understand her fervent belief that her own daughter was responsible for Michael's death. However, until the autopsy was finished and more viable evidence was gathered, no one would be charged with the murder.

And so Burke left, appearing determined and angry, but much more reasonable than he had been in the hours following his arrival on Euphora. He assured them that he would be back to conduct more questioning, but only after the autopsy was completed. Until then, he'd grieve in his own home and comfort his wife.

Euphora was, as expected, a somber place in the days that followed the mysterious murder. Curious and cautious whispers could be heard all hours of the day, speculating and theorizing over what could have possibly happened. It was only natural, Rhiannon supposed, that the people of Euphora would look at her and wonder. Certainly no one could argue that she indeed had the most to gain from Michael's death.

But what they didn't realize was that she had the most to lose, as well.

Michael's death had broken apart her family, with her and her father on one side, and her mother and Sierra on the other. Her parents were not speaking to one another, nor were they even sleeping in the same room. And while she knew her father had finally found his freedom, it still hurt her to see him suffering, worrying constantly over what would happen to her if somehow Burke could prove she had murdered Michael. There was little he could do to help her if that happened, and that helplessness and uncertainty was hurting him yet again.

And what none of the others had considered, or could possibly even understand, was that Rhiannon did in fact feel sorry that Michael had died. They seemed to be quick to assume that she was, in many ways, glad that the marriage she had not wanted in the first place would now not come to fruition, but none of them seemed to want to believe that she could actually feel sorry over it.

But the truth was she did. Maybe she hadn't liked Michael, had been insulted by him time and time again and had certainly wanted nothing to do with him. But the last conversation they had in the courtyard had opened her eyes to the good in him, had shown her that he was more than just arrogant and insulting. He had cared about his mother enough to go along with everything his father told him to do, despite how much he didn't want to, all because he knew she would be happier because of it. He knew that if he caused a rift between his father and him, that his mother would be the one to suffer. How could she not have admired that quality in him, not have recognized his selflessness, as least in this one manner?

But none of that seemed to matter now. All she could do was deal with the hushed whispering, the spreading rumors and gossiping, and pray that the truth would be uncovered as soon as possible.

She was surprised, but pleased, to note that Liam did in fact stay distant from her, more out of spiteful hurt than compliance with her wishes. But what did it matter, so long as he wouldn't be subjected to the same terrible scrutiny she was experiencing. She would spare him and Brogan and the others that at all costs.

On the third evening after discovering Michael's body, Rhiannon went to bed in a strange and oddly anxious mood. She couldn't say what it was about the tension that sparked in the air all around her, but it had her skin crawling and her mind restlessly wandering. Something bad was coming, but she had no idea just how bad it was.

But when she was startled out of sleep in the dead of night, a damp cloth clamped tight over her nose and mouth and a tall, silhouetted figure standing over her, she felt true, unadulterated fear like nothing she'd ever experienced.

And as she drifted dizzyingly into unconsciousness, the only thing she could think was that Burke Callahan had come to collect his revenge.

Chapter Nineteen

She awoke some time later, groggy and disoriented, her vision blurred and her body immobile. She wondered deliriously if she was paralyzed, her body weaker than her mind seemed to think it was. In her confusion, she swore she was telling her arms to move, and her legs to kick out. But her body was simply too weak to respond to the request.

It wasn't until she was able to blink her vision clear, and lift her head enough to glance around her that she understood herself to be simply bound and gagged. Not that this was a more welcome alternative to being paralyzed. If anything, being bound and still alive meant he wasn't finished with her.

Fighting back the first wave of fear, she struggled against the bonds at her wrists, ropes that were wound tightly around not only her, but the wooden chair she was sitting in as well. Her feet were also bound, which would explain why she couldn't move them. But, thankfully, her eyes were uncovered.

The room she was in appeared to be some kind of underground basement, with a sofa and a television set, along with a billiards table and stereo set up. Posters hung on the walls depicting various crime thriller movies and boxing champions, along with an entire wall filled with awards and trophies. The walls were paneled walnut, and the carpet at her feet was dense and a sickening shade of olive green. In front of her were stairs that led up to a single door, probably leading to the main floor. She stared at the door, suddenly hearing a shuffling noise on the other side of it.

It opened and Burke emerged, shutting the door swiftly behind him. He stared down at her for a moment, meeting her eyes, and flashed a quick, maniacal grin that had her blood chilling several degrees.

"I was wondering if you were ever going to wake up," he commented as he descended the stairs, his hands trailing down the railing, his eyes never leaving hers. "Chloroform is such a useful little tool, don't you think?"

Behind her gag, she kept silent, not wanting to encourage him. She knew that the likelihood of him releasing her, especially after her having known he was the one who took her, was slim to none. No, she would likely die here in this miserable basement, with its horrid carpet and testosterone filled memorabilia. What a shameful ending…and for what? For a murder she hadn't even committed…now she knew how Brock had felt, being accused of something he hadn't done. Of course, Brock's life had never been in danger. But her life undeniably was.

"Rhiannon…" Burke approached her until he was standing just feet away, his arms crossed over his chest and his head shaking sadly. "So beautiful…so deadly."

Without warning he suddenly reached out and struck her hard across the face, whipping her head around with a sickening crack. She winced from the stinging pain, her eyes watering pitifully and her chest heaving from the shock to her system.

When she managed to look at him again, he was no longer smiling. Now he just looked mean.

"You killed my son," he snarled, fury in his eyes. "My legacy, my child. Don't you see he was all I had?"

She tried to shake her head, wanting to scream to him that she didn't do it, that she was innocent.

"He didn't deserve to die, not like this. He was supposed to carry on the Callahan name, to join with me in cementing our legacy in the books of history. But you saw to it that that wouldn't happen, didn't you?"

Wanting a response from her, he ripped the gag from her mouth and smacked her again, this time cutting her lip and drawing blood. She let out a shuddering breath, too afraid now to look at him.

"Damnit, why? Why did you do this?" Burke demanded, miserable grief flashing through the hate he felt. He covered his face in his hands and let out an anguished cry so filled with angst and sorrow that the sound of it penetrated her to the bone.

Uncertain what he was going to do, she kept her mouth shut despite the gag having been removed. He looked insane and one wrong word could have him ripping her head off. No, she had to find some way to distract him, some way to free herself from these bonds…

Then it occurred to her, an idea so brilliantly obvious she nearly wept with relief at having thought of it. But just how could she pull it off without him noticing…

As if by fate, the doorbell rang hollowly from upstairs. Burke turned and looked in the direction of the front door, his brow furrowing with concern and worry.

"Who in the hell could that be…" he muttered to himself, stalking up the stairs and slamming the door behind him.

Seeing her chance, Rhiannon pulled apart her hands as best she could behind her, spreading her fingers out as she shut her eyes and concentrated on the floor beneath the vile green carpet. It was a long shot, but if she could make it work then she could get home.

She pictured the soil beneath the concrete below her, and imagined a seed growing there from nothing. In her mind's eye, she pictured it sprouting thin green tendrils that grew and shoved skyward against the surface. Urging it to grow strong enough to break through the concrete, she felt it slip through a crack and slither up, until it was stabbing through the carpet. Biting her bottom lip, she pushed harder, relieved when she heard it break through.

Her heart was racing a mile a minute in her chest, but she tried to continue focusing on growing the tree. Once it was just big enough, she should, in theory, be able to use it to get home.

But a sound at the stairs stopped her, and she stared up warily as Burke entered the basement again and thudded down the steps toward her.

She stared at him, hoping to distract him so he wouldn't notice the tiny sapling at her back. But there was something different about him now…he seemed stiff, strange…and when his eyes met hers, she saw none of his earlier heated emotions in them. Instead his eyes seemed darker somehow and glinted with what she could only describe as pure evil.

For a moment, he simply stood still and watched her, his lips spreading in an unsettling grin. Terror gripped her heart violently as she realized that the man standing before her, much more so than the miserable man who had left just minutes ago, planned to kill her. She couldn't say what gave it away, but it was there, in his eyes. There was a loathing there, a pure hatred and revulsion and a desire to destroy that shocked her with one glance.

And when he spoke, she shuddered at the sound of it, for it wasn't Burke's voice, not really. It was different, harsher and deeper and colder…

"The Earth Dryad…how intriguing," he said with a smile, reaching up to stroke his chin thoughtfully. "I wasn't sure who to expect when I came down here."

"What?" Rhiannon managed, looking perplexed as she eyed him. What in the world was wrong with him?

He chuckled, dark and sinister. "I suppose you wouldn't recognize me, not in this outfit, anyway." With another laugh, he suddenly lurched forward, expelling some kind of dark, shadowy mass from his mouth, hideous retching noises coming from his throat. She watched in horror as the shadowy mass formed a serpent, and then transformed almost instantly into a man.

Burke collapsed onto the ground, unconscious. But Rhiannon wasn't looking at him any longer, couldn't bother one single glance his way, not when her eyes were so feverishly glued to the stranger who'd just appeared out of nowhere. Because she knew exactly who he was, without even hearing his name. There was only one demon alive who could become a man, and though she had never seen him before, there was no doubt in her mind that this was him.

If she'd thought Burke was frightening, she hadn't considered what it would be like to be face to face with Dante himself.

He smiled at her again, this time in his own body, though the grin was identical. Darkly humorous, but slick and laced with an evil so heinous she shivered at the sight of it.

He was tall, much taller than she had imagined, and lean of body with thin limbs and a long, sharply angular face. He had long, dark black hair pulled back at the nape of his neck into a tail, and a crooked, broken looking hooked nose. His mouth was thin and wide, and when spread into a grin, displayed perfect white teeth that contradicted nearly everything else about him. And his eyes…the same fiery amber as Blythe's, but with none of her playfulness, and none of her heart. These eyes were just cold, and indescribably wicked.

"So you are Rhiannon, Rohan's daughter." He smirked as he stepped toward her, reaching out to cup her chin and tilt her face side-to-side, examining her. "Beautiful, but toxic, yes? I hear you've killed a man."

"I didn't," she replied coldly, her face carefully blank as she held his eyes. She wouldn't give him the satisfaction of seeing her true discomfort. A man like him, he thrived on seeing others suffer. She wasn't about to grant him the pleasure.

"No?" Dante's hand trailed down her chin to her neck, his fingers tracing over her skin, his eyes following the movement. "Pity. Tell me, would you have done it, if given the chance?"

"No."

His eyes flashed as he grinned, his hand resting at her collarbone now. "Would you kill the man who gave you these bruises?" His fingers ran along the blooming black and blue marks on her neck.

"No."

"Would you try and kill me now, if I threatened to kill you?"

"No." She saw the intrigue and the disappointment flash once in his eyes, moments before his hand clenched around her neck in nearly the same exact spot Burke had held her days before. She winced at the pain, but wouldn't plead for her own life. It wouldn't make a difference with him, that much she knew.

Dante tilted his head and stared down at her, his lips curving wickedly as he started to laugh. His body shook with it as he released her, standing back and reaching into a sheath at his waist and pulling out a demon blade. The razor sharp edge of it gleamed sadistically in the light.

After seeing the knife, she closed her eyes, and prayed it would be quick.

But when he shot toward her, the blade sliced through the bonds at her wrists and the bonds at her feet in two quick swipes. Her arms fell forward as the ropes tumbled to the floor, and she immediately rubbed her wrists, bruised and bleeding from her earlier struggles. She managed one quick glance up at him before he pulled her roughly to her feet, holding her in front of him, his hands clamped over her arms.

"I don't believe that you won't fight," Dante told her, releasing her so she could stand on her own. She wobbled a bit, having been seated for hours, her legs still weakened by the drug. But she managed to stand tall, and stared regally at him.

When she said nothing, he moved to strike her, only to stop his hand mere inches from her face. When she barely winced, he started laughing again.

"Nothing? Come on, I'm giving you the chance to hurt me. You're not bound any longer, you're free. You just have to hit me."

"I won't play this game," she said dully, standing her ground. "You're going to kill me either way, so just be done with it."

"You know, you are *quite* boring," he mused, scratching his chin again in thought. "Nothing like my fiery Blythe or faithful Capri. It's like there's nothing inside of you, nothing that wants to live. Blythe, she would have slaughtered me by now, or at least attempted. And Capri…she would be trying to understand me, to reason with me on why she deserved to live. But you stand here and do nothing. How strange."

Again she stood in silence, holding his eyes. So far he hadn't noticed the tree she'd started growing behind the chair, and if she could just get him to leave the room…

"There must be something that would get a rise out of you," Dante said, clearly losing his patience. He wanted to see the bitch cry, beg, plead for her life. On impulse, he reached out and grabbed her again, thrusting her against him and yanking her head back by her hair. His eyes bore into hers, violent now instead of amused. She braced for the pain, for the quick shock of it.

But behind them, Burke let out a muffled groan, and started to get to his feet.

"She didn't just run away, Thea, that's outrageous," Liam protested, running his hands through his hair in agitation as he paced in the parlor.

"Until we have evidence to the contrary, I have to go on what little we have thus far," Thea retorted, fighting back the uneasiness and the frustration she felt. Around her, Sebastian, Serendipity, Rian and Capri hovered, looking distracted and worried. "And hopefully we'll know more once Blythe and Jax return from investigating that lead that came in this morning."

"This is tied to Burke, I just know it," Liam snapped. "And I don't believe a damn word he says."

"He claims he doesn't know where she is," Thea began, shaking her head. "He's an Enforcer, not a kidnapper or a criminal. I don't see him acting so brashly."

"He's convinced himself of Rhiannon's guilt." Liam stopped and stared at her incredulously. "Isn't that enough to suggest to you that he is responsible?"

Thea said nothing, knowing that if she answered no that it would be a lie. Certainly she had considered the possibility that Burke had taken Rhiannon. But without any proof, she couldn't bring herself to accuse him. Not when he had just lost his son, right under her nose.

"Damnit, if I had been with her last night this wouldn't have happened." Liam started pacing again, misery cracking his voice. "I could have protected her."

"We'll find her, Liam," Capri said reassuringly, reaching out to touch his shoulder. "Maybe she just went shopping."

"No, she left behind her money, her purse, her damn calculator. She doesn't go anywhere without those things. She's neurotic that way." Liam groaned and held his head in his hands, feeling restless and broody. "This is stupid, I'm going out to look for her. I can't sit around and wait any longer."

He started to bolt out of the room, only to spot Blythe and Jax racing in.

"Holy shit, you are not going to believe this!" Blythe said loudly, her adrenaline and excitement buzzing in the air around her. Jax looked just as eager, but gave her the stage to speak.

Thea, Liam and the others all gave her their full attention as she launched into her explanation of what they had just learned.

"So we got that tip this morning that someone we knew down in El Paso might know something about what happened to Michael. We go down there, and meet with Ricky, a demon bar owner Jax introduced me to a couple months ago. He's a rat for the Enforcers and keeps a lot of the illegal drug and weapons trafficking down there under control. But what he told us was that the other day Michael came to him, alone, and was demanding that Ricky give him the names of his suppliers down in Mexico, and that if he didn't comply, he'd arrest him. Ricky tried to explain to Michael that he has an arrangement with the Furies that he and his suppliers will remain untouched as long as they follow rules and regulations and keep other demons from coming into the market. But Michael wouldn't listen, and apparently he kept rambling on about how this was going to be his big sting, and how he was going to expose and arrest all of the demons conducting business in that area. So, when Ricky tried to give him the boot, Michael pulled out his gun and tried to shoot him, but of course he missed, given he's a lousy shot. And so Ricky did the only thing he figured a responsible, Enforcer-obeying demon should do. He let Michael take him to Euphora under the guise of surrender, and then he killed him."

"Ricky did this?" Rian asked, eyes hardening with shock and understanding.

"Yup." Jax grinned, looking amused. "Said he figured he was doing a service to you guys by disposing of the prick before he could do more damage."

"I can't believe this." Thea shook her head disbelievingly, rising to her feet. "I'll contact Burke, let him know."

She left the room, Sebastian in her wake.

While the others began talking and discussing the newest revelations, Liam was watching Serendipity.

She had been oddly quiet and expressionless up until this point. Now she looked not only shocked, but panicked. It was in that moment that he understood she knew what had happened to Rhiannon, and probably knew where she was.

When Serendipity slipped from the room, he followed her quietly, keeping back just far enough so she wouldn't hear him. He wanted to see where she was going, and what she would do once she was there.

To his surprise, she went straight to the Greenhouse, where he knew Rohan was busy prepping Bane, Thea's wolf, who he was planning on taking on his search for Rhiannon once they had an idea where she may be. Liam hung back and watched in the shadows as Serendipity burst into the Greenhouse and went straight to Rohan, who glared up at her cruelly. Bane growled, low and deep.

"What do you want?" Rohan snapped, his anger and fear clear in his eyes. He wasn't convinced that Rhiannon had run away, either.

Serendipity wrung her hands in front of her, her normally cool demeanor shattered to pieces. There was honest fear and guilt in her eyes now, and perhaps it was seeing it that had Rohan rising to his feet and giving her even an ounce of his time.

"We found out who killed Michael," she faltered, her body trembling. "It wasn't Rhiannon."

"I could have told you that," Rohan said darkly, still wary of his cruel wife. "Who did it, then?"

"Some demon, I don't know." She looked away, unable to meet his eyes any longer. "I…I made a huge mistake."

Because part of him had expected this, he reached out swiftly and grabbed her by the shoulders, shaking her until she would look at him. "You helped him kidnap her, didn't you? *Didn't you?*"

"Yes!" she cried, tears flowing down her face now. "Yes, I did, but I thought she was guilty, Rohan, and Burke was hurting so badly, and we both knew she deserved to be punished. So I helped him get into the castle last night and showed him to her room, and he left with her. I don't know where he planned on taking her."

"Damn you," Rohan hissed, pushing her away from him bitterly. "Damn you to Hell."

With that, he whistled at the wolf to follow him and left to find Thea. He had to tell her what his wife had done so they could begin the search.

What he didn't know was that Liam was already on his way upstairs to retrieve the gun Blythe had stashed in her nightstand, a scribbled down note of Burke's address from the Furies' files already tucked into his pocket from that morning.

He just had to pray he wasn't too late.

It amazed her to see the gun, clutched shakily in Burke's hands as he pointed it at Dante. She stared at it, mystified, wondering what it would look like if he fired it.

For a split second, she thought she might get to find out when Burke suddenly pulled the trigger. But the answering empty click and his dumbfounded look told her something had gone terribly wrong.

Dante just laughed, releasing Rhiannon and pushing her back onto the chair as he rounded on Burke, knocking the empty gun from his hand and punching him hard in the face. Burke, still dazed, crumbled back to the floor, clutching his head and groaning.

"Fool, you think I'd leave you with a loaded weapon?" Dante chuckled, kicking Burke in the gut for good measure. "I thought you were supposed to be a big, bad Enforcer?"

He kicked him again, pleased with Burke's answering painful grunt.

"Who are you? Are you a demon? What are you doing here?" Burke asked, clutching his stomach in pain as he glared up at Dante.

"You could say that...and I came here to find out which of the Council you'd kidnapped for killing your son," Dante informed him jauntily, smiling back at Rhiannon. "But she tells me she didn't do it. So I'd say you're not a very good Enforcer if you're arresting the wrong people."

Burke looked at Rhiannon then, the violent anger back in his eyes. "She's lying."

Rhiannon stayed where she was, silent, hoping they would keep talking with each other and ignore her. Already her hands had snaked behind her chair, and she was ready to finish growing her small tree.

"You know, I heard a little rumor...it's probably nothing, but perhaps I should share it with you," Dante began, eyeing Burke with sick glee in his eyes.

When Burke didn't respond, he continued. "I heard that it was a demon who killed your boy, not one of the Council. Isn't that just delightful?" Dante clapped his hands together, grinning broadly as he saw the shock flash over Burke's face. "So, you see, Mr. Callahan, when I kill the girl here, I may just leave you alive so that Thea can punish you for making this one grave, deadly mistake."

"A demon did that to Michael?" Burke spluttered, staring up at Dante in stunned disbelief.

"That's the rumor," Dante replied lushly, grinning again. "Now, here's what we're going to do. I need to send a message to Thea, letting her know that I'm, shall we say, back in town and ready to rumble. I think it would be fun if I give you the honor of strangling our lovely Earth Dryad here..." He paused, eyebrows arched as he crouched down beside Burke. "That is your handiwork, is it not?"

He pointed up at the bruises on Rhiannon's neck, and she stayed still as a statue, hoping they wouldn't notice what she was doing. Just a little bit more...the tree was almost large enough. She just needed it to have a few branches and a couple of leaves, then it should be large enough for her to grab and transport back home.

Dante turned back to Burke, who scowled miserably. "Maybe it is."

"Ha!" Dante beamed, immensely pleased with how the whole situation was playing out thus far. "Well then, you should have no problem doing it again. Then, you'll carry her body back to Euphora, and tell Thea who made you do it. Tell her that I'm coming for her, for all of them, and that these last few months I've been preparing." His eyes glinted with sheer evil and wicked madness as his gaze held Burke's. Burke's eyes widened in terror at the swift change of mood, the rapid darkening in the air that fell over them, dismal and sinfully insane. "Tell her that I have an army, the likes of which she's never seen…tell her that all of the evil she's banished and locked up over the last several centuries has been released, and is now under my command. This time, she won't win."

Rhiannon's breath caught in her throat and she momentarily forgot all about her tree. An army? Good God…

Suddenly, there was a loud knocking noise from up above. They all stared at the ceiling toward the sound.

"Hmm…" Dante's eyes narrowed as he considered how to handle the situation. But before any of them could do more than acknowledge the sound, there was a loud crash, the front door more than likely kicked in, and the sound of feet racing throughout the first floor.

Rhiannon's heart was thudding in her chest, praying it wasn't Brogan or Rian, or any of them up above. And when she heard the steps come toward the door to the basement, she felt the panic and fear choke her worse than Burke's hands ever could.

Dante stealthily slipped his own pistol from the holster at his hip, a large, .45 revolver. Burke started to move, but Dante swiftly struck him on the head with the butt of the pistol, knocking him unconscious.

He pulled the Enforcer up by his shirt and dragged him underneath the staircase, where they would both be hidden from view. Then he pointed the revolver at Rhiannon. "You say a word, shout a warning, and I will kill you."

She nodded, and then braced for the worst. If only she'd known just how bad it would be.

The door was shoved open and Liam appeared at the top of the stairs, gripping Blythe's pistol in his hands and pointing it down into the basement.

Rhiannon's heart clenched hideously and she felt a single tear escape and fall down her cheek as she stared up at him in both horror and disbelief.

"No…" she whispered, her eyes immediately shooting to Dante, who was watching her from under the stairs, his eyes gleaming with manic discovery.

"Rhia." Liam rushed down the stairs, thinking no one else in the room. He went straight to her, not recognizing the terror in her eyes. "Where's Burke?"

She shut her mouth tightly, knowing Dante had the revolver pointed right at Liam's back. If she said anything, he would surely shoot him…

Liam reached for her hands, thinking she was bound to the chair, only to find she was sitting there, unconstrained. "What the…Rhia, why are you just sitting here? What is that?"

She met his eyes, knowing he just saw the tree behind her. She tried with all her will to convey to him silently to keep quiet about the tree. He sensed that there was something wrong, and when he heard the cruel laughter coming from the stairs, he knew he'd walked straight into a trap.

Turning around, he pointed the gun in the direction of the laughter, where Dante was now emerging from the darkness. Burke's body lay there, unmoving.

"I knew there was something that would make you cry…" He chuckled, his own revolver pointed directly at Liam as he sauntered forward, his eyes glittering madly. "Let me guess…this is the Water Dryad, come to save you from the big, bad, crooked Enforcer?"

"Who are you?" Liam asked, placing himself between the stranger and Rhiannon.

Dante only smiled wider. "I'm your worst nightmare, boy."

Knowing it may kill them all, but seeing no other way out, Rhiannon shot her hands forward and pointed them at the ground, instantly jolting the plates deep below. The floor beneath them trembled and then shook violently, knocking both men to their knees as the ceiling above them started to cave in. Dante scrambled away from the falling debris toward the staircase as the ground swayed sickeningly beneath their feet. She held her hands in place, feeling the earthquake down to her very bones, her eyes open now and shining with strength and power. This was her way of fighting back, her way of hurting him. And oh, she hoped he'd suffer.

With something close to a battle cry, she sent one last, jolting tremor that rolled visibly beneath the carpet, heading straight for Dante. His eyes widened and he fired at her, but missed by a long shot due to the shaking ground. He reached up to cover his head as the ceiling above him started to crumble down, covering him in a mass of dust and debris.

Knowing they only had seconds before the entire house caved in, Rhiannon reached for Liam, grabbing his hand and then the tree behind her.

"Mother, I seek to return to you. Grant me entrance, and I will always be true," she said as quickly as she could, shutting her eyes as the golden light flashed before them, and the house disappeared in a shroud of misty fog.

Chapter Twenty

When the fog cleared, she opened her eyes and saw her home. And, for reasons completely unknown to her, the sight of it broke free a need deep inside her chest, something that for so long lay hidden and secret. Perhaps it was a culmination of adrenaline and fear that freed it, combined with the knowledge that she and Liam could very easily have just lost their lives. But they were safe now…they were home.

She pressed the back of her hand to her mouth, the urge to shatter into pieces coursing through her body. But she couldn't fall apart...not now, not here…

"God, Rhia." Liam pulled her against him, shuddering as he breathed her in, knowing she was safe. "You were so brave."

"It was nothing," Rhiannon insisted, pushing away from him, not sure she could even bear to look at him. She had to be alone, had to find someplace to give in to this urgent need to do something she had never before been able to do.

She started to walk and saw Blythe and Jax racing toward them through the meadow, fear and concern in their eyes.

"Jesus, Liam, what the hell happened? Rohan said that Burke had her, we were just about to go over there," Blythe called out, running to him and hugging him tightly. He pulled away and handed her back her pistol, his eyes wide and uncertain.

"Yeah, he had her, but there was someone else there, some guy..." Liam managed, shaking his head, dumbfounded. "Ask her."

Jax had already approached Rhiannon, who took a deep, steadying breath and began to speak as calmly and evenly as she could, given the circumstances.

"Dante is back at Burke's house in the basement. I don't know if either of them are still alive. The entire place caved in."

"*Dante?*" Liam gasped, mouth open in shock.

Rhiannon turned to him and nodded once. Words were not necessary to convey how much more danger they were in than he'd realized.

Without hesitating, Jax grabbed Blythe and led her to the tree. "C'mon, Blythe, we gotta go dig them out."

"Hot damn," Blythe said, more out of shock than excitement as she ran with Jax to the tree and left Euphora with a flash of gold light.

Without a word, Rhiannon began to walk swiftly toward the castle, her purpose simple and clear. Liam raced beside her, stunned and bewildered. But he knew now was not the time to question just how Dante had found his way into Burke's home. Pushing aside the thought, he stared at Rhiannon and had to fight back the anger he felt at seeing what they had done to her.

"You're bleeding," he said as he noticed her wrists, but when he reached out to touch her, she dodged away from him.

"Leave me alone, Liam," she snapped, picking up her pace.

"Damnit, let me help you!" he shot back, glaring at her when she stopped and met his eyes.

"I don't need your help, I'm fine."

"Oh, that's right." He shook his head, his eyes narrowing bitterly. "You don't need a hero, right Rhia?"

"Right. Now leave me be." She turned around and started walking again, and this time, he didn't follow her.

To her dismay, however, by the time she reached the courtyard, the others were pouring out of the castle and she was immediately barraged with questions.

Her father swept her into a hug, stunning her momentarily when he gripped her tightly in his arms. Bane was at his side and let out a welcoming howl. She was promptly shuffled into the arms of Capri, Brogan and Thea, and none of them would let her get a word in.

She broke free and pushed past them, not caring that it was rude. She was on the verge of an enormous breakdown, and she knew it would startle them if she succumbed to it in the middle of the courtyard.

To her relief, they let her go, and she heard them begin to question Liam instead. Good, let him fill them in on the details, she thought. It would give her at least ten minutes alone. She couldn't ask for more than that.

And so she went straight to the back gardens, where the wild roses bloomed and the silence hung heavy and indefinite. It was perfect because all she wanted was silence.

She walked through the tall, wild grasses, going off the pathway and deep into the small meadow, walking until she found a good spot. She stopped when she noticed a small, royal blue wildflower, blooming haphazardly amongst the sea of roses. Seeing it, thinking of it as some kind of sign, she reached out to tenderly cup it in her hand, and suddenly pressed her other hand against her mouth.

This was it. Thank God.

The pain was incredible, but the release beckoned her with dizzying urgency until all she could do was crumble to her knees, and weep.

She covered her face in her hands, ashamed and startled and incredibly relieved all at once. Her back heaved and shuddered as she sobbed, her chest aching as warm tears poured like rivers from her eyes.

So this is what it's like to cry…she thought wildly, the dam inside continuing to burst from within, releasing years upon years of pent up emotions in one violent, flooding wave. Oh, it was so…*liberating*.

She didn't hear the sound of soft footsteps behind her, nor did she notice the arms enfolding her, pulling her close and giving her an anchor to cling to while she drowned.

Liam rocked her slowly, pressing her face to his chest as she let herself go. He should have known this was what she was coming out here to do…she was finally, *finally* free.

"I love you," he murmured, kissing the top of her head and closing his eyes. "You are the strongest person I have ever known."

Hearing his words only made her sob harder, knowing just how callous and cruel she had been to him. He deserved so much better…

"Cry, baby..." he whispered, reveling in the sound of her release, knowing how badly she needed this. "Get it all out."

And so she did, and he stayed with her while she weathered the storm.

He guided her upstairs to her room, avoiding the others. Even though her crying jag was over for now, she still wasn't ready to face them. She needed to clean up, to rest…but this time, she wanted him with her.

He filled her tub with hot, soapy water while she examined the bruises and cuts on her wrists, wincing at the pain as she cleansed the worst of the dust and grime from the wounds. He helped her out of her clothes and into the tub, which she sank into with a grateful, feminine purr of satisfaction.

"Is it too hot?" he asked, crouching beside her.

She managed a small smile and shook her head. "It's amazing. Thank you."

"No problem." He grinned, rising to his feet to find some clothes for her to wear and bandages for her wrists. She had a cut on her lip as well, and more bruises at her temple and on her neck. The sight of them and knowing that both Burke and most likely Dante had harmed her, had him vowing to Hell and back that he'd finish them both for this...if they weren't dead already.

And if they weren't, if Dante wasn't...then he would just add it to the long list of other reasons he deserved to die.

He helped her out of the tub after a while and watched her dress, mesmerized as always by her beauty. But it wasn't just her beauty that attracted him to her. It was her quiet compassion and her unbreakable steel spine.

He realized now she would have probably made it out of Burke's house without him, given that she'd already had an escape plan in the first place. All he had done was provide a distraction, but it might have made the situation worse.

And to see her in action, putting that clever mind to work to save them both, quite simply amazed him. She was just so captivating, so brilliant and so much stronger than she looked. So it was true that she didn't really *need* him. But as long as she *wanted* him, he vowed he would always be at her side.

"How are you feeling?" he asked quietly, sitting on the bed as she buttoned her blouse with her slender, capable fingers.

She turned toward her vanity table and ran her brush through her long mane of dark hair, unsure how to answer him.

"I feel...cleansed." She let out a small laugh, not quite sure why she found it funny. She met his eyes in the mirror over her dressing table, and held them as she continued to brush her hair, her smile fading. "I'm sorry you had to see me like that."

"Are you kidding? I wouldn't have missed that for the world." He rose to his feet to stand behind her, resting his chin on her shoulder, his hands coming up to cup her arms. "It isn't every day you see someone break free."

She let out a shaky breath, feeling her hands tremble as she set down her brush. "Is that what I am? Free?" she asked, instinctively leaning back against him, welcoming his arms that came around her.

He nodded in response, pressing a kiss to the smooth curve of her throat. "As a bird, my love."

"I don't even know what to say to you," Thea began as she sat in one of her cushy lounge chairs in the garden room, Sebastian at her side. Her dark eyes were focused on her Earth Dryad and there were tears in them. "You are now the third of my Dryads to have been terrorized by this monster. And I wasn't able to protect you from him."

"Thea…" Rhiannon twisted her hands together in her lap, uncomfortable to see the formidable and regal Thea look so weakened and afraid. "I learned a long time ago that you can't control the actions of others. You can only control how you react in response to them."

"And perhaps if my reaction had been harsher, we would have searched Burke's house immediately and Dante wouldn't have reached you," Thea insisted, her eyes hardening with both guilt and misery. "I don't know how he escaped from the rubble of that house…"

Sebastian had his arm over her shoulders, squeezing her gently. "We all believed Burke to be above kidnapping. But perhaps we should have seen the signs of his madness when he tried to strangle poor Rhiannon to death."

Rhiannon shivered from the memory, the glaring hate in Burke's eyes permanently burned into her mind. "It's over now. He knows the truth and he won't come after me again."

"Yes but when he gets out of the hospital, I'm going to have a long talk with him. We are lucky Brogan had the foresight to look through Michael's things at the Enforcer's headquarters in D.C., or we might never have known the truth behind his murder," Thea muttered, shaking her head with a mixture of relief and anxiety.

"Brogan gave Blythe and Jax the lead to El Paso?" Rhiannon asked, stunned. "I had no idea."

Thea managed a smile. "He cares about you. He wanted to do as much as he could to help prove you were innocent."

Humbled, Rhiannon sat quietly, lost in thought. When she spoke again, there was distinct concern and apprehension in her eyes.

"Thea, what are we going to do about Dante?"

For a moment, Thea said nothing and turned uneasily to Sebastian. "If what he told you is true…if he really does have some kind of army at his disposal…then I suppose we will have to fight."

Sebastian nodded assuredly at her. "It has been done before, we can do it again."

Thea let out a heavy sigh, looking uncertain. "I fear this will be worse than those times, my love."

"We are strong now, stronger than we have been in the past. We will handle whatever he throws at us and we will win," Sebastian reassured her and then eyed Rhiannon with purpose and determination. "We will all have to push past our petty disagreements and unite now if we want to survive what is surely coming."

Knowing he meant the feud between the Dryads, Rhiannon flushed and looked away, ashamed. "We will work it out," she murmured, staring down at Bane, finding comfort in his golden eyes.

"Rhiannon," Thea said, waiting until the girl met her gaze. "Your mother is truly sorry. I have never seen her more repentant in all her life than she is over this. You should talk to her."

Rhiannon grimaced, but nodded. “If you wish.”

“I do.” Thea sat up, her lips curving. “And let me just say that I am pleased to see that Rohan is doing much better. Would you believe that I actually saw him laughing about an hour ago? I couldn’t believe my eyes.”

“Laughing?” Rhiannon managed, startled. Oh, she wished she had seen it…

“Go see them both, dear. Your parents have a lot of selfishly wasted time to make up with you.”

Biting back a small smile, Rhiannon rose to her feet. With a polite nod, she swept from the room, eager for the first time, in a very long time, to see her family.

She wandered into the Greenhouse and saw her father sitting studiously at his drafting table, working away. It was the most industrious he’d been in a long time, and it brought both relief and joy to her to see it.

When he heard her approach, he turned and looked up, his warm smile stunning her.

“Rhiannon,” Rohan greeted, setting down his pencil and rising to his feet. He walked toward her and pulled her into his arms. “I was hoping you would come see me.”

“Why wouldn’t I?” she asked, relishing the familiar scent of his cologne and the soft feel of his dress shirt. Her proper and elegant father.

“I was so scared,” he admitted, pressing his face against her hair, his eyes shut tight against tears that threatened to fall. “I thought I was going to lose you.”

Feeling her heart swell, she sighed against him and felt her own eyes tear up. “You didn’t. I’m still here.”

“You’re my heart, Rhiannon. You always have been,” he whispered, more to himself than to her.

Feeling hot tears stream down her cheeks, she pulled away to look at him, impossibly moved. "I love you."

"I love you, too." He smiled, pressing a kiss to her forehead. "I don't know why it's taken me so long to say those words to you."

"Likewise." She shakily returned his smile, wiping away her tears. "Perhaps we have all been foolishly cold."

They heard the sound of footsteps behind them. When they both turned they spotted Serendipity hovering in the doorway, looking out of place and embarrassed.

"I'm sorry, I just…" she trailed off, seeing her daughter and her husband both staring at her distrustfully. Feeling unwelcome, she started leave. "Maybe I should just go."

"Mother, come here," Rhiannon said, pulling away from her father to stretch out her hand toward Serendipity.

She approached apprehensively, but clearly something was different in her demeanor. Thea was right. She did look truly sorry.

Rhiannon met her mother's eyes, fighting to push aside her ill feelings for the moment. "Do you have anything to say for yourself?"

Serendipity pursed her lips and took a deep breath, her head instinctively rising in an attempt to mask her embarrassment. But it was still there in the tears that silently streamed down her cheeks. "I'm sorry."

"You knew Burke was going to kill me," Rhiannon said, her head shaking disdainfully. "And still you handed me to him. I accept your apology in part, but it is going to take a long time for me to fully forgive you. I hope you can understand that."

Serendipity's eyes darted to Rohan and then back to her daughter. "I understand, Rhiannon."

"Good." Rhiannon reached out then, and to her mother's surprise, gave her a somewhat awkward hug. It was the most physical contact she had had with her mother in years.

Pulling away, Rhiannon turned back to her father.

"Well? What do the two of you want to say to each other?"

Rohan crossed his arms over his chest and stared warily at his wife. "For now, Serendipity, I cannot trust you. Perhaps, in time, you will earn back my trust. But until then, I feel it is best that we stay separated."

For a brief moment it looked as though Serendipity was going to retort in anger. But when she looked at Rhiannon and saw the disapproval on her daughter's face, she nodded solemnly.

"If that is what you wish, Rohan," Serendipity said quietly, turning to look at him with hard acceptance in her eyes.

"Hey, what's going on?" Sierra appeared in the doorway, looking a bit weary and cautious. She stepped forward, stopping beside their mother and eyeing Rhiannon thoughtfully. "Are you doing okay?"

Rhiannon nodded, oddly touched to hear her selfish, little sister utter words of concern. "I'm fine."

"Good." Sierra nodded, pouting as she glanced at each of their parents, sensing the tension in the air. "Is this, like, our first family get together or something?"

Rohan laughed then, and the sound of it had Rhiannon jolting around to face him. But his smile was real, and the relief in his eyes palpable.

"I suppose it is." He chuckled, reaching out with one arm to pull Sierra to him, and wrapping his other around Rhiannon. He met his wife's eyes and he beckoned her forward. "Let's all enjoy this moment. It certainly is a first for us."

Rhiannon sighed against him as her other arm wrapped around her mother, her heart, at last, content. Maybe they weren't completely whole, but at least they were making headway.

The first thing she did when she left her parents was to look for Brogan. It didn't surprise her to find him in the kitchens, tending to her vegetable garden.

She stepped inside the little greenhouse, her lips curving into a warm smile at the sight of him, crouched down beside her tomato plants, pruning and placing select tomatoes in a basket beside his feet.

When he heard her, he glanced up, and though he flushed a little with embarrassment, his answering smile was honest and open.

"Hi," he greeted, standing up to meet her as she walked toward him.

"Hi." She wrapped her arms around him, hugging him tightly, needing no words. His arms came around her as well, and she felt him relax.

Backing away, she smiled up at him. "Thea told me what you did. I can't thank you enough."

With a shrug, he let out a small laugh and averted his eyes. "I knew you weren't guilty. You're the kindest person I know."

"No, you're much kinder than I am." She reached up to cup his cheek, and turned his head until his eyes met hers. "Really, Brogan. Thank you."

"You're welcome." He grinned, then pulled away to reach down and lift the basket full of tomatoes from the floor. "Since you haven't had much time lately, I figured I'd come take care of these for you."

"Thank you." She took the basket he held out and retreated into the kitchen to set it on the countertop. Inspired and a bit curious, she whirled around to stare at him again, her eyes questioning. "Were you going to tell me that you had looked into Michael's things and found out where he had gone and what he was doing? Or were you going to let me go on believing Blythe and Jax had done it all?"

He smirked, leaning against the doorframe to the greenhouse. "Remember Boo Radley, Rhiannon?"

With a quiet laugh, she nodded. "Yes, I do."

"Well, like him, I don't do well in the limelight. But I still want to help."

She just smiled. "Your secret's safe with me. Now, come on, I'll walk with you to dinner."

She waved him over and he followed, pleased when she wrapped her arm around him companionably. They left the kitchens, laughing and smiling together as they headed down the corridor.

Before they could reach the dining hall, Blythe burst through the doors, looking agitated and more than a little frustrated. When she spotted the two of them, she let out a huff of breath and crossed her arms over her chest.

"I need to talk to you," she said to Rhiannon, an eyebrow cocked in irritation.

Rhiannon and Brogan stopped, both of them eyeing her strangely.

"Alright," Rhiannon replied, her face carefully guarded as she turned to look at Brogan. "I'll meet you there."

"Okay." He smiled a bit apprehensively, but left them alone.

"Outside," Blythe snapped before taking off toward the atrium and leading the way into the courtyard. Rhiannon followed behind, rolling her eyes. She had no idea what to expect but certainly it couldn't be good…

Blythe went straight to the nearest bench and plopped down on it, perched on the edge. Rhiannon followed suit, crossing her legs and folding her hands over her knees.

"Well?" she asked after a moment went by with Blythe saying nothing. Blythe scowled, tapping her hands on her knees restlessly.

Suddenly, she bolted to her feet and stood before Rhiannon, fists on her hips.

"Okay, look. This isn't easy for me to do, especially since its becoming somewhat of a habit nowadays, but I just wanted to say thank you." She paused, eyeing Rhiannon expectantly, as if daring her to laugh.

Instead, Rhiannon's eyebrows raised in an expression of polite interest. "Oh. For what, may I ask?"

Rolling her eyes dramatically, Blythe reached up to run her hands through her wildly curly hair with a frustrated groan. "Ugh, I hate the way you talk sometimes. So goddamn superior…"

Despite the insult, Rhiannon's lips curved slightly. "Much like I despise the blunt and careless way you speak, Blythe."

Her hands fell away from her head and she stared at Rhiannon for a moment, one eyebrow arched indignantly.

"Right…well anyway, I'm thanking you because despite what I think actually happened, Liam is claiming that you saved his life. So…thank you for that." She pouted a bit, looking annoyed and irritated as she scuffed her shoes over the ground. Rhiannon thought she looked kind of childish, but perhaps it was part of her charm.

"You're welcome," she replied, biting her lip as she thought. "You know, I should thank you as well."

"Hmmph, for what? I didn't do anything for you." Blythe snorted, crossing her arms over her chest.

Rhiannon smirked and met Blythe's eyes. "You stood against Michael, albeit for Liam's sake I'm sure, but you certainly didn't have to. It was a…humbling experience for me."

Temper properly deflated, Blythe rolled her eyes again and moved to sit beside Rhiannon once more, turning to the other girl with a knowing look. "As your arch nemesis, even *I* couldn't stand by and let you marry that prick, rest in peace and all that jazz," she said, her lips curving into a cocky grin. "And besides, my best friend...my brother...was hurting and I wanted to do all I could, even if it meant, for once, supporting you."

"It meant a lot, coming from my enemy." Rhiannon tossed back her hair and winked at Blythe, feeling more at ease than she had felt in a long time with the Fire Dryad.

"Well, I don't have to like you and I probably never will like you, but…" Blythe began, her amber eyes lit with fiery humor. "That doesn't mean I can't respect you. And, I gotta say, after you saved all our asses by uncovering what my mother was up to a couple months ago, and after you faced Dante and saved Liam… damn honey, you've certainly earned my respect."

Rhiannon laughed and in a sign of openness, settled back against the bench seat and shifted to face Blythe. "I definitely don't like you but I can't help but respect you, too. You faced Dante all on your own and you survived. I don't know how you did it."

"He's an evil bastard, ain't he?" Blythe joked, though darkness haunted her eyes. "He's gotten to all of us, in one way or another. It's time we take him out, once and for all."

They both turned at the sound of footsteps, and spotted Liam and Capri approaching, arm-in-arm and smiling.

"Hi girls," Capri greeted, sitting down between them and glancing side-to-side. She suddenly realized what she was interrupting and her mouth fell open in shock. "Oh God, were you two having a conversation? Shoot, okay...pretend I didn't sit down and that I didn't interrupt." She started to get to her feet only to have Blythe grab her hand and yank her back down.

"Calm down, honey, I don't think either of us object to you joining in." Blythe grinned, wrapping her arm around Capri and eyeing Rhiannon. "Right?"

"Right." Rhiannon smiled as Liam sat down on the other side of her and wrapped an arm over her shoulder, pulling her close.

"What were you two talking about, anyway?" he asked, winking at Blythe who stuck her tongue out at him playfully.

"Dante," Rhiannon said softly, tilting her head to meet his eyes. A shadow darkened his expression momentarily.

"I see." He attempted a smile and pressed a kiss to her forehead. "Well, we've all faced him now, in one way or another. I think we're ready to face him again, when the time comes."

"Do you think he'll try and attack us again, like last time?" Capri asked curiously, a hint of fear in her voice. Blythe hugged her closer, not just in a show of comfort, but also to soothe her own worries.

"I don't know. I don't think any of us can really say." Liam shook his head, reaching out with his free hand to hold Capri's. "But we're together now and we're strongest that way."

"Damn straight," Blythe agreed, meeting Rhiannon's eyes with a quick grin. "For better or for worse, right?"

"Oh, speaking of that…" Capri interrupted, her face flushing as she glanced around at the three of them, biting back a grin. "Rian asked me to marry him about an hour ago."

"*What!*" Blythe's jaw dropped as she gaped at Capri, eyes wide.

"You did say yes, right?" Liam asked, his mouth splitting in a wide grin.

In answer, she held up her left hand, where an old-fashioned looking gold band with a simple, emerald cut diamond rested.

With a hoot of laughter, he rose to his feet and scooped her up into his arms, spinning her around once before setting her back on her feet. Blythe laughed and got up to hug Capri as well. "Lemme see that rock. Ha! That boy did good!"

"It was his mother's," Capri explained with a soft smile.

While they admired the ring, Rhiannon rose to her feet, tears welling in her eyes as she watched her young friend, her lovely face filled with joy and promise. She blinked and a couple tears escaped as Capri turned toward her.

Capri's smile instantly faded, replaced by worry. "Rhiannon, what's wrong?"

"Nothing." She laughed shakily, brushing away the tears, embarrassed by them. This would take some getting used to, this crying thing… "It's just that I had this mental image of you in a wedding dress and it broke my heart. You're going to be such a lovely bride."

Capri beamed, reaching out to hug Rhiannon. "Thank you. You're the first ones I've told."

"Rightfully so," Blythe put in as Rhiannon and Capri pulled apart, both turning to face her. "We're the four Dryads, we're closer than family and we can't forget that, especially not now.

We've spent too long being torn apart by petty stuff and I'll be the first to admit it. I say we all make a truce–right here, right now–to never let anything divide us ever again. Deal?"

She held out her hand, palm down, between all of them. Liam was the first to place his hand on top of hers.

"Sounds good to me," he said cheerfully, grinning at her before shifting his eyes to Rhiannon.

She stared at him as one last tear fell down her cheek. "Count me in," she declared, placing her hand over his.

Capri, more than a little misty eyed herself, joyfully placed her hand on top of all theirs, binding them together, just as she'd always hoped she would.

"Deal."

Chapter Twenty One

After dinner, they walked hand-in-hand into the courtyard under the night sky bursting with stars.

Rhiannon had a blanket tucked under her arm, a small bag filled with snacks and a bottle of wine. Beside her, Liam carried a lantern filled with fireflies, his guitar slung over his back.

They went to the old spot where they hadn't been since they were teens, an open grassy area with a perfect view of the stars. Liam spread out the blanket while Rhiannon uncorked the wine with a sultry pop. He tumbled down onto the blanket, flipped to his side and grinned deviously up at her.

"You know how long it's been that I've wanted to take you out here again?" he asked her, his eyes shining brightly in the glow of the fireflies from the lamp beside him.

Rhiannon kneeled down and handed him a glass of wine, smirking. "Since the last time we were out here?"

"You're good." He took a slow sip, then sat up and leaned toward her, pressing his lips to hers. She savored the taste of wine from his tongue and delighted in the way his breath quickened as her free hand caressed through his hair.

"I merely used deductive reasoning, Liam," she corrected as she pulled away, taking a smooth sip of her own wine and eyeing him over the rim.

"Clever girl." He chuckled, setting his glass aside and reaching for his guitar. "So, what should I play for you?"

"Mmm…I don't know, surprise me." She smiled, enjoying the moment. "You know, I used to listen to you practice outside in the back gardens? I would hide just inside the doors and sit and listen to you for hours."

"Really?" He looked up from tuning the strings, eyes wide.

"Mmm hmm." She bit her lip, tilting her head and smiling. "You could say I'm your biggest fan."

"Well." Honestly surprised and honored, he laughed and strummed a few notes on the guitar. "Then I suppose I should give my biggest fan a song worthy of her devotion."

"Let's hear it."

He cleared his throat, strummed a few testing notes, and then began to sing a timeless Beatles tune about a blackbird learning to fly…

She shut her eyes and sighed, her mouth curving into a contented smile. Around them, fireflies danced in the night air as a gentle breeze blew by to trail temptingly over her skin. The moon up above, joined by the stars, shone incandescently down from the heavens. All she could hear was the sweet music his fingers made sliding over the guitar strings, and the lilting, caressing sound of his voice that she had loved her entire life.

It hit her then, this crazed moment of awareness, of feeling her heart swollen with this love for him. So it had happened, after all.

Stunned and breathless, she turned to him and stopped his hand with her own, halting the music and his singing. He lifted his eyes to stare at her, alarmed by the look on her face.

"What is it?" he asked, already pushing aside his guitar, thinking something was wrong.

"I love you," she told him, her head shaking and her lips curving as she let out an unsteady laugh, not yet believing it herself.

"Oh." He paused, his brows furrowed together as he pondered what she said. "Did you just now come to that conclusion?"

She nodded, though she felt embarrassed. "I've never said that to anyone before in my entire life and then today I told my father I loved him, and now I've told you." She tilted back her head and stared up at the stars, letting out a huff of breath and laughing at herself. "It's been quite the day for revelations and new beginnings. I guess it's all part of this…freedom thing I'm trying."

Without a word, he reached over and tilted her face so she was looking at him, and he silently kissed her, his hand cupping around her jaw line. Her body shifted and she wrapped her arms around him until he slowly laid back against the blanket with her curled against him.

He stroked a hand lazily down her back as he broke the kiss, his other hand still touching her face, marveling at her. "So I assume that this means you're going to tell your parents to shove it, figuratively speaking, in regards to selecting a husband for you?"

She laughed, pressing her face against the crook of his neck. "I don't think they'll be trying that again anytime soon."

"And in regards to you and me?" he added, more seriously now.

Rhiannon rose up to stare down at him, wondering how he couldn't see it. It was all so clear to her now… "Liam…" She reached out to touch his face with her fingertips, trailing them along his cheek, her eyes following the movement before meeting his. "Nothing, and no one, will ever keep me from you again. As long as you want me, I'm yours."

"You're all I've ever wanted, Rhia," he murmured, needing her to remember that. "I was only waiting for you to be free."

DON'T MISS THE EXCITING FINALE OF THE DRYAD QUARTET

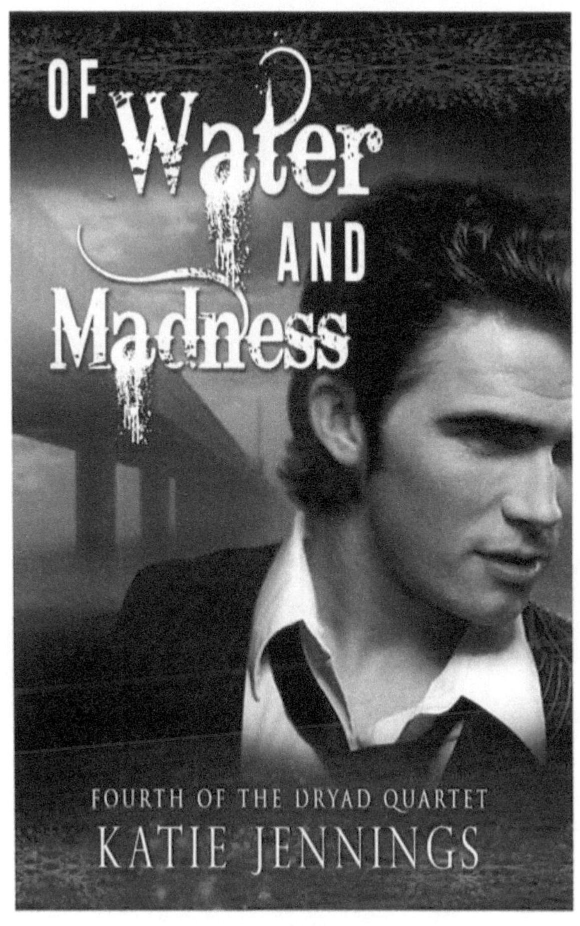

CATCH KATIE JENNINGS' NEWEST BOOK

About the Author

Nothing can compare to the exhilaration of discovering, at last, a mode of release for the imagination. Mine came, after years of struggling to visualize my creativity, in the form of the written word. I found myself with my nose constantly in a book, absorbing the life of the characters and the beauty of thc setting. It was intoxicating, to say the least, and the only thing I knew was that I wanted to give writing a shot, and take the thousands of characters and storylines in my head and put them down on paper and form them into something real and compelling.

In truth, I'm just a girl from a small town north of Los Angeles with an imagination for days and thank goodness a keyboard at my fingertips. And even though my husband thinks I'm a nerd and my mom is undoubtedly my biggest fan, at the end of the day I'm loving life and enjoying giving breath to the characters living in my heart and sharing with others all of the creativity I can harness.

I believe in true love and I've always believed in happy endings. And that is just the beginning of the story.

K

www.ingramcontent.com/pod-product-compliance
Lightning Source LLC
Chambersburg PA
CBHW031256170626
46807CB00001B/170

* 9 7 8 0 6 1 5 7 2 0 4 0 1 *